the As_____ __

Pemberley

A historical novel set in Regency England

MARELLA SANTA CROCE

Dedicated to my beloved grandparents,
Elizabeth May and Joseph Newton

First published by Marella Santa Croce
© 2022 Marella Santa Croce

ISBN 978-1-998980-25-3 (Print)
ISBN 978-1-998980-26-0 (eBook)

Cover, illustration and interior crafted with love by the team at:
www.myebook.online

---

*A*s soon as Elizabeth Darcy stepped into The Old Jamaica Inn, she knew that she had come home. If any restlessness remained in her soul from its incongruent days at Longbourn, it was assuaged by the fragrance of the beeswax polish, the smell of the old thatch and the base note to this heady mixture, the edge of tobacco in the ashes of the fire. Indeed, somewhat alarmed by the possibility of her eyes glowing like coals in her face, she dampened this little hymn to another time that was to her, The Jamaica. Insisting that this should be a short stop, the reputation of the inn notwithstanding, Darcy clucked around them like a tall, elegant cockerel, his long legs disappearing into his jacket, as was their wont. Elizabeth and Jane went about on tiptoes, such was the delight of each in the other and for the first time, the former realised how much she had missed the latter now that she was beside her.

The sun was coming to its late morning heat, flashing and sparkling into corners - the Inn was at her best for the ladies, the darker deeds present there from time to time wrapped around by light. Newly scrubbed tables still smelled of soap and the Delabole slate floor, also ready for the day, was the perfect backdrop for the pleasure of drinking coffee, whose deep aroma seemed to marry with the polish, which was even now being rubbed into the chairs behind the seated party. Elizabeth felt that she might swoon with delight at the orchestra of fragrances and longed to stay, but dare not say, as her husband busied with the preparations for their exit. She said, instead:

'Dear Mr Darcy, it is thought that King Arthur's sword was put into a small lake nearby; do we proceed along this route across Bodmin moor, for if so, we might have comprehension of the legendary spot.'

'Of course, my dear one, we may indeed, it is on the way that we must take, one which I have deliberately chosen to give prospect of the land and its ancient past.'

The words melted into the now continuing sea of delight lapping around Elizabeth's head and they all filed into the carriage, ready for the next part of the journey to Truro, their river port of call. Every person in the group felt a sense of gratitude for their being together; the conviviality between them; the place in which they were now gathered; the piquant smell of the mosses and lichens on the rocks; the sheep grazing wild and the dash and fling of the as-wild ponies. Soon they were in the presence of a King and the pool at Dozmary. Elizabeth felt curious, for here was the water of the *Lady of the Lake*, who was said to have given the sword to Arthur and to whom it was returned at his death: it seemed to her that so great were the King's powers that he would have been able to draw her to him when in need. Bereft of ken, for no one was about to enquire further of the history of the pool, Mrs Darcy was left musing on the idea of the great sword and, indeed, its owner, whose fame had not diminished in the area since his departure from it: she bethought herself, 'when a king is great, it is impossible to erase his efficacy.'

*M*indful of the pitfalls open to a woman of slender means bespoke to a man of immense material wealth, Elizabeth Darcy stood silently before Pemberley's lake, taking stock of the exquisite content of the moment.

'And so it is,' she thought, 'I am mistress of this great house and have come to share in the ancient heart that beats within it.'

Here was a woman who had never felt a sense of possession in her life, yet she had lived with its consequences and in full cognizance of her own apparent worthlessness in the eyes of those who judged her, indeed, whose own equally apparent *worth* had oft been flaunted before her. She had never comprehended what the word meant, it seemed absurd to have to bow to those who had sucked the life from the very persons who provided it – she had thought this many times but of course, never said it, outside of her private talks with Jane. Now there was no Jane to talk to on such topics, nevertheless, Elizabeth was observing and amassing -worth seemed too often to tally with material possession – she was endeavouring to learn without prejudice, her old friend. That she was neither possessive nor any longer oppressed by being at an inadequate remove from life was an immense relief to the new mistress of Pemberley, yet she felt strongly the anomaly of knowing that her husband owned most of Derbyshire.

Still shocked at the turning tide of her life was a woman whose own heart had returned to its natural state, she watched as the part of her that had lived for so long in the undertow of shame now receded, whilst the rest whirled around in some heavenly place, all pain surpassed. It seemed astonishing now to think that she had lived beneath the weight of others' censure but to have lack blasted through the air from noon till night, through breakfast and into supper, was destructive. Then there was Mr Collins. The great silence of Pemberley reassured her, yet its might came from a sense of both history and human industry – for her husband was a landowner - sometimes she had to bite her metaphorical tongue, for she was glad, eternally grateful about what had fallen into her lap. She found herself jousting with the old problem: if only the entail had been spliced with the justice of two sexes in the world and not one. The casting of the male lot had constantly spawned the apparent poverty resident within the Bennet family and was the foundation of much despair and vocal ferocity on the part of her mother. This having been said, there was nothing so educational as lack, especially when it ceased to function: such a thought seemed both distasteful and sublime at the same time.

How long, the mistress of Pemberley had asked herself, standing before its resplendent facade, must the stoicism attendant upon the spectre of poverty residing within the widows of lost husbands continue? Further, there was to be no discussion of this aspect of the past with her husband - she, Elizabeth Darcy, had flown to the other side but was duty bound to her own conscience not to forget what it was like to be under the table. There was a fireplace to be cleared within her soul, she thought: had she not poked about in the ashes for some time and now someone had re-lit her. Whilst the memory of shame stretched out before her, she could no longer give it claim or credence. Someone had flown into her life, initial argumentation notwithstanding, and plucked her out of Longbourn: it was real, like having a royal pardon. So used was Mrs Darcy to averting her gaze from the monstrous opinions handed out by the hour by her mother, that to live with Mr Darcy was a new experience in her life; first of all, it was a sort of bliss through the absence of that which had been for so long a torment and then there was the great felicity of tenderness. She resolved to perpetuate no more the feelings that had reduced her at a time when she was meant to be burgeoning. She comprehended, nevertheless, that the yearning for inclusion in a life without anxiety was a valuable tool of understanding; she would retrieve that which had fled.

Such were the thoughts of the living Mrs Darcy; she had much to delight her now as she stood in her favourite place in front of the lake, a place of great elegance and beauty:

'In all wonder,' she thought to herself, 'this has come out of a man's love: astonishing!' the fact that *she* was the woman whom he loved could not yet be comprehended. 'No matter! I am learning what being conscious of love means,' she thought firmly, 'and I know that here before me is a man who has come to it and not been found wanting.'

Only the arrival of her husband ended Elizabeth's state of reverie.

'My dear Mr Darcy,' she beckoned as she ran back into the warm sunshine to greet him, 'I was just deliberating on a small idea, which bethinks me to share it with you. It is to do with your tenants and cottagers, so you may tell me if you think that it is not my business – I wish you no ill-thought, of course, nor criticism – you are a fine landlord.'

'If it pleases you, then tell me,' said Darcy, without baulking at her particular interest in a domain that had heretofore been his alone.

'Well, we know that our beloved Lambton holds its weekly market on Saturday, but I wonder whether there is a way in which we might build a possibility of your own farm produce ...'

'*Our* farm produce,' interrupted her husband.

'*Our* farm produce,' she repeated softly, 'to be sold by the people who harvest it? I do not want you to think that I am trying to put us into trade, but I pondered on asking if it were possible to provide a small space in which your tenants and workers might sell some of the farm's produce and benefit from an exchange of the overspill, as it were? Is this too far-fetched, or incommodious to you, dear husband?'

'I think that you must not tell Bingley's sisters, we would never hear the last of it!' said he, smiling.

'It's just that *we* have vast and abundant fields, even kitchen gardens and perhaps it would be a way for those who labour for you to feel part of the greater whole. I am quite terrified to say more!' Elizabeth was also grateful that the name of Lady Catherine de Bourgh had not been mentioned.

'I do not believe it! Mrs Darcy terrified!' A tender kiss was planted at once upon her unsuspecting nose. 'Please let me think on it; you are not in trouble with me, I can feel the spirit of the times changing and, whilst I would not wish to serve behind a display of vegetables, nor indeed, be in charge of the running of such a venture, I might be able to provide some manner of station for their journey from field to table. Let us see.'

Elizabeth's body movements had grown wider and more expansive as she had been explaining out her idea with the natural care and enthusiasm for duty that her husband cherished. He found her small theatricality, with its own verve, both charming and delightful and he remembered at once that the estate owned a small building in the village in perfect placement and condition for the assemblage of both persons and the fruits of the farm: he would think on't.

*E*linor Ferrars stood in her small, upstairs parlour admiring her husband's hair: 'the colour of late harvest', she thought. Here, before her, the man she had not dared to make real to herself when he came to Norland. A man distinguished by his own nature: patient; slow to anger; a friend to all he met and therefore a defender of the faith, and a great *hearth* of comfort for her after the demise of Norland. For the hasty departure from her childhood home after the death of her father was, indeed, a *demise*, its very walls immediately and inappropriately impregnated with Fanny's vast and constant need for more, regardless.

Elinor's sister-in-law was never able to pull back after the death of her father and the inability of her mother to love anyone but herself, and in a family soused in wealth like a fat herring. Two brothers, Edward the elder, ruled by an overbearing matriarch with a vicious tongue, set the scene; when his father died, there remained only the grimness of his mother's snobbery and the invective of her spite. Always dressed in the most expensive garments (which Elinor had sometimes thought better fitted to someone more beautiful from within) Mrs Ferrars was mostly in sumptuous silk, whilst inside she grew to become like an old sack left on the greenhouse floor too long and sadly become the verdigris. Indeed, Mrs Ferrars' shameless tongue had become so slick, as charmless as it was sharp, that grandiosities became slanders and slanders became a sort of licentiousness of language itself: in short, she was a baggage.

In contrast to her mother-in-law, Elinor Ferrars was a sparkling beacon, like a graceful candle set in her husband's very hearth; she quietly lit every conversation, every visit, every dinner table, with her equilibrium, offset by a secret sense of fun. Indeed, so big was her presence in relation to the slenderness of her physical being that new acquaintances were bowled over by her carefully weighed opinions and unwillingness to throw at them any aspect of herself not valuable as a contribution. Elinor knew about exhibitions of temper, of tantrums, of drama and preferred to keep her own difficulties to herself.

In this way, the young Ferrars' household quietly sang its own song which all who came to the Parsonage appreciated; and many came, for Edward was a country parson who was steadily building a large following. His church of St Mary Magdalene was a place of peace in an area otherwise beset by a turn of the tide, for in England, as in France before her, change was afoot.

It was for this reason that at breakfast on that first morning of Spring, the Reverend Ferrars hugged his wife to him with anticipation:

'My dearest Elinor, I would like to put to you an idea that came to me, to help with the growing numbers of our parish at church on Sundays and, in particular, some who are in need of being heard at this time. I feel very strongly that some of the men of our parish need someone to hear them, before they grow into angry, rebellious subjects and find themselves in a worse situation than the one in which they started. These are curious times with a hard edge: the fact is that many of the farm labourers find themselves with little money at the end of the week, sometimes with barely enough to put food on the table. Their ill-will rises, and their ill-health grows and the harvest that they gather does not reach them.'

'I see that too, my love, so tell me, in small parcels, so that I may comprehend, how you mean to help them.'

Edward was aware of his good fortune, not only in redeeming the woman his head had told him was lost but in being able to do what he had long wanted in becoming a Pastor and living somewhere in the countryside. His church, in the parish of Delaford in the county of Dorsetshire, was growing – something that he had not even conceived of – and he was at last beginning to be himself again. Edward's memory of the spectre of poverty could not, would not be erased, yet he felt that such a memory would act as a leveller in times of its opposite – not everyone spent such a short time beneath its cloud and his occupation required the faithfulness of compassion.

Prising the gate hook off its slumped hook whilst marking the moment to mend it later in the day, Edward took his first steps into land husbandry. Never schooled in this latter, his natural bent was, nevertheless, one of mending that which was broken: he thought that the gate being out of kilter was a fine metaphor for what he quietly wanted to do in his parish. Steadily gathering a small list of things requiring attention, he walked on; his delight at where he found himself and his prospects there, and the warmth and equal skills of his wife for their home and its garden, made him feel a man rich in abundance. Nothing could have tempted him to adhere to any sense of loss, or of thinking himself in a place that was the lesser had he inherited the outer grandeur of the Ferrars' estates and the headaches that accompanied them. Here was a man already in heaven.

Heading pensively to the kitchen and the warm promise of his second breakfast, Edward turned only to regard the sheer beauty of the May morning, inspiring him as to what he was going to say upon the coming Sunday. Both the scent of warm bread and, let us say, that of his warm wife, drew him to the room where a small fire burned as part of the stove.

'I wanted to continue with you, dearest Elinor, on our project for a small hall, for the community to meet as an extension to Sundays.'

Edward mused on how it would indeed be possible to consider a project with this woman, one who had shown him the miracle of her burgeoning self; she was so much common sense dressed in simplicity and Grace:

'Of course! Do let us sit and consider,' she said.

4

'No ghosts for me,' thought Elizabeth as she avoided the usual routes to Pemberley's upper floors, this time taking smaller and less used staircases to her favourite wing. As she progressed, she observed architectural changes often presenting themselves in the hidden recesses of the stairwells, or their connecting passages, yet the ghostly never occurred to her, nor would she permit such an occurrence. As she slowly made her way, she thought, of those whose lives had been woven into the house before her. Always more aware than she let on, Elizabeth had often mused on the Tudors - only ever discussing the content of their reign with her father and in the quiet of the library. Judgement of them was, of course, suspended, the gloriousness of their courtly culture winning hands down over their darkly inhumane side.

Mrs Darcy stopped at a rather beautiful door just where the passage opened into an Elizabethan corridor, its beams silently revealing their age and allegiance. She still had to pinch herself when these moments presented themselves, why, she had not even begun to visit Pemberley's rooms, let alone find out what was within them. It was delicious to have been given *carte blanche* by Fitzwilliam, to explore, to 'go where you will in our home.'

The wondrous door of the room that had attracted her, its lintel and frame richly embellished by distinctive carving, gave of itself easily as she turned the handle, it was unlocked, despite the presence of a very large key on the outside. The chamber was dark and a little musty but behind the must a hint of sandalwood - enchanting. The large furniture was covered in dust sheets and the light seemed a long way off as she went further into the gloom. Proceeding to one of the casements, she deftly unlocked the latches and allowed in the first light that she felt the room had seen in a long time. The dust startled her somewhat, not by its presence but by its very absence – 'it must be age that I can smell' - she thought whilst stifling a need to run around the great furniture in the equally great room pulling off the cloths with some abandon. A daughter of a family living beneath the constant cloud of inadequacy, albeit in a very pleasant house with adequate rooms, insisted to herself that she had found a heaven in her Fitzwilliam and not just the man!

Further thought was banished as Elizabeth, recovering her steps, pulled off the cover on an exquisitely worked and quite long chest. As she bent to open the *kist*, silently acknowledging her sense of trespassing, a moth flew out from beneath it.

'Ah,' she thought, 'there is a gap in defences and the Lenten season has entered even into the inner and the undisturbed.'

Crossing to the other side of the chest to remove the caught-up cover, she realised that some initials looked to be almost erased but not a small star, sitting next to them. There was no lock on the casing and its lid gave way to her very quickly. As she opened it the smell of beeswax was both so beautiful and so strong that she drew breath and stepped back. It seemed as if the *inside* of the chest contained the smell and not the outside, until she could just see some stubs of candle beside something that was covered.

'O yes,' she thought, 'no tallow here, we are amongst the gods.'

As she focussed into the chest, she was immediately taken by the brilliance of its silken lining, a sumptuous fabric and one pressed carefully into every corner. Peeling back the cover over something well preserved, purple silk this time, she stopped with a jolt, feeling that she was intruding in someone's cherished place. Only the passion of it all drove her on to peep beneath the purple; her breath coming quickly and so loud that she felt almost dizzy, but she knew within a second, without any further unwrapping, that she was regarding the most beautiful musical instrument: a lute! Now dispensing with panic, she wanted to lift it out and inspect further but her greater senses, supported as they were by a love of the ancient music of William Byrd and some of the ayres and dances, held her in check: she was not going to go any further without her husband and she closed the *kist* quickly to fetch him.

5

*E*lizabeth's rapid flight down the staircase ended in a friendly collision with Mr Darcy as he was leaving the library:

'My dearest Elizabeth! What is it? You are quite flushed.'

The dearest's laughter rang out into the trumpet of the stairs as she clasped Darcy's hands with a child-like delight.

'I have been exploring and feel elated, I am astonished and a little foolish! I pray that you do not find me foolish.'

The great eyebrows raised a little as their owner absorbed the sight of this woman who had indubitably brought to him such joy. Certainly, Georgiana had brought much to him, had filled a big part of his life with the fealty of loving companionship but here was a full-blooded, full-bodied woman with whom he laughed and found love through the most inexplicable things – and each day a little more. Even in the split seconds like this one, Darcy bethought himself that what was called *love* was never, *could* never be discussed by men; too little tutored and too late, they floundered in the mire that was a shameful mixture of bravado and collected disdain. Amongst his far acquaintances there was only to be found the riposte of mockery, the female

being the explicit target of judgement and jackanapes. St James'
was full of astonishing debauchery and a seeming fearlessness for
its physical consequences in disease. He would sometimes have
not been a man, it was a desperate sojourn, there were too many
blind alleys and not enough said, or felt, or even thought. Set into
his own, finer context of riding out in Derbyshire, which he loved,
particularly the forest and always alone, the master of Pemberley
bethought himself of his masculine lot. Of course, there was
nothing to be complained of in his own past situation, the shoot
was not his delight, he was never equal to the way men regaled
themselves with laughter at it - an apparent addendum to the
killing - but it was to him neither demanding nor delightful.
Darcy was not squeamish, he put that aside, he had gone shooting
because it was there. Now, fishing he liked, it was peaceful, the
catch serendipitous. Were these distractions masculine? He
supposed so, the thought of Elizabeth at a shoot filled him with
discomposure, yet the ladies were beginning to attend, he had
seen them. Now there were simply other ways to feel and here
was one: within the conjugal. Astonishing. It had found him out!
Now, betimes, the benison of Elizabeth and the *privacy* they
shared outranked all other activities, in short, he kept to themselves and was glad.

The Darcy collision at the foot of the stairs promoted laughter
and that was the outward symbol of a great and inner pleasure.

'I want to know all! Tell me all, dearest, lovely Elizabeth.'

They sat at once on the stair tread, like the two children they
had become, an indulgence that Pemberley's master would not
have permitted unto himself until now. Pemberley's mistress sat
slowly recounting the morning's intrepid ascent to the chambers
of the east wing; her favouring of the Tudor atmosphere and
appearance of the inner windows and doorways; the great pleasure of being drawn to one chamber, in particular, its carvings on
the lintel attracting her - the acorn and the star. Then the fear lest
she were trespassing, her husband's solid invitation and bidding
to 'go where you will,' notwithstanding.

Darcy said nothing, dissembled at nothing, led by his wife to an inner room in his own house, he felt nothing but a boyish delight, one that had been lost this many a year.

6

The wind in the chimney sounded, whispered, roared and wailed and never found itself wanting. After the sea sounds of Barton Cottage, Elinor always found the noises comforting. In that time, when life had often seemed placed into a new version of storm, the likeness of wild water seemed so often enacted in the weather. Now Elinor regarded the man who, with his simple, yet serious absence of pretension, had joined her in their mutual release from an enforced misery: floundering was not in their character, yet both had felt greatly misheard and cut adrift from the heart of life itself, save for Elinor's mother and sisters. Neither had vilified the source of their discomfort yet had, ironically, shared one, namely that of Edward's sister Fanny, whose strong resistance to Elinor and equally strong censure of her brother coupled with an unpleasant influence upon her husband and mother, was consequential.

Edward was a real person to his wife, he was to her a complete answer to the unspoken requests of her being, he was, indeed, a panacea to all ills, yet her observance of a little obduracy, or, let us say, reticence, on his part, quelled the pedestal effect. Further, she was not inclined to be doting; nevertheless, each of this partnership knew where it had landed and was glad.

This said husband, also in a soft *reverie* across the table, mused on the period in his life in which he had felt like a cuckoo in the wrong nest. Always his father's son, a gentle, a kind a man as he, the memory came each day as a daily reminder of his absence until the advent of Elinor: leaning across towards her, he explained:

'My dear one, it has long saddened me that I could make no communion with my mother, only my father held that place for me – they were so utterly opposite – so that all the adjustment in the world could not bring mama to the place she should have held. I speak no ill here, it is simple observation, a matter of fact that our two worlds collide, they are too polar; I am not surprised that she has been recalcitrant to the *private* authority housed within Love, to which I adhere.'

Elinor still retained the sight of her mother-in-law stoutly leading the ladies out of the dining parlour in Berkeley Street at the time of their marriage. Of course, none of the Ferrars family showed any warmth about the wedding, although thankfully, softening was at last evident there, for the gift of some funding for Edward, and therefore his wife, came out of the blue and was gratefully and necessarily received.

'My dearest,' said Elinor, competing with the buffeting in the chimney, 'tell me what you imagine for your new hall.'

'No, no, no! you must tell me your proposal first,' the smile unique.

'Well,' continued Edward, 'I should like there to be a place where we could build on what we do on Sundays but in a more worldly context because the men must have a place in which they can be heard. I would not, could not be involved in politics, but only a fool can see that there is much afoot just now that is incendiary. I had not realised it until coming here, such were the closed circles in which I moved previously and then the visits to Mine-stock alerted me to what was already happening before my very nose. Where there is omission, let us say, on the part of the landowners, there will inevitably be resentment and, in these times, even calamity. I know that there are clergy helping a bit further north, but I will only listen, not act, I cannot take up a political stance: I was not entitled to my wealth through any other way than birth and in the last moments of my time in that family I was beginning to struggle with the oblivion in which it lived, in which it mocked those who kept it.'

As Elinor heard these words, her able and loving heart quickened by her husband's eloquence and passion, she leapt to her feet and encompassed his body with her smaller frame. Quickly the stairwell heard the sound of feet on the treads, the chamber windows closed against the wind and the silence of two bound together in parity.

7

$\mathcal{U}$pon the receipt of as much information as Elizabeth dared to give, Mr Darcy's eyes indicated that here was no mere conclusion before them but the start of an enquiry. Pemberley was filled with treasures and this was one of them; as a boy, its master had visited most of its corners but it was only as a man, as a wearer of the badge of full responsibility, that he became interested in his entail. Both he and Elizabeth could see that where they abided was indeed a house within a house, now a distinguished mansion but once a place of smaller proportions: the Tudor character, central to the demesne, was still exceeding visible two hundred years after its time.

'You will find a world within a world in Pemberley, dearest Elizabeth and you are welcome to examine its contents, as I have said, so very welcome. Indeed, there are corners of it which are crepuscular to me but I think that it appertains to the times in which I saw them: perhaps grief, as it is being digested, informs us through what we see and feel. Both Georgiana and our late mother loved to look through the house, but I left it alone. Entire apartments long shut, or chambers too full of a history which I could never accommodate, slowly evolved in my mind as I grew older. I say to you: please look, be a seeker in your own home; I keep you from nothing; you are my own one.'

As they reached the top of the first set of stairs, in sight of the acorns and the star, Darcy suddenly stopped and reached out for his wife's hand.

'You know, it bethinks me to ask if you might accompany me to Lambton and let us return to this chamber presently; there is more in it than you might imagine.'

Elizabeth, far from being taken aback by the sudden swerve in intention, took the beloved hand, pivoted herself to the right and, in this new and symbiotic dance led them both back in the direction from which they came. In the moves of this new-found intimacy the master of Pemberley took its mistress by the waist and kissed her with all the ardour that his once-inadequate words had framed – and that a long time, ago.

Mrs Darcy was thinking how very attractive it would be to sit together in the inn at Lambton once more, perhaps in a more withdrawn aspect, so that she might tickle her husband's knees, an action which would send many Derbyshire ladies into a spin, were they to have comprehension of it. Elizabeth loved to be playful and she had been bidden to a most interesting place for its practice: one obviously inconceivable in the days when they faced one another like two opponents on a chess board. Her absolute trust in the massively good fortune in finding that which she thought she had lost, never ceased to ignite in her the burgeoning of both gratitude and fun: in short, she could never have believed that such a pompous-looking man could now be her deepest friend and lover.

The small, private dining room at The Lamb and Flag had many times witnessed the subdued, even the dramatic but now overflowing laughter sounded from behind its closed doors and the waiting staff, who knew and loved their own Mr Darcy, were in approval, because complicit, in the great joy emanating from their kindly patron. Elizabeth and her husband liked nothing more than hiding at this inn and an occasional blush from the

former flew past the waiting ladies who had known their landlord from a boy, since when they had quietly suffered with him in
his losses. The fine physique of Darcy, his height, proportions and
handsomeness, had always charmed the ladies at the inn, yet so
generous were they in abeyance of all possessive tendencies, that
they took his wife to their ample bosoms as soon as she arrived.
So aware was The Lamb of the master of Pemberley's generosity
and justice over a long period of time, that it encompassed Elizabeth with goodwill – where once there was a master there was
now also a mistress.

Having made swift surveillance of the small but well-kept hall
in part of Lambton, the Darcys had walked to the inn to drink a
small cup and feel contented with their morning's work.

'Elizabeth! I do believe that you have brought me into trade!'

'Not at all Mr Darcy, I was simply led, on one of my many
walks in *our* beautiful fields, to see that it might be possible for
the good people whom your family has cared for through generations, to sell their own home produce, as well as yours. My bold-
ness does bethink me, however, pray forgive.'

'I do see that times are addressing new ideas, my love, I do not
wish, have never wished, to see my tenants in any way behind. I
think that you are voicing what I have been musing over for some
weeks now but did not see. There is nothing counter between us,
Elizabeth, in ways that you may never imagine, you have been a
revolution all of your own to me.'

The knees, so tempting beneath the table, received a delicious
tickle.

'Would you that we take this hall, free at this time, for your
good social purposes?'

Elizabeth showed her appreciation through the knees.

'I would, indeed, my husband,' the hands now firmly clasped
and back upon her lap, 'I would that you be so good as to help me
procure one or two pieces of furniture, for the actual sale of
goods. Yet I do say with a heartfelt respect, that if you retain any
doubts, then please to say 'no', I will not be offended, nor act with

any difference. I am sure, that with your assent, Georgiana might help me to start off this venture, this bringing together of the excesses of harvest of the Home Farm and any fare from the tenants' land pockets, that you have so graciously provided for generations. You know, I was oftentimes so full of my own pride at Longbourn, I would never have thought of this activity but as I walk around Pemberley and visit your people, I see how doing something like this would benefit them in the gracious manner which your family has shown for many years.'

Mr Darcy's face did not move a muscle, but he silently took Elizabeth's hands and placed them firmly upon his knee; each looked at the other and laughed and laughed, the moment only arrested by the arrival of the soup.

8

This was the Sunday in which the inhabitants from Rosings arrived; Elizabeth always thought that the name was ironic given the propensity for sharpness of its owner; perhaps the latter was the thorn rather than the petal - she was most emphatically not the scent. Lady Catherine de Bourgh had still not openly received Mrs Darcy as the woman whom her nephew married and she had continued to refer to her as *Miss Bennet*, even and especially as she sat at her table. Status was all to the elderly aunt, privilege and its many and convoluted components were natural to her and to avoid resisting this usurper, for that is what Elizabeth truly was to her, was a sort of blasphemy. It was not simply a matter of the reality of Darcy failing to marry Lady Catherine's daughter, it was that he had married someone so apparently ill met by the standards of his own magnificent position in society. Still thoroughly furious about the affront made to her own Maria, Lady Catherine would brook no bending and there had been many assaults upon Elizabeth's wellbeing and from the start of her marriage, yet she bore them without retaliation: she did not own a policy of revenge. Having been the outspoken one between herself and Jane, she had nevertheless learned much from her elder sister and saw that in her (now exquisite) circumstances there was *nothing* to be gained from answering back to a woman of little consequence to her. It was, however, important to realise that Fitzwilliam and Georgiana had no other family than Lady Catherine and Colonel Fitzwilliam, her nephew, thus, every effort was made to furnish her needs whilst the latter was a guest at Pemberley. In aspiring to good manners even under duress, dinner was always a matter of the provision of the best, even if conversation was trying:

'And what, pray, do you do with yourself Georgiana?' asked the dowager aunt as soon as the ritual of seating was complete.

'Well I, well, I study at the pianoforte,' said Miss Darcy brightly. 'You know, aunt, that my brother bought me a most beautiful instrument a while ago and it has been my intention to learn as much and as well as I can.'

'That is admirable, Georgiana, I always say that to be able to play well is of the *utmost* importance and indeed, significance.'

'And you, Miss Bennet, what do *you do*?'

Elizabeth paused and in her sometimes-diffident way, a form of defence when met with rudeness or impertinence, replied,

'Well, I try to remind myself of the enormous privilege it is to be married to a man of such noble spirit, I am sure that we could live together harmoniously in a cottage consisting of a single room.'

'I do concur, dear Elizabeth. I wholeheartedly concur,' said Darcy at once, a faint smile spreading across his lips.

At this Lady Catherine's jaw dropped, firstly that Elizabeth should suggest an opprobrium of Pemberley's glories and second that she should offer her husband's spirit, whatever that was, before the magnificence of the house's architecture; or its situation; or the vista from the lake, or indeed, the hills; or the excellence of the furniture or the way in which the gallery outshone any other within miles; or *anything comprehensible,* notwithstanding.

'Why, madam, you do put forward such a strange idea, are we to be talking of our *souls* soon, or the best ways in which to embellish them whilst upon this earth?' ejaculated Lady Catherine.

At this slight rift in proceedings, Georgiana put forward:

'O but aunt, let us tell you of our new project!'

'*PROJECT*,' boomed the aunt, '*new project*, what *do* you mean?'

Darcy looked at Elizabeth, who thought that she might faint, and Elizabeth looked back at him as she asserted:

'O, we, we thought we might decide to help the tenants a little more, that's all ma'am.'

Not even a shadow passed across the face of the mistress of Pemberley, something which said much of her maturity, as she addressed her words directly to the mistress of Rosings:

'More potatoes Lady Catherine?'

At the pronouncing of this sentence, one of the dowager's dogs burst through the door of the dining parlour with a half living rabbit in its mouth and all was at once diversion and fluster. Elizabeth accordingly bethought herself, 'Heaven be praised for intervention: I am satisfied.'

The week of the great divide passed quickly enough, all forbidden subjects well-managed, yet the stay was mercifully short lived, curtailed at a drop of the hat pretence of some matter to deal with at Rosings, and the party vanished - Elizabeth felt, because the dowager was clearly not winning in the bullying stakes. The effect of departure was delicious, each of the Darcys regarded the other as the barouche box rounded the corner from the great doors, gave polite bows as the farewells were bade and turned slowly on their heels to a certain relief and the resumption of their freedom.

'Well, that went considerably better than I had anticipated, *projects* notwithstanding,' said Darcy, smiling from ear to ear.

'I cannot imagine, sir, to what you allude!' said Elizabeth, a beautiful smile creeping across her face.

9

*L*ove had come again to both Colonel Christopher Brandon and the Reverend Edward Ferrars by surprise, taking them both unawares and which did not flow smoothly from the first but became a river at the turning of a bend. For the former, a military man of substance, honour and reputation, love was not a stranger, but it had devastated him before and left nothing in its path unscathed. Amongst his closest, he was a man who had never forgotten the power and majesty of the heart but after the finding and then the dying of the woman he loved, he had known no other. That is, until Marianne Dashwood, whom, before she even placed one beautiful finger upon his pianoforte, he was ready to love. It was only in assisting her, in extremis, as death hovered in the antechamber, that salvation occurred – his through heroism in finding her in the storm and hers through the realisation that the calibre of love is not always to be found in an immediate cataclysm of physical delight.

It was Marianne who came to greet her brother-in-law coming into Delaford Hall:

'Edward, we are *so favoured*!' - wrinkling her nose whilst looking down it, in the mode of his sister, Fanny; everyone laughed, her husband coming down the staircase so that the three were in a perfect triangle - all held hands out to one another with pleasure, they had journeyed some little way to find such commonality. It was interesting for Edward to see how comfortable Marianne had become; once a firebird, she had grown into a sleek and lovely wife, appreciating the Colonel and all that he provided for her whilst retaining her love of life and a jaunty sense of humour.

'O, Edward, it is so delightful to see you, I cannot imagine what I've done to deserve you as my brother and to live in such proximity to you and Elinor,' she said, warmly, 'do come in, we are awaiting your presence for a late breakfast, there are freshly laid eggs from the home farm.'

Edward was profoundly grateful for where he had landed and it never ceased to amaze him that things could have been so different in a loveless marriage to Lucy Steele. Here was a man with all that he really wanted in life. They quickly sat to table and he began.

'My friends and family, I have come to ask your counsel but first I thank you for the warmth of your welcome and for my second breakfast!'

'The welcome we extend is heartfelt, Edward,' proffered the Colonel with an inclination of the head which was most charming.

'I wanted to ask your direction about an endeavour close to the hearts of Elinor and me. We would like to find a small meeting place for an extension of what happens in the church on Sundays, but it will be for neither political nor religious purposes: in short, we strive to provide a place in which men may be heard. There is a full house each week and I am moved to try to create another place where hope may further dwell: it is as simple as that. I have long felt that every person should have someone who listens to them and the atmosphere about here at the moment, especially a bit further north and in the south west, is one of impatience boiling to something more, in terms of farm workers' pay and conditions. It is not that there is any question about men being patently unable to take home enough recompense for the labour they provide, any one can see that, if he cares to look. Such a place will not be political, but I have felt this unrest circulating for some time and it must be heard in loving quarters before it catches fire and burns to pressing consequences.'

This was the inspiration of the message given out by Edward to his lately acquired family and such the comprehension of his brother-in-law, a commander of many men and witness to a multitude of sometimes terrible sights, that Edward's request fell straight into the open hands of possibility. He could see this happening as he spoke and was indeed glad. The words exchanged and the manner in which they were harvested made a great gesture out of harmony with the spirit of the speakers' times: the three made a small, unprovocative history, yet one which contributed to a greater whole with consequences to come.

'If you will be so good as to leave your plan with us, Edward, we shall do our very best to find accommodation for it; I, for one, am very much in agreement with your assessment of the times, the idea of a place in which to be heard seems splendid.'

At this all rose and with a mutual affection that comes from journeying together along bumps in the road. Edward was bid farewell with felicitations to Elinor and as he left, he bethought himself how much life had changed and how very much such change was to be welcomed.

*T*he Pastor walked back from the Hall considering every good morsel of delight that had come from his visit there. He loved Marianne as his sister and could see, from the luxuriance of her skin and hair, that she was deeply cared for. He breathed in the beauty of the morning and the intense green of everything in this forested countryside that ran down to the sea. As he walked to the Parsonage, their more than ample home, his heart was full. The heat of the day had not yet arrived and the leaves were like balm to a man come through; it did not obtain that he and Elinor lived in a smaller demesne than the Brandons, the fact that they were here at all was due to the kindness of his brother-in-law: this was a hard fact. There was never any counting of possessions nor of status for Edward Ferrars, a cynic would say that his privileged upbringing had neither required it, nor spawned it but he had long felt lonely in a vast mansion and knowing that he was the *heir apparent* to it had never saved him from either crippling melancholy or loneliness.

Elinor was sitting pondering on life's difficulties for the labouring man. Not given to lengthy abstraction, unlike her husband she was, nevertheless, thinking of the privilege of her situation and the happiness of 'the quiet country parish' that had fallen upon them. Thinking of her own life with Edward, their relative proximity to her mother and Margaret and now the wonder of having Marianne next door, she perused the pleasure that the hatching of these eggs had created for them all. There was not one part of Elinor that was mean or miserable: she was naturally optimistic, practical and fair; she soon knew in life that among its imponderables was the ridiculousness of 'wishing for the moon'. She never set her store on any one thing, or anyone; even when she knew that she was falling in love with Edward she left to him the development of what would occur: a blessing in the circumstances since he had been engaged, albeit unhappily, to Lucy Steele. No! things and persons came of their own volition into her garden, or they did not come at all, there was no dreadful conniving.

The young Mrs Ferrars did not espouse all that she knew of her husband's beliefs, but she had eyes and could see what poverty could be and that it was alive all around them in the English countryside. Edward saw first what was happening; in his own childhood there had been fun, the fealty of at least one parent being aware of his needs and through that a sort of justice within the family, yet here, here was the spectre of hunger and a lack of justice by its very presence, because the fathers of the children who looked so ill worked hard and long and were paid inadequately. Edward was coming to a watershed in his life as he settled into a parish of both the rich and the desperately poor: he was the fulcrum. He was not interested in any legalism in his church community, what happened there was to be about Love, about circulating what could be *made available* and to facilitate the traffic in between. He had not been truly out in the cold for long but the *threat* of it and the constant, gypsy-like existence made to avoid his family of critics was never very nourishing, on the contrary - he was not a man who weighed his life in what was fashionably known as *the diverting*. Thus, as the Reverend Ferrars walked home, he was much inspired and not a little excited by the prospect of support for his small venture.

*N*o sooner had the sound of coach wheels of Lady de Bourgh's barouche disappeared from the drive, the square shoulders of the rear coachman perfectly aligned with his coach, than Elizabeth excused herself with a shy wink and a short curtsy to Darcy and ran upstairs. Her husband's quizzical expression spoke volumes. 'Back to her lute,' he thought, with the genuine pleasure of a good heart. Meanwhile, Elizabeth was anticipating a return to her *moutons* and the unbridled joy of discovery in her own home. Ever the favourite of her bookish father, she loved to read, so these new finds in the upper floors of Pemberley ignited within her a million fires of inquisitive and historical passion.

The Darcy outing to Lambton concerning the new hall and the subsequent occupation of Mr Darcy with his steward had postponed discussion of the lute, but nothing hung upon that head, Elizabeth had eyes too, did she not? The room was just as it was, the great key - where on earth was such a key procured? – in the keyhole on the outside of the door where she had left it.

The darkness this very morning was suffused with shards of light coming through the heavy curtains, she had not pulled the vast gauze panels back as she left. The effect of these light shafts was dazzling, it seemed as if the whole room were dancing with poniards of light beams: an astonishing sight and one which she only much later felt as a warning to be careful with what she had found. The routine of discovery began in earnest– this time she was faster at it – and she soon sat before the chest slowly considering its opening.

Lifting the long lid with two hands and not a little care, she came at once to the sensuousness of velvet. 'If owners of things had an atmosphere,' she thought to herself, 'here would be his.' Part of her already ignited sense of the lagging behind of women silently reported that the owner of this beautiful instrument was a man. With the same silence, Miss Bennet moved her hands back to the lid, still retaining its beeswax patina and thus a little of its delicious scent.

'My heavens,' she thought, 'this is turning out to be a most particular experience.'

Whilst holding the wood mid-air, she noticed for the first time a lock, quite small for a long *kist* and again, the presence of initials which were unintelligible.

'Well,' she mused, 'who was this man and why is his lute here?'

Before she could continue any further, her beautiful *reverie* was disturbed by a mighty clanging of the dinner gong downstairs in the hall, a strangely disconcerting sound since it was but ten in the morning. Quickly she put down the lid, slid the white sheeting back onto the chest and ran from the room, leaving only the sunlight behind to witness the dream. As Elizabeth approached the start of the first landing she was met by the figure of her husband, running up the staircase two by two.

'Elizabeth, please come quickly, it is an emergency because your sweetheart pointer has fallen into the lake and seems trapped by weeds.'

Pemberley's mistress paled significantly at these words and her heart raced with her more than capable legs, for this was Bess, her dearest dog.

Gathering up servants, whose heads had popped out from everywhere at the sound of the gong, the whole house seemed bound for the lake. Darcy's long legs took up speed as he went and he was soon at the water's edge; as he arrived he could see that the alarm was real, firstly, that the dog was indeed trapped and secondly that she was the mistress' favourite. Before there was any time for reflection a jacket and boots were removed and Pemberley's master was about to wade into the shallows when Joshua, the youngest stable lad, beat him to it and was fighting to free the struggling creature. Cheered from the side and soon assisted by the arrival of a fire ladder, one weighted by some of the bigger coachmen to provide Joshua with some leverage, progress was rapid. Elizabeth was pale and breathless in this, a magnificent demonstration of the esteem in which she was held by the staff of the great house, now her community. Surviving for so long beleaguered by a constancy of lack; the want of money; the want of status; the want of connections; even the want of a husband; Elizabeth was overwhelmed by the sheer living kindness of her Derbyshire *family*. All of these people, led by her once seen-as arrogant, separate and aloof husband, were come together for her: the fact that Mr Darcy, now in the water up to his knees and about to collect a very green and not a little frightened hound, added to the intensity of the moment. Bess, whose enormous pleasure at being rescued by her master, was so great that she had accordingly deposited water weed, not only over his leggings and coat, but also in sweeping arcs of green all over his face.

In a matter of moments, a small roar went up for the success of the operation and all was dear and bright. Darcy thanked everyone profusely and his wife simply wept and nodded. No sooner had the servants resumed their posts and the door to the small morning room shut, than the two fell into each other's arms, Elizabeth laughing and crying at the same time, for not only had her sweet dog been saved but she had witnessed the very funny sight of her husband wading up to his knees in green, to save her. How they both laughed as they sat on the leather fenders and regarded one another: she still pale and he become a green man! How much, Elizabeth thought, would her husband's erstwhile dissenters say, could they but see him now. As they both mounted the staircase to change their appearance, Darcy was reminded of Robert, Earl of Leycester, being known – amongst other things - for the utter discipline in which he kept his dogs. Chuckling at the preposterousness of a Dudley dog falling into the water at Kenilworth, he realised that even he, his long-term hero, would have indubitably waded out in the green water for the woman he loved.

Having repaired their dress and spent the day in various domestic pursuits, the Darcys sat down to dinner, the servants amicably dismissed for the evening. They chose, unusually, to sit in the long dining hall, a very grand setting, which Elizabeth had filled with as many candles as housekeeping and a good conscience would allow. She had not returned to the upper floor of the east wing but there was perfect adequacy in the drawn gauzes, and she would go up again tomorrow. Sitting next to one another at the head of the long table, the couple would have provided another comical sight for their dissenting neighbours, the top and bottom being usually attended by the master and mistress separately. There could be no separation on this night, this beautiful evening of early summer, when all was both delicious and well.

As she sat to dinner, gratitude poured from Pemberley's mistress, for her home; the rescue of little Bess; for the burgeoning of her friendship with Georgiana and, of course, for Fitzwilliam Cadogan Darcy himself: she knew where all of this came from and she did not want to issue scant praise therein.

'Mr Darcy,' she began, as was the custom, only to correct herself, 'my love, shall you please furnish me with some comprehension of your family's heritage here?'

The joy in Elizabeth's face, perfectly lit by candlelight, said all – her real interest in life, in the place in which she found herself now and its history - all those days sitting with her father were not wasted.

'I would like to tell you about a part of my family who lived in this house in the sixteenth century, their name is often found hidden in the folds of pages, yet it is, nevertheless, most real. Before we look at the past however, I would like to invite you, and indeed, your sister and Charles, to accompany me on a special excursion. I have been pondering on the idea of taking you to visit some most dear friends in the deepest of Cornwall. I know that you might attest and rightly so, that it is a good way away from here, but you will remember that Sir Richard and Lady Maria Tremayne were unable to attend at our wedding, thus, it seemed to me a perfectly lovely idea for us to go together to see them and to ask the dear Bingleys as our guests. I will, of course, ask the Cornish folk if we may bring our family but they are so generous, so open and kind that I am sure that they will not mind. What do you say my dearest?'

In a startled moment, Elizabeth found herself near to tears, so unused had she been to sweeps of the hand which offered small parts of heaven, that the idea of spending time with her husband, with her beloved Jane and Mr Bingley, was beyond comprehension.

'Old habits die hard,' she bethought herself and spoke aloud their equivalent:

'It is with profound joy that I accept your wondrous invitation and ask myself whatever I have done to deserve such treatment. You are quite miraculous, Mr Darcy!'

'Perfect! I will begin to plan a special itinerary and alert your sister and Charles to it, with an invitation for their accompaniment. It is also a delight for me you know, to prepare something of this nature, the like of which I have been a stranger to all these years. Pray, let me surprise you my dearest, lovely Elizabeth!' He held out both hands to her as she replied:

'I entreat you, sir, I am filled with joy at the prospect!'

12

The sound of boots on the gravel woke Elinor's *reverie* which soon coincided with her husband's arrival at the table; he was fresh from the green of summer and aglow with enthusiasm for the possibility of his conjecture being made real. Edward had flown into the kitchen of Delaford Rectory to a loving and appreciative wife, the walk from the hall took only minutes but was long enough for all sorts of thoughts to take root.

'How did you fare my dear one?'

'Well, thank you,' said Edward. 'We all sat together, the three of us and both the Colonel and Marianne spoke very warmly about our idea. You know, I feel keenly the need to provide a place where the men can speak in safety. I know that the sermons on Sundays – isn't *sermon* an awkward word? – raise morale but at the end of the day, if there isn't enough money to live on, then there isn't enough money to live on.'

Elinor decided to move around the other side of the table, nearer to her heart.

'I say this to you privately, my dear wife, I am not an ignorant man and have lived for too long in a family bereft of any form of compassion, or, indeed, any form of *consideration* for those who create the wherewithal by which they live. It was always a matter of historical fact that the *laird* set the tithe and the tithe remained, no matter what. I know these are harsh words and that there is speculation now and more speculation still but at the end of yet another day, the miners pay for the flow of the mine owner's life! Isn't that a grim reality? I am not sure that I know what to do with it. I do not wish to be the founder of any movements or break any laws but my late father's heart tells me to provide a place where ills may be heard and that is what I seek to do. You know, Elinor, the very *minute* that my father died, all the good-will payments stopped. Harvest, Christmas, Easter, all STOPPED. And it was *my mother who stopped them*. Can you imagine that all through his life he gave extra benefits for his people and then when he was dead the payments were dead too – I found it then and I find it now, completely nonsensical. It is no good going about in a *barouche* in the greatest of fancy and knowing this Person and that Person, when it is all balanced upon the backs of men who can now no longer feed themselves. It is simply time to redress the balance before it becomes impossible to do so.'

Elinor sat motionless but alert through all that Edward told her; she was no stranger to straitened circumstances and the laws of society which cut out all but the eldest male in family entail; she had always thought that it was hardly conducive to good rela-tionships but never seen this side from that of the eldest son who was, unusually, cut off from his legal rights. It sometimes seemed extraordinary to her that she had a lovely house, albeit someone else's house and a home within it of her own: the rapid flight from Norland to Barton Cottage, with no means of transport and initially no known community, was not yet fled from her bones. She got up abruptly and stood above her husband, hugging his head, strongly espousing the content of what he had spoken with his quiet passion. Marianne had at first criticised Edward for this quietude, seeing it as an apparent lack, yet here was passion alive, strong and consequential, if not the flamboyant variety for which her sister had then wished.

'I am in full accord, Edward, there is no need for an explosion,

it is not in our way of doing things, but the men need their grievances to be heard. We must tread a careful line though, must we
not? What do the Brandons say?'

'They applaud the idea in principle and will talk to each other,
then let us know. I simply want to bring people together, why! I
keep our hens in better conditions than many here who eke out a
poor living – and where should we be without them? No! there
must be a better way.'

13

*N*o sooner had the small group taken tea at *The Lion* and rested awhile, than it was time to go out into the town to the recital. Truro lay in a beautiful valley out of which flowed the river Kenwyn; despite some ancient buildings, much of the architecture was newly constructed: Truro was a Regency town. This latter gave the place a crisp attention, especially with the sound of the sea gulls and a breeze often coming from the nearby coasts. The Red Lion sat at the bottom of Lemon Street, facing up this hill lined from top to bottom with Georgian houses, some of which were prestigious. The hill was beautiful, the houses built with style in an echo of Bath, its not-too-distant neighbour and *The Lion* gave onto a most attractive vista. The summer light fell softly on the beauty of Lemon Street's construction, its sharply rising approach from the Inn enhancing its atmosphere of elegance and grace: Darcy particularly liked this small treasure lying at the end of England.

The reception awaiting the Bingley-Darcy contingent was to be held in the Assembly Rooms, the quietly imposing façade of which welcomed the friends on this lovely summer's evening in June. As both Elizabeth and Jane were in a complete dream of anticipation, pleasure given through all that surrounded them in a time that all newly married may remember well, the group walked as one into the Rooms, which lay just at the end of the Red Lion's stabling. The world they inhabited was in the throes of much growth and the current of its higher society was palpable in the very fabric of the vestibule in which the visitors found themselves. Beautifully decked with welcoming pedestals of Cornish flowers and a circular marquetry table of exquisite design, the floral arrangements complemented the wall decoration which would have been at home in London. The party was processing to its seats when Mr Darcy, normally of a clear and decisive step, suddenly made a sharp turn to the left, an action which both confused and startled the group's forward motion. There, however, standing in front of Darcy, not yet quite taken into the Hall, was a face they all knew well: Colonel Fitzwilliam! How they all whooped for joy at seeing their old friend again and the serendipitous nature of the meeting. All agreed at once to return at the end of proceedings, to the very place in which serendipity had occurred.

What a transcendence of earth's plane was the sheer delight of that evening – the choice and equilibrium of the pieces so well placed; the perfection of the cadences and the party's inclusion in comprehending the truthfulness of them and then a sort of mesmeric effect of wonder at finding themselves all together in a place of beauty. Then to meet up with an old friend who knew their history, who knew of what had passed before in life's sometimes turbulent winds! The master of Pemberley's face was filled with the delight in which he found himself - and his wife came not far behind him.

'Colonel Fitzwilliam!' shouted the two sisters rushing upon their friend with as much *gusto* as the occasion would permit. 'We are utterly delighted to find you here!' said Elizabeth. 'Whom are you visiting, pray tell?'

Further hand-shakings and whoops followed amidst the amusement of the now onlooking crowd.

'Why Fitzwilliam, you have a fine gift for appearing in the most unexpected places,' said Darcy, all smiles.

'I am truly delighted to see you,' said the Colonel, further aglow with merriment.

'But come, how are you here, most esteemed cousin? You have not given us intelligence of the details of your visit!'

'My dear friends, since I no longer have the delightful charge of Georgiana - upon whose very situation you must now inform me – I have more leisure to indulge my oft-times constrained desire to travel for pleasure. I am in the area for a week, staying in Falmouth with no more to do, officially, than to absorb the history of a place to which was carried the news of the success at Trafalgar, but the death of beloved Lord Nelson. I am an army man, through and through but could not contain my wish to come here to pay homage to my hero. There you are! a man's regard, nay, *love* for a fellow servant of the people.'

14

This time the Brandons came to the Rectory. The warm summer was proceeding with ease and grace, the weather a little held back, rendering the blossom its perpetuation – a delight for all as they walked in the garden. Both couples were animated in discussion and appreciation of the watershed in their lives into which they had surprisingly arrived.

Edward's Orders completed; he was a confident young Rector surrounded by so much simple abundance that the two facets, bound by his infectious warmth in a kind and loving nature, drew in many, many people. Since his ordination, his name was quietly spoken of roundabout as a sincere man of good heart who proclaimed his beliefs in his doings. The new pastor believed that only Love mattered and that this mighty power was all inclusive in its ability to encompass and supersede all rules. This Love was palpable and it was not a soft touch, instilling, as it did, so much respect in its owners and wearers that there could be no breaking of the heart's rules, impregnated by the state of loving as they were.

Expansion without its requisite balance was already besmirching many, when agriculture was getting bigger, braver and its masters lacking in the third 'b' – benevolence. Edward found the most terrible arrogance amongst some of what was his own landed class, out of which he could not forget, he had come. As machinery and its intrinsic power reared up to dissolve some of the inconveniences of needing to house, care for and organize a human workforce, it was becoming evident that much (and many) fell through the net of even the scrapings of conscience within the land lording communities.

Had Edward less moral awareness himself, he might have thought the motion of the new mechanical wave wholly propitious. He had heard much from friends in Cornwall, tales concerning the continued ills of working in the tin mines. He knew that such news was not exaggerated and that the certainty of more machines, fewer men, was simply a fact.

Such a fact also rubbed hard upon Christopher Brandon, a heroic man known and loved by his men and who carried them with him, often to their terrible and violent deaths. The leadership that the Colonel knew and made real, for the men and for himself, was what Edward meant by the paradigm of Love and he said so to his brother-in-law and the small collective in Delaford Rectory Garden that summer's eve.

'Of course,' Brandon began, 'there is no doubt that sufficiency in the production of food will replace the insufficient but there must be no lack in housing and helping those who struggle - as the land's best army they must live reasonable lives. I have no sympathy for those who merely pocket – it is parasitic from where I stand - and there can be no praise for raking up the takings to the greater impoverishment of those who create them.'

Despite years spent as the darling of local society, Brandon, whilst appreciating the gift of social acceptance, and the hard-won pleasure of his home, was still an army man. He had seen enough suffering in his life to fill the pockets of so many social dandies, even *dilettantes*, who remained alarmingly oblivious to social division and the recency of the guillotine. No! this was not the time for complacency.

As they came together, four people somewhat buffeted by

life's rougher winds, they all recognised the sheer delight of this tenure - even in discussion of a serious nature, even in debate now about 'Edward's sounding room', the members of this *quadvirate* were appreciative of what they shared. Even the youthful Marianne was not exempt, for her wrangle with death had given her a remove from the frequent pleasure-orientations of a youthful young lady.

Brandon was the first to bring up the subject of the meeting place; Edward had earlier explained that he felt it necessary to accommodate those who needed to air their views, to release pent-up feelings about hardship or treatment from their masters. Both men were acutely aware of the real possibility of friction and neither was in want of a political career nor its potential dangers. The Colonel began:

'Edward, Elinor, we have thought long and hard about finding a place for you to extend your Sunday discussions and feel that it is possible for you to use a small barn here behind the counting room. It is not a large room – perhaps fifty persons at the most - but that might be adequate for you. The overseeing of cleaning would help me, there are old benches in there and otherwise straw bales. What do you think?'

Edward was quickly and clearly delighted and Elinor with him and the look between them said 'we are in this together!' The Colonel had every comprehension of what was intended in the mind of his new rector and was not afeared that he was creating the provision of some tinderbox of political intrigue in his back yard.

It was therefore agreed that the room would be prepared over the next week or so and that, mindful of numbers, a place of relative safety would be given to help restore unquiet minds. As the four sat together at table, the beauty of the surroundings was mirrored in that of two contented new wives and mirrored again by the balm of an English summer's eve. Dining in country abundance: new potatoes, fresh asparagus and a fowl, all from the glebe in which they abided, the friends toasted friendship, love and the prospect of a new member of their party – for Elinor had surprised everyone, including her husband, with news of the arrival of a little Ferrars later in the year. Edward smiled - like a man who already knew the secret.

Leaving late, the moon's span across the garden being wide, Colonel Brandon turned in radiance at his own good fortune and left a parting word:

'Dearest family, for we are family now, I cannot thank you enough for what we share and what we are to one another: I sometimes cannot believe we are all here together!'

15

*T*he small party, now wholly replete with friendship, fellowship and food returned forthwith to The Lion. Colonel Fitzwilliam ambled along Boscawen Street with them, the sun not even setting yet, well after ten o'clock, and then ascended Lemon Street to his lodgings. All agreed to meet on the morrow, perhaps to peruse the town but also to ascertain where their mutual interests would carry them next. Farewells were said and a commitment made for the hour after breakfast.

The group of four was happily silent as it turned lightly into the Inn. The Quay could still be heard, lit and busy. Two years ago, no one in the party could have imagined the profound delight taken in each other in the trip from Pemberley and good accommodation superintendent upon them along the way. Now came this evening of sheer and unexpected delight!

'My cup is indeed brimming over,' said Elizabeth, smiling, a *certainly for my husband* smile.

'Mine also,' a sisterly acknowledgement of the same proportion came from Jane.

The group wheeled into The Red Lion, bade each other a warm good night and all retired – the clock chiming eleven, the last sound they all heard.

The morning came round with the alacrity of summertime, the sunshine speeding into the Darcys' chamber as they drew the blinds and greeted the hill of Lemon Street. There could be no complaint of such an early -bird dawn, the gulls on the Quay already shouting for the catch. The church clock did, however, proclaim five and a half hours, a little early to be moving about. A leisurely start was thus only punctuated by Elizabeth's sincere wish to visit the town before the roads became full of carts and gigs and even the odd barouche, for today was market day on Lemon Quay. The market presence always drew many to Truro – for the purchase of country delights as well as necessities and for the purchase of bigger fish than to be found on the Quay – for Cornwall's landed gentry came into town to trade in shares, to talk of new matters to be comprehended of dealings in more than tin mines and the content of local estates.

Despite the buoyant daily round of Truro port, it had not yet become prolific in human trading as its closer neighbour Falmouth and the more distant Bristol – the latter being in recent danger as much from Wilberforce's huge work to snuff out the flame of human trafficking, as the usual presence of extreme poverty.

Elizabeth and Jane were not ignorant of Wilberforce since he was known to them, incredibly, through Aunt Philips whose net cast wide. There could be no greater sense of sadness for these country girls than to consider the lot of such wounded mortals as slaves. Elizabeth had long known about this latter through so many private interlocutions with her father. She reflected upon the portrait of herself she had painted to Lady Catherine, for despite her mother's social incompetence, Lydia's deeply inappropriate behaviour, the total oblivion exhibited by Kitty in public at the pianoforte and Mr Bennet's lack of will to the correction of all three, the Bennet household was neither unintelligent, nor without curiosity.

Unwilling to allow his wife to set out alone, Darcy availed

himself of more than adequate facilities and they both went into the now-active town. After the awakening of his previously sleeping heart to Elizabeth, Darcy was no longer in receipt of quite such a bank of snobbery. Proceeding from a small phaeton loaned from the inn, they at once became participants in the busy hub of activity by the waterside.

Everywhere was a-bustle! The small lanes were laden with porters and box carriers and horses were being led away as the contents of their carts were disgorged. The start of brisk trade was evident as the local dwellers, living in small regiments of houses giving off Lemon Street, came out to buy for their mistresses.

As the Darcys approached the Quay, the cacophony of sound letting up a little, there stood two fine ships embarking: one of them, *Lady of the East Indies*, provided enormous delight to Elizabeth when she bethought from whence it came. Darcy, no stranger to the London docks, which fascinated him, also observed the vessels with delight.

Here, in Truro, the combination of early morning sunshine, the bustle of the men unloading their cargo, the aroma of ship's breakfast and the collective incantation of (enormous) seagulls, was a painting to be relished and remembered. All of this was clearly visible from the little phaeton, which whipped about with speed, weaving through both the clatter and not a little detritus.

After a good repast, the ladies both professed the desire to visit the shop adjacent to the Apothecary at the bottom of Lemon Street, in Boscawen Street, which abutted their inn. Persuasion was sought and granted by the two husbands, alert for the correct procedures in a strange town – and since the shop was in sight of The Lion, all was well. A promise was made to be swift enough since the party had agreed that after breakfast and with Colonel Fitzwilliam to accompany them, they would all to Falmouth.

'Such an expedition could perhaps prove valuable to us,' Darcy had put forward, 'since we would then be on the appropriate 'leg' of this peninsula from which to continue.'

For the jewel in the crown for Fitzwilliam Darcy, was the visit to his old friends at Tamara, a house tucked away in a creek of the Carrick Roads, which were, in fact, *sea roads* of the river Fal and to which they were all invited.

16

*T*he road to Falmouth was easy, straight up to the top of Lemon Street and straight on. Straight, all straight. Passing through villages that must have been there since the Domesday Book, the small party was excited to be on its way again, even if the carriage were a little compact with the addition of Colonel Fitzwilliam.

'It is exquisite, my husband, the prospect of the land here, a matter of rejoicing,' said Elizabeth, musing at the countryside going by. 'How fine the woods are, and many still covered in the flowers of late Spring – I love the wild garlic,' she continued.

'I also rejoice, my wife, you know I planned this diversion because I have long known and loved the beauty of these ancient places.'

Darcy was thinking of his long years alone, years in which it was simply easier to distance himself from almost everyone; it had not occurred to him until now that he had lived a life behind a mask, not the kind that he saw and abhorred in St James', but it was, nevertheless, the same sort of dissembling.

Colonel Fitzwilliam was all accord and still repeating his appreciation and delight at their falling into one another in the left-hand foot of England.

'I am sure that you will be delighted in Falmouth,' he said, 'I would show you the Packet, its historical significance being so dear to me but let us first to Mr de Wynn's where I lodge – it has the finest cake, and coffee right off the ships!'

Darcy sat in such pleasure that he hoped that he did not look ridiculous; he had lost almost all the sedateness of his former days, retaining only his natural air of dignity. He reflected that this version of himself bore little resemblance to the man of old.

The road suddenly dipped and fell toward the Fal estuary and water could again be seen as they traversed a small bridge on the way into the town. The sea, or the river, or the sea-river could be seen from almost everywhere in the vicinity, and for the party, so used to being inland, this was a diverting matter. The views of the river's tributaries provoked great excitement, not only because of the sheer beauty that emanated from them but because of what Elizabeth called *'mes escaliers de terre et mer'* by which she meant the steps of land going down to the water below - an idea which had a truly seductive effect on her that bore not one jot of reason in its being. There was something about Cornwall; first her feelings on entering The Old Jamaica, then the pool on Bodmin moor and then the wonders of Truro Quay and now the fall of the land to the river: it all made her shiver in the happiest way.

'If I were a smuggler,' she said, 'I would hide here! Why! there is room enough to hide a great galleon in the waters below.'

All laughed at the idea of their sister as a buccaneer whilst she herself did *not* find the concept amusing at all but rather, very real.

The carriage came slowly down into the town and at once into Church Street and the celebrated windows of de Wynn's, the gulls were wheeling as they came into the inn yard. Protocol thrown to the same winds that carried the big sea birds, the ensemble tumbled out of their carriage with pleasure as yet another beautiful place unfolded before them.

Colonel Fitzwilliam was heartily welcomed back and the

luggage taken care of by the willing hands of Darcy's own men. Both Elizabeth and her sister felt that they would burst with the luxury of it all, the greatest of which was the continued presence of their two husbands and the fact that they now had the fillip of an old friend.

'Well, Fitzwilliam,' said the other Fitzwilliam, 'we are now in your capable hands, pray, show us the way.'

So glad were the staff of de Wynn's to see their friend again, that they broke ranks and showed their appreciation for the return of the Colonel and now his friends, with applause. Soon the small party was comfortable again and seated before hot coffee - now a firm favourite of the mistress of Pemberley. They had all loved the Red Lion but now a new delight: Sally Lunns at the seaside! The warmth of the welcome; the smell of the salty sea air and the madding of the gulls all contributed to the favourite that was this Falmouth hotel. The fact that their friend, the Colonel, had as his hero one of the world's most beloved Admirals only contributed to the *frisson* that was the town! a sea dish that was piquant to them all and for different reasons. The ladies requested leave for the shortest of walks alone, as guided by Mrs de Wynn and it was agreed that they would return by two of the clock, when the menfolk would leave to regard the famous Packet.

The sisters were so taken with Falmouth's charm and its small streets, so many dotted with handsome and whimsical figure-heads of famous ships, that their heads felt quite turned with the delight of it all. Such pretty ideas only gained progeny, not least about beloved Lord Nelson and there was much talk still circulated about his last words to Lady Hamilton, spoken at his death. Whilst being very *proper*, both Elizabeth, and especially Jane, quietly continued to sympathise with the Lady Emma abandoned, with their beloved daughter Horatia, to an entirely uncaring English populace who could only judge and sneer, when the very opposite had been promised to the Admiral as he died. No! the sisters were too bound to the remarkable effects of love to embark upon a critique of so noble a man who once so dearly loved a woman…

'I bethink me in a dream, my dear Jane,' offered Mrs Darcy.

'I too, my dear sister. How many times did we sigh at Long-bourn, accepting our increasingly gloomy lot yet always believing, beneath our very skin, that we would come through the befoulments waiting to be cast upon us by those encased only in wealth and prejudice. O! those long times lived in the absence of love and, dare I say, *comprehension*, of our estate.'

'Or *lack of it*!' added Elizabeth. 'E'en in those seemingly luckless times, I believe that we grasped what it meant to love and to be within the boundlessness of it. Jane, we are in some sort of Utopia these last days and no one is here to explain it to us, not even our father: but we *mark it*, my dearest sister, we mark it.'

'Yes! I think that all that we really felt was doing its best not to fade within us. When I did not see Mr Bingley in London, that time, my heart could not truly believe that he had vanished from my life: otherwise, all that had passed between us would have simply been untrue – and it was not. Yet, the only way that I could survive his disappearance was to sweep over what had happened and bethink myself that there was some sort of explanation.'

'My Jane, you were so very courageous. Pray, what happens to our poor hearts when thrown into a pit, if the person whom we love either does not inform us of what is happening or just vanishes? It is surely like a death, the grief that follows, only without a funeral, or proper means of helping the wound to the heart to close.'

A return to *The Wynn* arrested all further conversation and created a succinct rush of the limbs as it was nearly two of the clock; mounting the stairs with alacrity the two separated to the rooms they shared with their husbands. As Elizabeth entered, a small red packet lying on the bed at once caught her eye and Darcy, alerted by her unusually noisy entrance came round the corner of the dressing room to meet her.

'Whate'er is here dear husband?' she proclaimed, straight 'way.

'Open and see,' said the twinkling eyes and she was not missing those long legs.

Elizabeth Bennet Darcy opened the little package with tender care; her eyes sending puzzled information to her brain – for there was, in the red, something made of soft purple silk and upon which were printed small, creamy coloured stars. Her eyes asked the question.

'Take it out, take it out!' said the master.

'*Upon my word*, it is so very lovely!' said the delighted mistress.

Lifting the silk from its red envelope, Elizabeth saw that it was a small scarf and as she put it to her throat, she could see that its shape was a beautifully made triangle.

'Why! I think that you have stolen this from one of the ships!' she said.

Another look between husband and wife.

'I just thought that it was perfect for my *pirate*.'

17

𝒩o sooner had the Sunday service come to an end than an extended group of men could be seen gathered in front of the church porch.

'Father Edward!' exclaimed Ned Rust, a large man and so well-proportioned it was as if he had been made bigger than the usual size but to a very straight pattern. Edward found it amusing that 'his men' as he termed them, called him 'Father' since he was years younger than they and was not under the rule of the Pope.

'Father Edward, we would speak with you.' Edward came forward.

'We are heartened to hear that we can come to meet in your barn and we wanted to tell you that there will be no trouble.'

'Thank you, Ned,' said the pastor.

'You can come on Wednesday evening at seven, if you would, all together. You know where to go.'

Deferent bobs of the head fell in a small wave, Ned Rust's at the top, his appropriately coloured hair at its peak.

Wednesday came around quickly.

The Colonel's barn room was long but narrow, extant benches had been placed by Edward along the front, then some straw bales behind and the rest was 'let us see who comes'.

It was the second week in June, so harvest had not yet begun but Ned, clearly the leader, had wanted at least one meet before the evenings were taken in working, he stood up.

The men gathered were about fifty in number, more than came regularly to the Magdalene church but these latter attendees had brought friends. Edward, already standing, spoke first:

'Gentlemen, you are most welcome here. You know my heart-felt position - this place cannot be political in the strongest sense of the word, but you may get off your chest what ails you so heavily.' At this a low 'aye' sounded out.

The sun was still shining strongly and the group of men before him, some still very young, touched Edward's heart deeply. His own youth, even curtailed as it was by the death of his father, had none of this cut-throat anguish, so clear in the faces of the men before him. Many had lodgings with other labourers, all worked in the fields or on the farms and all could not manage on what they earned.

The stark contrast between his own life, now so abundant in every way, was not lost on Edward, who said little but observed a good deal.

The 'meet' did not last long but it was agreed that all tempers should be left at the door. There was to be no raillery or shouting, since this was a gift of place from Colonel Brandon and a gift of heart from Edward, but it was a forum where a man could be heard.

As the sun was beginning to consider moving along to the west, the group disbanded, all with a lift to their spirits, and glad that there was a spark of hope come into the bleakness of their lives.

18

The journey from Falmouth to Darcy's old friends was beautiful, tucked deep in the inlets of the Carrick Roads; Tamara was Darcy's magical gift to his wife in the sharing of somewhere that he held very dear. In his past bachelor life, he conceded to himself, he would never have believed it possible to inform another living soul of this place and indeed, its people. That he had found a pirate's kerchief for Elizabeth seemed perfectly apposite, for here they were in smugglers' territory and she was indeed taken by the idea.

Darcy had not included the trip to Falmouth in the inventory of his plans, but the appearance of the Colonel had reminded him of their visit there some years ago. In that town he had discovered that it would be possible to take a sailing cutter to St Mawes which stood almost opposite the creek to where his friends lived. No matter that the party would divert from what was a simple journey from Truro to Tamara, the curiosity of the sea village with its own castle, the beauty of the water and the descent down again toward Tamara was reason enough for this romantic assertion to be made real. The idea of arrival by boat made Fitzwilliam Darcy thoroughly elated and he laid his plans most carefully to avoid detection until the very last moment.

The Falmouth Market Boat was not an elegant affair, capable of taking all manner of small cargo, livestock, market traders and farers and it had been in existence since the earliest times when intrepid merchants traded tin with far-away places. This very fact bowled Mr Darcy over, such that he was determined not to furnish Elizabeth, in particular and the small party in general, with any mite of information that should give him away. Having spent two nights at de Wynn's he concluded that it was possible to send the horses, carriage, luggage and coachmen on to Tamara without them, awaiting their arrival by boat later in the day: he would have to be very careful that none of the information got out!

The morning was yet another made in heaven, the sea wind light and the swell small and kind. Everyone left the hotel in good spirits and the briefest but most sincere of farewells was said. The entire staff of the inn turned out to say their goodbyes to one of the warmest small parties they had cared for in many years. All agreed on a return whenever it might be possible. A special goodbye was bid to Colonel Fitzwilliam as the contingent set off for Darcy's friends and there was a general air of appreciation at the serendipitous nature of having discovered him in Truro.

Elizabeth and Jane, arms linked, sat in the carriage on the way back inland, the two men chatting quietly. It was Elizabeth who first noticed that they were setting off in what seemed to be the wrong direction - going further into the town instead of out of it. She spoke in a gentle tone:

'Dearest husband, are we to swim to Tamara?'

'Yes dear,' said Darcy, straight faced.

All regarded about them except for Pemberley's master, who seemed wholly taken with a small piece of paper in his hand upon which seemed to be a grid!

'Yes, yes, all is inordinately well, we can swim across from the Roseland peninsula in half an hour,' said he.

More raised eyebrows whose sequitur was a large 'aah' as the carriage rounded into the ferry quay and they could see that there was a boat waiting upon it, already loading persons. Nevertheless, where were they heading? If once astonished at the sight of the cutter, the little group, excepting of course, its leader, was again taken aback at the thought of embarking upon it. Falmouth, known for having the most profoundly deep waters in Europe, was going to take them on a relatively small but long boat, with a large company of people, and place them down again on the other side – 'but the other side of where?' Elizabeth asked herself. They seemed to be going in the very opposite direction to the one in which she *thought* Darcy had said they were to go. Doubt notwithstanding and trust upstanding, the party obediently filed onto the vessel and, as they disembarked from the carriage and embarked upon a boat more used to carrying cattle and market sellers than the master of one of England's greatest houses, more and more laughter rose into the warm air of a summer's day in Cornwall.

But yet! This was not all! As the party followed their leader on board, they could see that their carriage was wheeling round and setting off in the very direction they had once thought to be espousing. No! this was neither a mistake nor a mere visit to a small vessel; for the coachmen, their very own coachmen, were waving them goodbye! The look of confused questioning and not a little anxiety on the part of all but Darcy, was comical. The master, their leader in this, shall we say, *adventure*, boarded last and with a 'see, I am coming with you', to add to his party's amazed faces watching their own mode of transport begin to pull away from the quayside.

Everyone was now firmly on their way to *somewhere*, a novel thought. There was a distinctive and noisy atmosphere: hens in cages clucked and scratched and at least three dogs, one apparently alone – perhaps the ship's pooch – woofed and whined at the pace of the now rapidly sailing boat. They all found a seat - a great relief - and then a moment of utter disbelief and this time it was Bingley who saw her first: in the far corner of the boat, if boats have corners, there sat under a small cover to the leeward side, a baby *elephant*. As soon as Charles' gaze alerted the rest of his fellows, they could not stop the flow of laughter striking them as a piece of divine judgement on so many reproaches to their leader. Not even Darcy himself, already seated in the most extraordinarily dignified pose, would ever have entertained such a trip in his bachelor days. No! not even Fitzwilliam Cadogan himself could have arranged this one! There could be no immediate explanation for the presence or destination of the small creature, yet since reality seemed delivered of an exeat from life that summer's day in Falmouth, there seemed little point in asking too many questions.

It was again Charles Bingley, who, having glimpsed a small but potently present keeper, dared to ask for information:

'Pray sir, do give us comprehension of your wondrous charge.'

'O she be on 'er way to Plymouth sir, to the circus and we s'all drop 'er off at St Mawe' for 'er to further 'er journey up by road.'

The party's face was a composite painting. Sadly, all hopes of further inquiry were instantly dashed by the captain's entreaty to be ready to go ashore.

'We are entirely abandoned to your trust, dear husband,' said Elizabeth, composing herself after another rising volcano of laughter and rocking a little in her heretofore stable seat.

'Indeed, Darcy, you have excelled yourself, it must be some sort of pact with the angels,' added Bingley, carefully regarding the clear, deep waters below them.

The cutter glided into St Mawes, its Tudor castle standing strongly to the left and, with a sigh of relief the party disembarked. Now finding themselves in an exceedingly pretty harbour and busy village rising sharply from it, they all praised both heaven and their leader for a safe arrival.

'Well! A little adventure!' whispered Jane to Elizabeth as her husband was still chuckling to himself about the content of this latter.

All surged forward into a most attractive inn on the quay side, which was still busy with fishermen. Avoiding the lobster baskets hanging by the door, the men led the way and good food was discovered to compensate for suspended expectation and to add to the feeling of joy. Even Darcy himself, never in any doubt of the veracity of the captain in assuring him of their safety, felt gladdened to have his feet on *terra firma* - ne'er had crab sandwiches tasted so good.

The party rejoiced at its good fortune; the beautiful weather; the calm sea; the light breeze; the salt spray and the presence of each other to each other – all in a safe harbour, the elephant *inclus.*

'Just regard these ships' bells, dear friends and the sweep of the view, quite the thing for us as landlubbers,' said Bingley, bursting with happiness and wellbeing. 'I never saw such a charming and invigorating prospect!'

'Indeed, the air is crisp and warm at the same time and so welcome, especially since we have ceased to sway, why! my being is so unused to going along on water, however brief, yet I thank you, brother, for the most *interesting* experience.' Jane concluded whilst Elizabeth heartily agreed, the small cup of wine having already made inroads into her head.

Darcy, who had been in some silent ponderance, thought that everyone should make a little haste now, so that they might reach their destination before mid-afternoon. He had also written to Georgiana from Falmouth and was thinking of her; Mrs Reynolds was of course at Pemberley, as well as a young friend from London but he was duty bound, as well as bound by blood, to take care of her.

Leaving the harbour, the group re-embarked into their now-awaiting, hired carriage. The ladies were a little disappointed to leave such an active and pretty little town but delighted to see a carriage again – it was lovely to be once more amongst the known and besides, Darcy had masterminded a wonderful detour! To the sisters' delight there were many small shops giving onto the quayside itself, even a tailor! The latter provoked Elizabeth to say:

'Dearest Jane, it is a long way from home but perchance we

shall come again one day, it is perfectly lovely, and I would do a little poking round these places, were there time!'

The party regrouped and the small carriage set off, taking the near-vertical climb out of town very carefully. They were soon bowling along, not without some relief to be horizontal, when the coachman called, 'away, below there,' as he took his charges immediately left and into a sharp descent. The move was nothing if not surprising! the sisters returned to their wary regard of each other, even Bingley raised an eyebrow and then winked, for he could see that his long-time friend was in perfect mind and even chuckling to himself:

'Well, you see, the adventure is not yet over!' said Darcy.

To Elizabeth's great delight they were descending into a dense forest which was falling away fast before them. Narrowing and steepening, the road was becoming more and more wooded and thick vegetation surrounded them: it was delicious! Squints of sunshine came through the canopy of the leaves and lit the way in the most beautiful, satin light.

In a flash, the canopy gave way to the river, leaving everyone a little startled - for the river's territory did not encroach upon the trees, it simply stopped in a delightful surrender – at one moment there was forest and then there was water, fathoms and fathoms deep, water: all regarded the scene as if spellbound.

It was immediately evident that they had arrived at a small chain ferry manned by two ferrymen who were going to wind them across the river!

'Utopia again, my Jane,' whispered Elizabeth, wondering when these fairy tale days would end.

The captain of the vessel bade them welcome as they came aboard his boat, their last means of transport waving them a sincere goodbye and leaving them on the waterside like so many parcels waiting to be collected. Indeed, they had to wait a little for the ferry to fill but the clanking of the chains soon indicated that all was ready for departure. Bingley found their mien as a group particularly amusing:

'Why! we have become tourists proper, it will be The Grand Tour next.' All sat in a row, the parcel theme continued.

The two couples sat closely together as they drew in the wealth of detail: the great depth of the water; the distant scent of honeysuckle tumbling in the still salt air; the birds flying alongside the craft and the sand waders beckoning on the nearing shore. The ferry glided across, silent human effort and energy notwithstanding, the clank of the chains below becoming louder as the other side approached. Elizabeth was moved by the brilliance of the sun in the narrow channel and the dark profundity of the water below – she persisted in thinking of this inlet as holding some of the deepest in Europe and found the idea considerable and unwieldy. Both sisters loved the steep fall of the trees, the packed forest running down to the water's edge, as if each territory sealed and then separated into its own, potent dominion. Elizabeth could not help herself from further dwelling on smugglers!

19

*T*he parcels lifted from their shelf just as the ferry was pulling up onto the small embankment; all marvelled at the fact that two mortal men had worked the chains to bring them across with other passengers and even a cart. Darcy thanked the men profusely, quietly pondering a life that was so unlike his own; his friends at Tamara had sent their own phaeton to collect the party since it fitted the smallness of the lanes, and it was a very short journey to their destination now, say, ten minutes, even five. The master of Pemberley felt this to be a sort of homecoming, even a bringing home of his wife for a man bereft of parents; since he had known Sir Richard and Lady Tremayne for a long time, the arms of their friendship embracing the death of his parents and the grim time with Georgiana and Wickham.

Climbing into their seats the atmosphere was all anticipation and delight at the prospect of being in the small inlet of the Carrick Roads where Tamara lodged. The trip on the Market boat; the unusualness of its passengers; the fascination of St Mawes; the castle therein; the same King's ferry; the magical feel of the waters beneath as the men pedalled them along and the final arrival at Tamara on a fine summer's day in June: all, all led to a sumptuous concoction of love and time woven together, as if by Queen Mab herself.

Their finely tuned means of transport frisked along, so elevated was the spirit of the people within it. Turning after the Manor whose grounds gave onto the ferry, the group came in minutes to the Tremayne household standing at the head of the most beautiful and silent creek. Elizabeth felt her breath draw in at the sight of the trees' descent to the water's edge, just beyond the garden. Utopia was doing her best to establish her presence:

'We love it already Mr Darcy!' she cried. 'Here we are with the smugglers in the bowers of the forest, the water below, see! the boats are waiting for us!'

Fitzwilliam Cadogan Darcy turned onto his wife a look that spoke the exultant passion of the man.

Tamara was cradled halfway up a small creek, a world between the water and the trees; sitting in a bowl, like a jug in an ewer, its stern granite exterior did not belie the human warmth within. The house felt royal, its geography and its occupants made it so. Such a feeling was further expressed in the party's arrival into the small, inner ward that was both protective and charming.

'Darcy!' - a thunderous shout from the doorway clapped the air. Jane, who was in a sort of reverie, was at once startled back to earth. Something in the increasing retreat of the real world, from Falmouth to St Mawes, from the ferry to here – they were all increments of separation, of the falling away of years of constraint felt at Longbourn.

As they processed indoors, Elizabeth's eye ran at once to a corner of the great hall, a chapel, a working chapel since there was the slightest catch of incense upon the air.

'Come!' continued Darcy's friend. 'You are all so very welcome. Come in at once! Your carriage is here already and your luggage awaiting, with good hot water, upstairs.'

All was noise. Dogs (four), rushing and huffing; children (five) running and weaving, the eldest at the back (hovering) the youngest caring not to tumble between so many feet and so sudden.

Introductions were made informally, as the occasion demanded:

'Sir Richard: my wife, Elizabeth, her sister, Jane, and her husband, my dear friend, Charles Bingley,' said Darcy.

Laughter and glee and warmth everywhere: real human affection.

Then the arrival of the mistress of the house. All names precisely elocuted:

'You are most welcome, the Darcy party! Here, Emma, two years; Piers, her next brother; Sophia, his sister; Paraminder their next sister (you know, my mother and father were in India) and our eldest young person, Charles.' Then to Elizabeth and the Bingleys, 'I am Maria, at your service.'

All was a small chaos of friendships, of persons known and well-loved and now new friends, joining with the old.

Observing little Emma gingerly making her way through all the legs, Elizabeth bethought herself, 'yes, when we have a little girl, perhaps we may call her Emma, Emma Elizabeth!' She mused on the sound of the name as they moved toward their chamber, beauteous in its aspect of the garden, a white garden, full of new leaf. It was obvious why her husband loved the Tremaynes and their house, tiny in comparison to Pemberley, yet encompassing and almost magnifying its charm and substance. Mr Darcy was, indeed, a strange and wonderful fish, why! he had this lovely place and its kindly inhabitants secreted about his person all that difficult time around Longbourn, when all that he showed was the outer shell of a frostbitten bachelor! For here, here in a secret pocket in Cornwall was Pemberley decanted and its owner in his proverbial cups with it! All that the world could not see in him was here and in existence.

The little party was quickly united with their belongings and the ladies were disposed to a change of dress to accommodate them to the still rising heat of the day. Elizabeth wanted to explore a little but did not wish to appear rude. After the taking of tea and wonderful saffron cake, the like of which had been found at de Wynn's all agreed to meet again at six o'clock and she was able to have her wish. Mr Darcy applied to stay close by and speak with Sir Richard, Jane and Charles to rest. Recovered enough to be without the requirement of repose, Mrs Darcy, still very much Elizabeth Bennet, donned her sensible shoes and set off through the garden to the creek below. Never had she found herself so immediately enchanted – she must surely have been here before! Passing the little chapel, which again spoke to her as she passed, she went directly down to the water's edge, whose call was louder, greater, more poignant.

Six or seven paces away from the river, she came to a halt, arrested by her strong sense that someone was watching her – there was no fear, simply the knowledge that she was being regarded. She stood stock still and quickly saw that a young doe, completely slender and vulnerable in her regard, was before her. Standing amongst the ferns, the creature was well matched in height to the vegetation that surrounded her. Elizabeth thought of the deer she saw at home in Derbyshire, this one was different in colouring and stature but as delightful. She waited until the moment passed for intrusion to be irrelevant, the two looking at one another with an equal curiosity. Then timelessly, the sense that was between them parted, and she was left alone, almost bereft, the creature melting back into the green from whence it came.

Slower now and more cautious with her feet, Elizabeth thought to go to the water's edge where she could hear the sand waders and even, majestically, the call of a heron. The river's opening to her was breath taking; as before, first the intensity of the forest and the ferns and then suddenly the wider aspect of the natural world – the ancient waterway with its uncanny depths. Descending further, she saw that there was a small, gravel ridge, just as the tree canopy stopped and the water started; she was a little taken aback at the strength of her sensibilities, finding the grandeur of the effect overwhelming. In places, the gravel was powdery and held glints of crystal which caught the light, itself drawn into the trees, so that there was a sun picture on the bark of one, even upon the collective of leaves fanning down from it. Elizabeth was further mesmerised by the possibility of sound in the natural world, such as poets like Lord Byron and Wordsworth were endeavouring to explain; it all seemed to be tied to the visit of the small creature: she was in a veritable dream. Then, suddenly realising that the sun had now moved, and that late afternoon was approaching, she roused herself from the rock upon which she had been sitting, noticing a small rowing boat moored in the river cove.

'All a wonderment!' she bethought herself, 'clearly a wonderment,'

and with that, she set on her way again, back up the hill.

20

The party came down to dinner at 6 o'clock but not before Mrs Darcy, looking ravishing in purple silk, the very colour of her pirate's scarf, had peeped into the chapel. Drawn to its place in the corner of the Great Hall (even for such a compact house) it was immediately obvious to her that the family had once been Catholic recusants: she had not once visited Ashby St Ledgers for nothing. Whilst all manner of dips and dimples in the walls gave way to a sound comprehension of practices that had not followed into King Henry's Reformation, there was much here that was not part of The Great Divorce. Mr Bennet had absolutely neither time nor truck with anything to do with churches or their occupants, but his daughter had always lived in the Faith of Love, as she and Jane called it. Romantic they might both be, but this was a love of and a faith in the heart and both sisters had found much compassion between them for those who fought for such a cause.

The chapel had an upper window, a small storey window, which obviously gave off the main chamber; she knew that this was so that the lord of the manor and his family could attend the mass without descent to the little church. The seating in the latter was black with age and polish; the altar table was 'slight' she wanted to say, yet strongly present and the paintings looked at if they had fallen straight out of Florence. There was a small *reredos* on which was the most beautiful exposition of Mary Magdalene, kissing the hand of the man she loved: 'there you are,' thought Elizabeth to herself, 'there is more of *that* about which we do not know.'

The hum of the family gathering in the dining parlour unseated her private regard for all things lovingly secret and she slipped out nonchalantly, as if she had just been looking at a flower.

As the Darcy party came down the staircase together, so the home party stood before them in the sort of rank arrangement peculiar to the time. Just as the visitors were concluding their approach to their hosts, the latter opened its lines to reveal someone behind it who was not a Tremayne. There: Colonel Fitzwilliam!

Both sisters rolled their eyes upwards as the younger proclaimed:

'Of course, you are here, not where we left you, in Falmouth!' Both sisters and their husbands greeted their friend as if they had not seen him for months. Laughter dotted the old beams and the sconces on the walls, the children now dispersed all-about and even the dogs flown away: the family was complete.

During the journey through Cornwall, Mr Bingley had kept everyone well informed on the geographical changes and even some details of the Civil war, Cornwall being the last of England to surrender to the Parliamentary cause. The ladies observed, on Bingley's say-so, the difference from Devonshire and it was the same gentleman who now struck up the dinner conversation.

'Sir Richard, we are so glad to have been included in your invitation and thank you greatly for it; we are delighted with the setting of your home and wonder if you might furnish us with some of its history?'

'Of course, sir, I am your willing servant,' replied the host. 'We came here through an ancestor who fought bravely for Henry

Tudor at Bosworth Field and was given land in gratitude, accordingly. When Kingship arrived for his friend, our ancestor was knighted, and our future here became mapped out. We are the continuation of a line and proud and pleased to be so. As you see, we live simply and we do the best that we can for our tenants. But Darcy, we have been friends for a long time, do tell us of your family in the past, of which we know but little.'

'Dear friends, we are in your home and I should not really be in the business of telling you of mine!' said the Pemberley master.

'No, no, we desire to know, do we not, Maria?' replied Sir Richard.

Nods of assent followed. Darcy complied.

'Well, the most famous ancestor, for me, at least, was on our mother's side and was Sir William Fitzwilliam, of course there is also relation to the Colonel seated here, my cousin. Sir William married into one of the great families of the north, the Nevilles, so significant in the time of King Richard III and of northern descent and, indeed, power. Fitzwilliam was a soldier, and he too was also in the court of King Henry VIII and, Sir Richard, like your ancestor, a friend of the King: perchance they knew one another!'

The table thought this possibility both amusing and exciting. Darcy continued:

'Our Fitzwilliam was Treasurer of the Household after the demise of Anne Boleyn's father, as well as holding some other posts. It is curious because this man, Fitzwilliam, was, at one point, Lord High Admiral and wore the symbol of office accordingly, a small boatswain's call about his neck.'

The children thought this a very fine idea, perfect for hailing one another when down at the river and there was much laughter and conjecture as Maria lovingly shepherded them into the hands of the nursery. A fond goodnight was bid to the departing offspring – only young Charles remaining - and with all men and women staying at the table equally. The port was thus brought out with a full complement of persons of both sexes and no withdrawals!

'Forgive us, dear friends, that we include our children until quite late, but they gain so much by being present with us,' said Sir Richard.

A small concurrence of approval passed around and the evening continued with further reflection on country life in Cornwall, the hosts recounting all sorts of stories about being a humane Justice of the Peace. Elizabeth found herself tongue tied when the subject of smuggling came up, for her manners always came before the conquest of intelligence or self-interest, yet it was discreetly revealed that Sir Richard and Lady Maria were both painfully aware of the grinding poverty within the county: no more than this was said.

Conversation continued until nearly midnight, when Colonel Fitzwilliam recounted some of the amusing moments of being a single man in the Army and for many years, so that at twelve everyone retired, well dined and indeed, well wined.

21

The next evening followed at Tamara with the grace of the one which pervaded its predecessor. This evening there was only the taking of a cup of wine before dinner and the children soon went off upstairs with their guardian ladies, like a small charge of retainers. Conversation came in with the soup and it was not long before the previous night's subjects were reclaimed.

'I hear that you have all passed a restful day about the woods and the water?' said Sir Richard.

Bingley answered warmly: 'We have, sir, with such pleasure and interest – there were some quite large vessels to be seen further up the river, by the ferry, there.'

'Yes, certainly! It is such deep water, you know, that large vessels have been coming for a long time, to be restored and refurbished, or sometimes simply to rest. There are often boats from other countries.'

'Yes. We noticed a flag from France and another that we did not know.'

Indeed, I must watch my maidservants sometimes, you know,' said Sir Richard, winking softly, 'the crews of the visitors can be very, shall we say, *attractive*! Of course, our local men hardly care for it!'

Elizabeth spoke next, swerving the subject a little:

'We do appreciate what you have done here, for the hamlet of your people nearby and the making of the community that serves you. We hear that there is also a little bake house!'

Sir Richard and Lady Maria positively glowed, the latter continuing:

'You know, my parents were not in the easiest position in life, my father was a missionary. It was hard for them in their postings and the life they showed us was a far cry from English polite society, either then or now. When I met Richard, he just avoided all judgement of us, of me, let us say and we have made a fragrant marriage since!'

As Lady Maria stopped speaking, Elizabeth and Darcy acknowledged the core of what their host had said in a look of great comprehension. Elizabeth often thought how courageous her husband had been to marry her; what he said in his famous Speech on the Bennet family was *utterly* true, yet he had disregarded all of these matters because he loved her. It was a daily miracle that he had done this and in so doing marked himself out as a man of great tolerance, inhabiting, despite his previous and apparent tenure of its very opposite, a territory where prejudices could be overridden.

Mrs Darcy spoke back, 'might we know more of this wondrous demesne, ma'am?'

'You may, you may! We love being here and we almost eschew everywhere else, in order to be so. This whole side of the peninsula is in the lee, you know, so that weather, climate, soil - all sorts of things are different from the other side. When we came here, we came to a family who had been rebellious to the church – at this Elizabeth's ears pricked up – and were Catholics, rather a fierce position to take in a place where everyone knows much of what is happening within it. As time went on, they were also supporters of King Charles I and, it is said that he came here on a visit to the loyal town of Lostwithiel, a Cavalier stronghold. You know, there was much support for the King in Cornwall, many little castles and many folk who did not wish for a republic: they called it the ruffian's rout! Anyway, the spirit carried on all around because the place where we live, particularly the creek side, has been a place for fugitives from smuggling for many a year. But I will let my husband continue!'

'I will, my dear. Yet I must be most careful as a Justice and so I say this in utter confidence. The land of Brittany is very close to us, you know – it is not called by that name for nothing – and it resembles Cornwall strongly in weather, in geography and in its language - *Bretonne* – a tongue that is very similar indeed to the old language still spoken here. In time, we believe, many connections were made between local people and the French – I mean, how would they know that a certain boat is coming in at a certain time and with what? In a way, we are the same stock, the Bretons and the old Cornish: I have been able to hear both languages together and can see how each might be understood by the other.'

All was slight astonishment to those north of the Tamar, at this quietly given observation.

'Tell a little more, my love,' said Maria.

'Yes, yes! you may know that there are certain, *visiteurs,* shall we say, in our creeks and inlets, and in our coves. We are aware of the desperation of the great poverty here, even down to the mines in Redruth and beyond: having work does not always equal being able to put food on the table. I do not condone smuggling but am I not a man with a warm bed and a wife and our home that came with my birth? I have been able to learn enough of India's poor through Maria to know that grim truths lurk in our pastures, why! have you not seen the men out in the late of the night poaching rabbits? Of course, I am secretly thrilled that my population of vegetation destroyers is reducing, so *I look away* - a bit of night blindness - but it is not legal. I judge when I am at the Bench, but I prefer to comprehend the nature of the offence and the reasons for its occurring, rather than perpetuate the cruelties so often found in the administration of the law. Perhaps you will think that I do not do my job well, but I see such grimly harsh measures being taken against crimes that come from hunger, so that I try to persist in that 'quality of mercy' of which we have heard spoke.

As before, the conversation changed to more light-hearted subjects and for a while the group found again the mesmeric effect of the house and garden in which they stayed. The gratitude that Elizabeth felt for the visit was expressed in the hall, under the little chapel window that she now so loved – next time she would ask if she might see the window from the other side - and all retired again content as the clock struck midnight.

In the upstairs corridor, Elizabeth caught her sister:

'O, my dearest Jane, it is *adieu* to Utopia, for this time, at least, have we not been truly blessed? We have been in a happy state for hours and days, out of life and in another place.'

'Indeed, we have, my dear sister, it will be quite hard to return to our already wondrous lives after this encounter with it, I am sure.'

22

*T*he carriage rattled along the lanes on its way up country; the day was still warm – the good weather had been their friend and it remained constant.

'Thank you, my dear friends, for agreeing to pass quickly up through this leeward side of the county, until we reach Devonshire – it is a completely different aspect from the way we came. I am sure that it will inform you further to travel through the edge of Dartmoor, not only because you will witness a different landscape, but you will feel this part of the world from another perspective.'

After his informative speech, Darcy raised an eyebrow about which the party laughed but also understood: the captain was at the helm and didactic in his purpose. The days of their sojourn in the south west had been so blessed; they had loved everywhere they stayed and, Elizabeth felt, everyone they had stayed with. She marvelled at the man to whom she was married, still elegant and reserved in public but there was no more of the once-remove that he had previously carried with him – so heavily, she realised now.

Bingley entertained the group along the way, noting the many ports on this side of Cornwall and the manner in which history had woven well with the natural provision of the land. There were good, safe harbours rising from which a level terrain, making roads possible and navigable. There was no doubt that trade to these ports was brisk and settlements were burgeoning. The brief stop at Lostwithiel was charming, the party were Royalists, to a man. For the want of acquaintance thereabouts to visit, it was decided to head toward a small town on the river at the top of Cornwall and the bottom of Devonshire. The forests accompanied them as they ascended and the vista became magnificent in parts, showing the inner ward, as it were, itself often a plateau from where a great vista could reveal itself.

'Darcy,' started Bingley as the carriage found itself in the middle of one of the latter openings, 'would that you continue with another of your ancestors, we are greatly diverted by these stories.'

'Indeed, dear friend, I will continue for a moment because the lady in question, whilst not living in Pemberley, was nevertheless related and, I feel, had influence of some of the furnishings and content therein – she was a woman who made her mark!'

'We are ready!' affirmed Bingley for them all as Darcy began.

'You will recall that the there was a famous duchess who started the leaning to *grandeur* at a nearby house in the sixteenth century: it seems to me that she was a gorgon in one part and an angel in the other, nevertheless, she was increasingly powerful, popular and quite brilliant in making houses!'

Knowing a little of the reputation of the lady in question, the group smiled and continued with their attention.

'She was, indeed, fierce, but the life that she created was magnificent and she excelled at it! I shall call this lady Nella, for propriety's sake, though I tell you little that is not public knowledge. Now, this lady was married to a man who was high in the Tudor court and with him five extant children; these latter became part of my own ancestry. The Lady Nella had several husbands for she married older men and they died before her. Thus, twelve years after the death of one of them, she married again to a courtier who owned large estates, one near to where we are now and one higher up country. Through this husband Nella was elevated to Lady of the Bedchamber in the Royal household, a most prized possession.

At these words, Elizabeth sat up particularly straight for she loved talk of the royal line:

'Huff, dear husband, I am listening carefully!'

'Well, it is not only in my opinion that this lady made good marriages but in the one of which I speak, she was so dearly loved that when her husband died, she was the sole executrix of his estate (rare then, and even now, ladies) and he spoke of her and 'of the natural affection, mature love and assured goodwill' between them'.

At this both sisters exchanged looks of knowing pleasure.

'Now, my Elizabeth, this courtier was an able musician and I feel that the lute you have found came to Pemberley through him, or through one of his children. There you are my dearest!'

Elizabeth, by now so taken with the story of the ancestor and the possible link to her now-beloved lute, that she raised herself a little in her seat to kiss her husband on the cheek. At this very moment there was a terrible feeling in the carriage as it swerved sharply and slurred to one side, the senior coachman was at once shouting, and the rear coachman had been knocked from his holding position. The horses could not pull back. The carriage started to shudder and roll, the noise was inexplicable to those inside for they could not see the great stag in front of them – the cause of this havoc. In a second there was a terrible bang as the body of the massive animal collided with the now turning barouche.

Then only silence.

23

*E*linor and Edward were at Barton Cottage, they loved to be there with Mrs Dashwood and Margaret, Elinor thought that her husband looked happy within the bosom of this, her family. Everyone savoured the time they had at Barton, walking on the downs with the huge panorama of the sea below.

'My dear ones, Mary, Elinor, Margaret, I thought that I would just to Minestock today, to arrange a delivery of some cloth and to talk with some of the miners. I hope that my absence meets with your approval, I will be back by three.'

The prospect of three ladies chattering together half the day was favourite with them and their male was given leave. As he set out, Edward recognised and acknowledged the gratitude he felt to Colonel Brandon for the living of St Mary Magdalene. He was never sure what he would have done or even been without the generosity shown to him through his now brother-in-law. Certainly, the change of heart incumbent upon his mother at the marriage of his younger brother made all the difference to the stipend he gained – they would have been poor church mice had they not received what she gave them. It was the understanding of a precarious moment in life, such that time had provided for Edward, that was concomitant upon the comprehension of the spectre of scraping an income and now, the experience of the labourers whom Elinor called his 'Barn Men', continued the informing. The latter were in his consciousness as he rode steadily down to Minestock, where, indeed, he would meet with some miners extra to his purchase of cloth.

Edward dwelt much upon the mining situation – the mines around the town to which he rode were flushed with all manner of minerals and especially tin. He knew the owner of these mines and made a note in his mind to go to see him; whilst the acquaintance was not strong and the man's reputation as a sound manager of his business, Edward knew nothing of the man as a man. 'Talk is cheap', he thought to himself as the idea of being in the dark the day long surfaced to the front of his mind, 'I will just endeavour to meet with Lord Gallhope and see if he will support my schemes for workers' hearings.' In the very act of saying these words to himself, he knew that the outing may prove fruitless, but he was, nevertheless, willing to try - he had not come from all that wealth for nothing.

In hoping to see some of the miners, their shifts not of that day, he sought to hear what they thought of his plan for his own 'Men'. Not wishing to encroach upon their time, nor to effect any form of distrust, his own full situation in life notwithstanding, Edward needed to make clear that he was not a political man but that he was a supporter in his wide heart and wanted to say so. Here, and all around, so many and hardworking and still in poverty.

The two men that he would meet that morning were miners of exceedingly high position in their communities – well liked, upstanding men of good nature, they were not usually rebellious. Minestock, its ancient heritage stretching back into times when minerals travelled from St Michael's Mount to Phoenicia, had been mining copper, manganese, silver, lead and tin for ever. Even after a lapse, copper was being taken from the ground again as French prisoners of war carved out canals to carry it: there was much happening in this, his world.

Edward was not a man to take others' suffering lightly; someone who understood carefully that which he saw, he could not recant to himself the seeing; even if he just sat and listened, then it was, for him, doing *something*.

Quietly going along on his horse, he was beset by impressions of the mine owners from visits to his mother in Berkeley Street, where some were part of her circle. It seemed bizarre to the pastor that he should be on the edges of acquaintance with men who possessed such lives. Normally being distant from or indeed, choosing to distance himself from the big landowners, his parley with the spectre of poverty had laid bare a new layer of aware-ness: since he had faced the possibility of homelessness himself, he could never look at it again and leave. Too silent and for too long, his conscience required that he do something.

In these matters Edward was a rare fish. He remembered that at one of the last gatherings with his mother's *persons* as he called them, there were two, heavily built men whose material wealth went before them like a flag in a gale. In such moments, Edward's well-known lack of ambition went before *him*, so there was no question of his wanting to emulate them, further, his mother's harping on their success in life whenever he was in their presence made him feel nauseous. He would, nevertheless, have liked to ask these men about the welfare of their charges but would not bestow upon his mother the inconvenience of the dialogue. He admired the Reverend John Wesley very much, now *there* was a man to emulate, but he, Edward, was too new along the route and too uncertain of it to follow in his hero's footsteps.

Continuing in this vein of thought, he determined to listen as carefully as he could at Minestock, when a most tremendous bang shattered his calm. Turning the corner which sheltered him from the abrupt cataclysm, his astounded eyes met a carriage upside down on its roof, the horses already pulled off the shafts and bolted. He quickly put his own horse onto a branch and now, beset with anguish, started to run toward the wreckage.

24

*A*s Darcy crawled out of a side window, he could see Elizabeth at once. Flung several paces, she looked dead. All colour was leeched from his face as he painfully extricated himself from the carriage, the door of which had extraordinarily shut again after Mrs Darcy had flown through it. He could not move himself fast enough since one leg was dragging like stone; his mind was as racing light.

Before him, the still body of the woman he loved, the woman who had ignited love within him, a woman that, indeed, he had vowed *not* to love. Here a man who was first visited by feeling, then who stood back from feeling, then was rejected by talking about such feeling to the person who was its source and now she was so still as to be certainly beyond life. Darcy knew that his leg was damaged, but it stood for nothing, his only care to get to Elizabeth – the limb dragged behind him like the mute appendage that it was. He started to call her name, a calling that seemed strangely outside of him, like another man shouting from somewhere else; yet as he reached her, she moved almost imperceptibly. The only sound that could be heard around them was the spinning of one of the carriage wheels and the wheezing of his chest - letting out sounds that he could only sense to be making.

He could no longer call out, he was not able to alert the others, wherever they were; he began to sob – for the first time in his adult life – he sobbed such sounds of strength and indeed, veracity, that what little he could hear of them seemed to be those of an animal in pain.

'Elizabeth! My dearest, loveliest, Elizabeth, speak to me.' Again, the severed voice outside of him.

She seemed to have hurt her hip because blood was flooding from it, or below it, into the ground beneath.

Then the miraculous voice of Bingley:

'Jane, where is Jane?'

'She is not here my friend, try the other side – for God's sake try to alert someone.'

Bingley and a grey-faced coachman behind him returned to the far side of the carriage, returning Pemberley's owner to the silence and his lifeless wife.

He dared not touch her but moved closer to her face, to the side of her face, to an ear, into which he began to whisper:

'Elizabeth, my soul, please speak to me, do *not* leave me here without you. Elizabeth! my own one, you vowed to love me unto death, but it will *not* be on this day, surely.'

Nothing. Only the blood seeping and seeping, scarlet on a pale summer dress. The wound, wherever it was, must be massive, the blood was new, continuing to be new and so very bright.

At last, voices coming closer to them, the sound coming through the thicket which was so dense it seemed to be matted. Now more help, another coachman and a man looking, or perhaps feeling to Darcy, like a priest.

'Can I help you, sir? I can see that you are in very great need.

The voice, at once so kind and the presence of this man so very calm, like a balsam.

'My wife is badly hurt. Can you please get some help and perhaps a doctor? I fear the worst, but I am not certain, I am not certain.'

Tears fell in a torrent from Darcy's eyes, a flood brought on by the kindness of this stranger, who felt like an angel to a man who did not believe in them.

'We are near to our dear friends, I will send at once and return quickly, to help you further,' said the angel-man.

The voice, the very voice and the powerful presence faded into the bushes and Darcy was once more alone with his worst fears. He dared not move Elizabeth, hardly dared to touch her but kissed her hair, her face, her hands, which he felt were the last thing in the world to him. This lovely woman had moved away the stone from the sepulchre of his frozen heart: he would not let her die, fade into death as the kindly man had faded into the undergrowth.

Suddenly, sharply, Elizabeth tried to sit up, barely opening her eyes as she did so; the movement was so abrupt that her husband's first reaction was that she was having some sort of seizure, but he gently restrained her and could now see that their eyes were closely aligned and in conversation.

'My heart, my dearest heart, where are we?' - a voice lit by the wonder and love in her husband's eyes.

'My Elizabeth, my own one, we have crashed; our carriage has fallen but never mind, you are alive. You are ALIVE. Tell me where you are hurt.'

Mrs Darcy looked blankly at her husband: 'I feel no pain, my beloved' and then a moment of recognition as she followed his eyes looking down at her gown. She whitened more, looked more ill, if that were possible, and in the faintest voice, barely audible, whispered to him:

'I was going to tell you this morning my beloved, I am with child.'

25

*E*very part of Darcy froze and then shattered before him in the morning sunshine. The intolerable silence continued, exacerbated only by itself. He knew that Elizabeth was in the act of losing their child, the sense of loss to him was overwhelming, somewhere between the incomprehensible and the eternal; he held her hand until he thought he might be hurting her, but she was as still as the grave. Here was the greatest irony, almost a blasphemy to the heart; he had never allowed love to touch him and now it knocked him down. No one had ever talked of a man's love, save the poets – here he was in an unknown land – how could he feel what was occurring? Yes, he would talk to someone but to *whom* would he talk? His head rushed with questions, he wished fervently that the flux of everything would stop. Here was a travesty of something, if he were religious, he would pray. Here was a terrible end, he dared not think, to *someone*. Yet Darcy also found himself in a state of wonder, that this morning there had been the possibility for him of being a father and now, now he could see with his plain eyes that this possibility was gone. His mind ran through the inadequacy of what he was doing, he had dreaded this moment his whole life, never a complacent man, he was, nevertheless, stranded: his inadequacy ran through him like a knife. O that the kind man would return quickly so that help could be made certain.

'Elizabeth, Elizabeth,' he pleaded to the air around her.

His wife made a long, drawn-out sigh and then suddenly she was starting to struggle, trying to sit up, trying to get up. He took off his coat to make a pillow and as he lifted her a little, he held onto that beloved head, as if holding onto it might prevent her from slipping away from him.

'Do not try to move, my love. A man has gone for help and will be back directly. Thank God that it is not winter.'

The look between them, inclusive, eternal, brave.

'I will not die my beloved, I am not able to die yet!' she laughed weakly, a small flash of sunlight in an otherwise grey face.

Noises in the undergrowth, first Charles and then a coachman following – two faces that Darcy knew well, now equal in disaster.

'We have found Jane, she is not hurt, just badly shaken. Are you hurt yourself my friend?'

'Not I.'

'It is only Elizabeth then, who is hurt?' He was going to say 'badly' but stopped the word urgently in his mouth.

'Bingley, there are blankets in the back of the carriage, under a seat, please.'

Further rustling in the undergrowth and the return of the kind man.

'Hello there, I have brought assistance. How is your – er – wife?'

'Yes, my wife, I fear that we must try to move her. Are you able to help me?'

Darcy as never before, imploring, floundering, falling.

'Yes, we can. I have brought two men with me and a small pony and trap, but my own wife has made a bed upon it and there are blankets for a little more comfort.'

The master of Pemberley, beyond belief that they could be helped - he wanted to say 'helped so tenderly' since that was what it felt like - a very fine sort of assistance from this calm man, his very presence a panacea.

Slowly, slowly, as if they were carrying a new-born, Darcy's thoughts cruelly thought, they moved Elizabeth and what was left of their child; he had covered her body specifically so that no one may see the grim truth.

'My love, we are going to lift you slowly to safety. Please let us move you with great care, e'en to your own precision, so that you do alert us if we are causing more damage to your beloved person, undiscovered.'

The moments went well as Mrs Darcy was placed onto the padded splint in the cart and re-wrapped in the blankets; it was a warm summer's day, yet her body felt cold to the touch; her head was still upon her husband's coat.

'I am sorry ma'am, that it is not comfortable for you, but we will proceed with absolute care,' said the kind man, his eyes, so strongly blue.

As the men carrying the litter wove their way out of the thicket, Darcy was limping badly behind – his gratitude that Elizabeth was still alive greater than the need to worry about himself – a small phaeton arrived with more help. One of the three upon it was obviously the master of the house, the other his coachmen, still dressed in their livery after a morning excursion with the ladies. Carrying more blankets and concerned faces, they watched silently as Elizabeth was placed onto the cart.

The principal gentleman came across to Darcy, at a respectful pace:

'We shall get your party to our home, sir, it is but close by. You go ahead, my son-in-law will take you. We will find the horses and bring the carriage along.'

As Darcy turned toward the kindly man, now seating himself at the reigns, he felt that he had never before experienced such benevolent eyes. He held out his hand.

'Fitzwilliam Darcy, we thank you beyond esteem for your services to us.'

'O, you are truly welcome, sir, I am Edward Ferrars.'

26

*A*s the trap pulled away in a reverence requisite to life, the master of Pemberley could only feel that nothing mattered save Elizabeth – he would infinitely rather be stripped of his great house and all its acres, to ensure the return of the woman he had come to love so much. In the last moments she had looked a little better, but he knew a haemorrhage when he saw one and was deeply unsettled by the continuation of the spreading red.

'Go on my friends, go on home,' said the older man, 'we shall see to matters here and I shall bring your belongings back with me whilst the carriage and horses are reassembled. Please return to Barton Park, it is closely at hand and we shall assist you further, most of all, try not to perturb yourself. I have sent word to my wife to expect your party.'

More persons converged whilst the pony and trap set off at a sedate pace. Darcy was without words, even without sensation – another moment in his adult life of helplessness and surrender: he would remember it forever.

The cart processed slowly, even gracefully, as the noonday sun cast its warmth on two frightened occupants, somewhere between crisis and comfort. After a short distance, the horse turned into the drive of a great house - all was truth about the nearness of the abode – a place of dignity with lovely gardens in full bloom.

The driver of the cart, Mr Ferrars, called out in a soft voice as they arrived. Two ladies came at once from the portico where they had been waiting, an older, perhaps the mother of the man now down at the place of the accident and another, perhaps the wife of the cart driver; all was calm and quiet about them.

'Welcome to our home dear sir and madam, we hear that you have had a calamitous occurrence, but you are in safety now; we are here to assist you in every way that we can. I believe that my son is with your carriage, I am Mrs Jennings, his mother and here is Edward's wife, Elinor. Let us help to move your wife slowly indoors; please direct us as we proceed, to ensure her wellbeing.'

At the renewal of such calm kindness Darcy started to feel unwell himself, it was as if he were with Georgiana's family who was not even yet in existence, such was his feeling of being with kinsmen - and all of which took him completely by surprise.

'Dear sir,' said Mrs Jennings with a soft voice, 'let the coachman advance with the litter and pray, dear lady, do tell us if we move in any way that will bring you discomfort.'

As Darcy tried to get up, he realised that there was, indeed, some injury to his leg; gradually the party was got inside, thus his palpable relief served to take away the effects of the pain in the limb. Both Mrs Jennings and Elinor had already observed his demeanor and resolved to assist him as soon as was tolerably possible. The litter was brought into the salon, a small, lemon-coloured room with exquisite chintz drapes in yellow and turquoise; Darcy thought that in normal circumstances he would have expressed much pleasure in the décor, but his groin was throbbing and Elizabeth required perhaps less light and a doctor. He realised that he must speak to the older lady:

'Ma'am, your kindness is excessive in this painful time and we are glad of it, indeed; it is exigent for me to tell you that there is much loss of blood, you see my wife is with child.'

'O my dear sir,' said Mrs Jennings with a stifled gasp, 'we are so sorry, we shall do *all* that we can; whilst we await the doctor, I will call upon my housekeeper, Mrs Dolby, for assistance.'

Pemberley's guardian was left alone as everyone busied to bring into effect all the necessary arrangements for Elizabeth's welfare; her colour was returning and she was clearly alive.

'We are safe, my dearest, the doctor is on his way,' whispered Darcy.

'Beloved Fitzwilliam, I am so sorry that this should happen today of all days.'

'*Sorry*! Most dear heart, pray, do not be *sorry*!'

'I want you to know that I am well enough, I know it. Please know also, that if we have lost our child, then I shall be well again and, with Love's blessing, we shall make another child. I am young and strong. This time we shall send this little girl into the stars, for I am sure that she is, *was,* a girl and we shall ask, as she goes, that we may have another child as lovely as she would have been, as the fruit of our dear marriage.'

Just as Darcy thought that he might splinter, a soft knock at the door announced Edward:

'Dr Jago will be with us very shortly.'

A call from beyond took the Reverend away again at once.

'My beloved Elizabeth, you are forbearing and courageous.' The two held one another in a long regard.

'You know, also, that I love you with the ardour I felt in that time when I asked you to marry me, nothing has changed and now I love you with the protective love of a man who is coming to know his wife more and more with each day's passing.'

At least now Elizabeth was able to weep and she also began to tremble - for the gift that this man was to her, for all that he stood for and for being alive.

27

*T*he ladies of the house quickly gathered in the parlour, Mrs Jennings affirming that the lady on the splint was poorly (she gave no exegesis) that the doctor had been sent for and that there were two more passengers on their way:

'Edward is with the carriage, with Sir John and they will attend to its repair and return here with the luggage. The coachmen are bid to lodge with us in the servants' quarters.'

Elinor, who was painfully aware of her own child safely within said nothing but felt deeply and sought Edward's presence as soon as he could be spared.

'Mrs Dolby, please organise some food for all those in need and their appropriate accommodation. I am obliged. Make all comforts available. We shall wait to see whether Mrs Darcy can be moved upstairs,' said Mrs Jennings.

Just as she had finished speaking, the doctor arrived and was shown forthwith to Elizabeth. At the same time Edward appeared at the kitchen door having come from the stables. Everyone re-convened within the parlour to assess the situation and gain comprehension of its needs. No sooner had these latter been established than each person went to his own tasks. The Reverend

Ferrars moved swiftly into the library wherein Elinor wept and wept:

'Most beloved husband, I feel so very much the pain of this lady and, indeed, that of her husband. Is it not anguishing enough to experience this crash without the loss of a first child?'

Together they stood hands firmly locked.

'Yes, we are one with them, stand one with them, in our comprehension and our compassion,' said Edward.

The voices in the hall communicated the departure of Dr Jago and the Ferrars-Middleton family put their heads out of the doors in which they were standing. All re-convened now to the dining-parlour where the group stood silently, in reflection. Just as Mrs Jennings was about to ask everyone to consider the next step, the door of the morning room could be heard opening and Ellen, the maid for that room now posted outside it, being addressed by Mr Darcy. Mrs Jennings left her own post at once to go to him.

'Mr Darcy, dear sir, may I be of any assistance to you?' she asked.

'Yes ma'am, I would be most grateful. May we withdraw?'

'Yes, indeed sir, come with me.'

Leading the way to a small anteroom off the library, Mrs Jennings offered her new guest a chair, which she could see that he needed.

'Mrs Jennings, we are so obliged to you. Indebted. I would like to appraise you of what Dr Jago has informed us and ask, if I may, for our continued dependence upon your charity for a few days longer?'

Nods of solemn acquiescence required no language.

'My wife has indeed, lamentably lost our child, but she is brave and I am only beginning to understand this double act of nature – for you know that it was the bolting of a stag in the concourse that created this occurrence.' Darcy looked down quietly, then continued. 'Nonetheless, the doctor feels that a few days' rest and then a slow drive back to our home and then more rest, will heal all. Mercifully, there is no break or bruising to defend. I do ask for your further kindness and reception of us, for which we are boundlessly grateful.'

'Mr Darcy you are very welcome. We are so sorry for your news and will employ complete discretion in all quarters. Please continue with us. If you feel that Mrs Darcy might be able to be moved upstairs to a suite of rooms, you both might be more comfortable. We will bring you something nourishing just now and when you are ready to see us you must do so.'

At this moment, Charles and Jane Bingley arrived in the Great Hall, escorted by Sir John Middleton, their host.

'My dear *family* you are all right?' called Mr Darcy softly from the staircase.

'We are dear Darcy, we are shaken but well, however, Elizabeth?' enquired Charles.

'Come, pray, to a quiet corner with me,' said their friend.

The three went into an annexe of the hall, the Bingleys sitting whilst their brother-in-law told them of Elizabeth's situation. Silence fell like a sword. Jane paled visibly at the sight of her brother-in-law dragging his left leg and, like them, in a pallor that was almost green. Darcy explained about the loss of their child, at once reassuring them that the worst was passed, despite all, that their sister was alive and being well cared for and that the most significant damage was to her heart and not the physical one. He somewhat shocked them further by continuing:

'But this heart is the beating heart of two people and two people can mend it.'

Jane, now weeping in a flood, took his attention but he added:

'Dear sister, do not distress yourself. As Elizabeth said at the place where we crashed, she is young, strong and resilient; we will drive home slowly and find all the rest and renewal there that we can.'

Now Bingley spoke.

'We are glad, dear Darcy, we are glad and, indeed, grateful that she is alive, that we are all alive; nevertheless, we are deeply saddened and deeply sorry that this has occurred and you must give her our love.'

'Yes, yes, of course, yes. And I feel that she might need Jane to help her with some small tasks. I will ask.'

As he started to leave them Bingley called out after him:

'But Darcy, what of your leg? You are dragging it horribly.'

'It is fine, thank you, the Doctor does not think it broken, just wrenched in several places and gone into a spasm: it will be quite fine again with rest.'

The Bingleys stood stock-still as their friend limped pathetically back to his wife; he was like a great stag himself, whose antler had been ripped off in a fight – it was a dastardly sight to see such a man brought so low.

'It is difficult to see our friend so wounded, my dear Jane,' averred the one, standing close to the other.

Jane nodded silently. They both remained mute for many minutes in this parlous state, pondering the situation and the experience of the collision; its noise and shock; the immediate chaos incumbent upon it and now their miraculous removal through such kindness and from a family they had never met before.

28

*O*n the second morning at the Park it happened that Mr Darcy was taking morning tea in the *Orangerie*, unusually to be found away from Elizabeth, when Edward came in to enquire about Mrs Darcy's health.

'I do not wish to disturb you sir, but how does your lady fare on this beautiful morning?' he asked.

'So kind, so kind, she is coming along very well indeed, thank you, also for having us here and for all your care, for which we are indebted. Pray, sit with me.'

Darcy, who was not a sociable individual, welcomed the man who had helped him in the grimmest of circumstances, a man he had taken to – by his very presence – before he had even spoken a word.

'Thank you,' said Edward sitting down amongst the ferns.

'Mr Ferrars, this is the seat of friends of your family-in-law, are you situated nearby, may I ask?'

'Yes sir, we are, near enough, at least – we are barely above two hours, in Dorsetshire. I am a country parson in a parish abutting my brother-in-law's home at Delaford Hall.'

'But forgive me, Mr Ferrars, do I not know of your family name in connection with London?'

'Yes, yes, you probably do sir, I am not here entirely by chance: I chose not to take the seat usually occupied by the eldest son, it was not my way – a quiet country parish was always my heart's wish, whatever the circumstances consequent upon its choosing.'

'Might I ask you, with not a little impertinence, what led you to such a decision?' asked Darcy, leaning toward his life-saving friend.

'Of course! I am not a lover of big social gatherings or the long list of connections one must inevitably foster within them – it all seems either false, or hypocritical, or both. It is not in my character to gush and ooze to please another! All that I ever wanted to be was a country parson, to keep bees, care for my parish as well as I could and now, as Elinor will tell you, we have our parish and our 'Barn Men', as she calls them.'

The term amused Darcy who asked who they were, these men of the barn.

'Well, I will gladly tell you, since we have met in such serious conditions, but I do not over-publish what we are doing, lest it be misappraised. After I had started to settle into my Sundays at Mary Magdalene, I realised, swiftly, that more and more persons were coming, particularly men. I say this not to proclaim my own doings but rather to illustrate my belief that there was some sort of need functioning there. I am not an evangelist in the sense of liturgy or regulation but only in the purpose and significance of the spirit of Love. I hope that you don't mind my saying that sir?'

'No, no, please, pray continue Reverend Ferrars,' said Darcy.

'Thank you, I felt that I wanted to make a place in which these men might be *heard*, such a place was not to be a political matter. However, I soon realised, as the men started to speak, that there was a deep fracture appearing in their lives and its consequent misery – I saw that as the weeks passed, the men were becoming more and more downward-looking, some looking ill, others speaking ill. Yet, Mr Darcy, you are a landowner and employer - and I do not wish to speak disrespectfully - but I see and hear that the men must be heard to avoid further remonstrance, and, of course, damage to their health.'

Darcy, who had been listening carefully, smiled.

'Reverend Ferrars, I applaud all that you have said, you are a man after my own heart, I also do not enjoy society – and I have made it my business to be as considerate as I am able to my tenants, without whose labour the produce of the land could not exist. Indeed, there have been particular strictures lain down for generations in our family; my father was always a good husband of the land and I have been taught to do the same, it was instilled in me, to be inclusive in my praise, organisation and payment. Why! I know every single family on the estate and they me. The difficulties come, I fear, when there is a lack of knowledge and mutual respect.'

'Indeed, sir, indeed, my own father was also exemplary on this head, yet he bore the concerns of the estate alone, and worried excessively about it: the result was that he died of a heart attack when I was seventeen. You understand, I do not seek to place blame upon any member of my family – it is a matter of lack of understanding, of that comprehension that comes from, shall I say, a less separated life - and when he died, the systems of generosity and mutuality died with him.'

'I see, I know myself that these matters are most perturbing, but may your venture in the barn go well – you have been most enlightening as well as coming to our rescue!'

The two men stood up and shook hands warmly.

'Please come to see us at Pemberley in a while, you are both most welcome.'

Darcy left with a small flourish, turning at the door:

'You know, my father always used to say, 'there but for the Grace of God go I.'

he days passed by silently, the Middleton household like a hospital with all its attendant rules and charity. Elizabeth improved with alacrity and on the fourth day came down to supper. Sir John greeted her warmly:

'A most felicitous welcome Mrs Darcy, may we gently enquire of your health?'

'I am becoming well, sir, thank you, and that is not a little in part to the vastness of your kindness and generosity; my husband and I, my sister and her husband, we are beyond gratitude to you.'

'O ma'am, ma'am, you are so very welcome, to help others when we can, do a good turn when we can, it is our way in this household. Please, enjoy a little wine with us and first a good soup, shall you?' said the patron of the table, all smiles.

As these latter were delivered by careful hands, Elizabeth struck up.

'Sir John, Mrs Jennings, I will not put myself forward to speak too long but I would like very much for my own familial party to tell you a little of our recent visit to Cornwall, which we so enjoyed and which was so diverting.

Thus, the journey through the soup, the roasts and the start of some wondrous puddings was upheld by the recounting of tales about elephants, beautiful and furlong-deep rivers and the changing character of the countryside along the way.

Just as Elizabeth was excusing herself to retire, a note came from Colonel Brandon to say that he also could give of his service to the distressed visitors were he to be needed. Further, that he and Marianne sent their most sincere wishes for the recovery to good health of Mrs Darcy and comprehensively warm wishes to the rest.

Sir John, who was always the executor of bringing persons together, was tender in his consideration when delivering the cordial message.

'My dears, our family, Colonel and Mrs Brandon are acquainted with your difficult time and send you all manner of condolences and heartfelt thoughts for recovery from your ordeal. The Colonel has been a friend of ours these many years and, to our great joy is married to Elinor's sister Marianne. We feel blessed to have encouraged their liaison, let us say, been enthusiasts for it!'

At this Elinor positively perked up: 'Say rather for bringing my beloved sister into a harbour of love and protection after being in a sea of harm!'

At which very moment all of those with comprehension nodded and sounded a knowing 'aye', to a man.

A most pleasant evening at Barton Park was thus concluded in concord and hope, for out of a short but fierce wave of trouble, both Bingleys and Darcys were beginning to be brought back to life.

---

30

*W*hen Edward and Elinor resumed their life at Delaford, that same life thrust them into doings with the Barn and the Barn Men. No sooner had the couple come through the door than a message came that Ned Rust wanted to see the Reverend Father. The latter was a little weary from travelling and even his compassionate care of Elizabeth in the shock of the crash. Much in Edward was said, even prayed for, in his own private way; he had been affected by the harrowing experience in which his presence was critical, but he rejoiced in the meeting with Elizabeth and her husband, and felt that he shared much with the latter, acreage notwithstanding.

Edward sent a message to Ned, through a faster service than the feet of the latter in bringing one to him but the affirmation was firmly made that it would be possible for the farmhand to come again the next evening.

When Wednesday came round, the barn was unusually full - word had spread that there was much afoot and Edward could feel, the moment that he walked in the door, that something had changed. As always, the gathering began with a prayer. All sat, all bowed their heads. This time the prayer was The Old Sarum, 'God be in my head and in my understanding... God be in my heart and in my thinking…' Apart from the very fact that Old Sarum was along the road and the prayer was one of the most beautiful and ancient addresses to the Divine, Edward always marked that it was the *heart* which was doing the thinking in these eleventh century words and not the parrot on the shoulder which seemed, so often, to be the content of the head. Yes! he completely agreed, for him the heart did indeed, think.

Edward asked himself how he was going to steer the group on this particular evening – he could feel their tension – how, he thought, was he to bring comfort to them when the hard facts were hard facts: hunger is a terrible thing and even the fear of it, for some, more terrifying than the reality.

As the time progressed, it was evident that Edward's 'own' men, those who worked on land nearby, some which even gave onto his home, were less defined in what they wanted, whereas those from an area further away seemed fiercer. The Reverend marked that a few came from not an inconsiderable distance – a thought which perturbed him greatly. Father Ferrrars, as they called him, did not have a judgemental bone in his body, he had simply wanted to make a place for a voice to be heard but it was rapidly becoming evident that there was a greater dynamo here than a voice and whatever, or *whoever* was fuelling it was doing something malevolent - and malevolence was not what Edward had in mind, or indeed, in his heart. This group was visited that night by an incipient rebel, Simeon Fawke – Edward blanched a bit at his name in these circumstances, for the man was, indeed, a potential troublemaker.

The Reverend always began by asking his men how he could help them:

'Gentlemen, I bid you welcome and ask you, as usual, how I might be of service to you, cautiously reminding that I cannot take a political stance here.'

Ned Rust came to the fore, a man well known to both the Colonel and his brother-in-law:

'Father, we know that you a'n't politicul but we need some of yore might as an edocated man. We mun' needs to go forrard.'

'Thank you, Ned, for your trust in me. The answer is that you have to be most careful, for in the last place, you do not want to lose your work, I…'

At this Fawke rose sharply from his seat and cut in:

'Mister Ferrars, we an' wish to cause you trouble but we need you to seek out some oak, as yerself, some 'igh up who wode 'elp us, listen to us an' 'elp us.'

'Simeon,' said the Reverend, quietly but firmly, 'I am a mere country vicar, not a political man and I would that you make no injury for yourself, or indeed, any other – that is *first*, Simeon, *first*. Yet I will cast my net amongst the gentry to see if there is someone to whom we may appeal.'

As the evening rolled along, the men seemed to cluster more, so that they appeared as one body, perhaps a federal body. In the moment that Edward stopped speaking, a great cheer rose from them, something which surprised him, but which was also a reminder of the limitations and constraints of the working man and the desperate and blocked nature of the situation in which he found himself. Whilst thinking that he would not like to fight with some of those within his immediate care, he also knew that a watershed had been reached: such was the urgency of their situation that these men needed, indeed, positively required, solid assistance.

Others felt able to add to what Fawke had said, albeit in a gentler manner but soon enough all became quiet and the meeting was ended. Each man filed out in silence, the air a little less thick than when he entered. The convenor resolved to go the very next day to someone of his acquaintance but not his pleasure, who might, possibly, possibly assist them.

31

*I*t was not beyond Edward's intelligent nature to miss that which was droll, thus, when he wrote to Lord Gallhope, he chuckled nervously at the nomenclature. The recent mention of this name, in Berkeley Square, had reminded the vicar of the not-so-quiet country parish that there was always power to be found if one were brave enough to search it out. The question was, would *this* power be receptive to his cause – he doubted it but dared, nevertheless, to make endeavour.

Gallhope the man, seemed unique, for he held huge lands, a good deal of which were given over to mining for tin and now, copper again. Edward felt it quite useful that this 'higher-ness-ness' (as he called the gentleman to himself) was also involved in farming, so that there might be a possibility of comprehension of the fire of revolt being ignited just now around parts of Dorset and, it should be said, potentially in Devon.

As Edward set out at eight in the morning the day after the meeting of the Barn Men and with his wife's full comprehension and not quite so full blessing, he acknowledged that he might run into a big wall. He knew the Gallhope family through his mother but not in any other manner than as a nodding acquaintance and, of course, they knew him and *all* his doings, since, above all else, his mother loved to chatter. Edward's late father had not liked the mining entrepreneur, he did not realise any ill will upon him, that was not his way - like father, like son - but he knew of the resemblance to inhumanity that was the mine and sometimes said so: a distinctly unprecedented soliciting in polite social circles.

The Gallhope household was but two hours' ride away. As Edward rode, a man deeply happy with his lot and forever grateful for the goodwill that had created it, he dwelt upon the relative simplicity of his situation, his wife growing now with their child and, that it was incumbent upon him, therefore, to help others - he who had been helped himself. So very recently an exile, the pastor knew a little of its taste: cast out by family and connections; closed out by his own mother and her way of thinking; ridiculed by his brother and sneered at by his sister and her husband who dare not say other; this priest who believed in the *power of love*, had to follow his heart, without compromise, to Dunford Castle.

The morning was crisp yet warm, riding fast through the forest and avoiding towns and villages, Edward wound his way across to the estate of his acquaintance. The magnificence of the bridleways lay before him at the approach into Somersetshire and the presence of a different geography, with some broad, flat sweeps of plateaux, spoke its own language. Arriving at the castle just before noon, Reverend Ferrars crossed the drawbridge, observing its marks of fortification. Small it was but its owner was lacking in neither wealth, nor, it would seem, the means of expanding it: the building was eloquent as a written log of material success. The servant taking Edward's horse made the country rector reassured of at least some sort of welcome and, safe in the knowledge of this he strode forward, as best he could, striding being the least of his skills in the library of his gaits. Uniting his long familiarity with the overt trappings of wealth with a humility that was both real and rare in these surroundings, the man from Delaford Parsonage - via Berkeley Square - armed himself ready for a different sort of human being from those within his compass just now.

'Sir, please come this way, his Grace awaits you,' urged the retainer. Reeling a little from the thought of a mine owner with a reputation indifferent to compassion being called 'his Grace', Edward nevertheless accelerated his pace.

Lord Gallhope was high in the fashion of his time; a veritable peacock, he was seated in a huge and voluptuously upholstered wing-back chair – cerise spots on deep mustard, the effect in tandem with the sartorial statement was astounding. Although the visitor was received into the library, a type of room he generally loved, this one was not so pleasant and a veritable *froideur* hung over it.

'Ah, young Edward, come in. Be seated. How is your mother?'

'Yes, she is well sir, thank you,' replied Edward, briefly pondering on his mother's continuing cantankerousness but scotching the thought as unkind!

'Is she in town just now?'

'Yes sir, she enjoys London life, the opera in particular.'

'And to what do I owe this kind visit, pray?'

The Reverend felt a small surge of panic as he knew well that the reason for his coming was far from kind.

'Yes, indeed, I have not been here since I was a boy (he did not dare to think that it was with his father) - it is beautifully situated.'

'Indeed!' said the spotted chair.

'Your Grace, I am mindful to be as plain speaking as decorum will allow. I have come to ask your advice.'

As Edward heard these words coming from somewhere far away behind him, the crows in the trees were making a huge commotion which reverberated around the inner ward and he felt that he must surely be at The Tower.

'You know, sir, that I have a small country parish in Dorset-shire and am married now. Well, it has been my desire, for some time, to help the local labourers in some way and I have been talking with them and most importantly listening to them.'

At this the *Grace* cut in at once, 'O, if you have been sent to ask support for this sort of nonsense then you have come to the wrong place! Do not tell me of every Tom, Dick and Harry who is puling, or inconvenienced by a fine day's work and pay at the end of it!'

'With all respect, *sir,*' Edward parried quickly, 'the men I have in my care as a rector are indeed, fine men, country labourers and true, the fact is that at the end of the week there is not enough money to put bread on the table for the next. I know that you have much experience in the field and so wanted to ask you a question.'

Silence. The speaker continued:

'Lord Gallhope, I have no comprehension of your views on the subject of the welfare of men, but I need someone powerful to lend support by hearing that the current, just now and locally, is becoming both fast-running and loud.'

As the speaker spoke, the hearer was turning an increasingly deeper shade of puce – most inharmonious with the decorous aspects of his chair – and leaning forward as if pushing into the magnificent facilities of the coal seams themselves. Edward could see that he was on dangerous ground but hoped that some learning could come through induction if no other means presented itself.

'Sir!' returned the magnate, 'do you expect me to have sympathy with the lot of such men? Why! they are little more than a rabble and were I not to be offering them the privilege of this work for me then they would be on some street corner, or other, don't you know? I follow all the usual channels of philanthropy in town, where they are fashioned for the best and most virtuous. These men are not my relations, they are a commodity and a commodity is a commodity, above or below ground.'

Edward knew that he was firing the last bullet:

'Yes sir, I hear what you tell me, but I ask that you might

remember the recent enough events in France; there is now, albeit a little later, a change afoot here, your *Grace*.'

Edward could hear the still, small voice within, echo, 'a very big foot' but he deferred to the Peacock's bristles; the luxury of the surroundings; the startling presence of the Tower outside the window and the increasing heat of the day.

Gallhope puffed and wheezed and edged himself off the seat; standing there he was barely taller than the wings of his commodious chair, nevertheless:

'I give you good day sir, my regards to your mother.'

Edward made a sharp bow. All was at an end.

As the pastor rode back the way he came, he bethought himself how easy it was to fail to serve when there was inadequate comprehension of the misery of another man's lot: he had tried but he was not going to give up yet.

32

*E*lizabeth and Darcy arrived home from Devonshire at a slow pace; the coachmen handled every matter within their jurisdiction with the utmost care, led by their master, whose fealty to his wife's experience was feather-light, almost within the authority of heaven itself. Many would have been brought low for weeks by the consequences of their ordeal but neither Darcy had it in them to cut into life's distinctive knocks with a hacksaw and parade the results to the world: had Elizabeth not said that she was young and strong? Nevertheless, the husband who loved his wife told the tale:

'I postpone all that I have bethought me to do in the next weeks, in order to do my best for you my dear one – do you greet such a wish with anguish or pleasure? I do not wish to swamp you.'

'I would be profoundly happy to be with you, my beloved Fitzwilliam; I am not ill, just a little shaken and wonder whether we might go along as two snails for a little while, as we settle after our emotional flurry. Shall we creep along together, my dearest?'

'I think so, it would please me greatly to sit with you, perhaps walk a very little way, when you feel able?' said Darcy, allowing himself to spread out in a beautiful, lemon covered chair, next to the bed.

They were both resting in the sunshine in a newly appointed room in a small corner of the front of the house, where the vistas were remarkable. First the lake stood straight before them and then the woods rolled down to meet the water and behind them both, the greater sweep and majesty of the forest. Darcy had created this small space, once a dressing room to one of the bedrooms, with homely comfort in mind. The morning sun was delicious and, in summer, there was a moment when the after-noon light caught the colours of the refurbishments in a most romantic way: the effect was one of being in the parlour of a honey bee – sweetly light brown oak tempered with warm mustard upholstery and deep blue dots.

Elizabeth loved this new hiding place: the dots spoke her. Knowing how much his wife loved to sit and read, the master of Pemberley had commissioned the placing of a small day bed built into the window seat – which of course had been expanded for the purpose – and across which had been hung a second set of curtains, so that at once, the bed was like an Arabian tent, cut off from the world and with a sublime privacy. In making this wonderful gift to his wife, Darcy had no idea how soon it would become useful, for it was to this place that he and Elizabeth repaired after their tumble in a Devonshire forest.

'I will bring us back to ourselves within this space,' he thought, drawing the first set of curtains back for Mrs Darcy to lie in comfort. Placing his own self - in both appreciation and prox-imity – into a big chair that would have accommodated them both, he stretched out his great length, not as a cat, thought Eliza-beth but the lion that he indubitably was.

'I do believe that I have never rested in all the years of my life so far,' said the lion.

'O, I can imagine that you have not!' replied his wife,

completely enveloped in a finely spun shawl the colour of his chair, 'such a pleasure must have been beyond your life itinerary! but now the interminable wait is over: it is *de rigeur to rest*!' The shared laughter was precious for the appropriate softness of its timbre and the peaceful renewal that it brought.

'Peace was something that could never take place within the walls of Longbourn,' she continued, 'it was an unknown and unknowable concept, possible only in long walks with Jane, you know, those about which you teased me – the bridleway to Meryton and sometimes beyond.'

The man before her smiled, remembering a certain second proposal on a walk to the same village and he took her hand tenderly, almost imperceptibly, in response. For the first time, Elizabeth felt the equality of human standing sweep over her; here was someone who had drawn her to him in a novel form of parity: it was, indeed, both curious and breath-taking.

'My beloved Fitzwilliam! said a seemingly far-away voice, 'I thank you for bringing me to a new place of self-respect, one in which I am no longer confined to the inadequacies of my parenting or a lack of entail in my favour, or the excessive irritations of having two persons in a whole household with whom to share good conversation.'

'Do not speak, my beloved, against the guiding principles, e'en intelligence of my heart – an intelligence so structured as to bring me to the harbour of your own. Do you not observe that the self-same arrogance that you accused me of in our first encounters, provides me with the wherewithal to extinguish objection to anything but a marriage with you into eternity?'

As the two came closer together, the reality of what they had created became real in a long silence.

'Further, my dearest,' Elizabeth broke in gently, 'I am also pleased to discover repose! But where did you find some minutes for yourself of true reflection?' asked Elizabeth.

'Upon my horse, of course!' exclaimed Darcy with aplomb.

Laughter was as uproarious as it was voluminous – in this marriage the panacea to all ills as well as the communion.

In a moment all was silence as the two looked with passion at each other: it was not yet time for earthly love, but the feelings had not fled with the grim truths of the stag on the concourse.

33

*E*xtreme insights came for both the mistress and master of Pemberley from their interpretation of what had occurred in the top of Devonshire, but this latter had also had some effect upon Georgiana. Absent when her brother and sister arrived from the south, it was only when she received belated news of their arrival in Derbyshire that she began to worry; they both met her in the Great Hall - she had been faster at entering her home than they anticipated.

'Dearest Georgiana!' the couple sang out to her in neo-unison as they came down the last steps of the staircase and she stepped through the great door.

'My dear ones! I have been missing you and worrying about you. Something felt strange in my stomach, are you both quite well?' called Georgiana, straightening her skirt a little whilst fending off Bess who had escaped and was vying for attention from her favourite sister.

Mr and Mrs Darcy stood stock-still at this somewhat telling question, Elizabeth answered with care:

'We have been in a little, shall we say *debacle,* our dearest sister but all is well now. Come, take some tea with us now and we can exchange news.'

Georgiana, who could already see that something had indeed occurred to them both, would not be put off by tea:

'My dearest ones, let us sit at once, I can see, or rather feel that you are a little *something*, by your very faces; I will eschew all else that is not direct, pray tell me all that has passed whilst we were gone from one another.'

'Well, let us retire to the small parlour upstairs, it is warm in the afternoon sunshine,' said Elizabeth softly, taking her sister's hand as carefully as she could, for the colour was already fading from Georgiana's sensible face.

'Please, do not be worried, our dearest,' said the master of Pemberley, 'all is well now.'

An imperceptible nod fell between the married couple, the telling was first to be on Darcy's part. They drew closer around the soft cushions of a small sofa by the window in the upstairs sitting room which they all shared, Georgiana's brother on a separate chair – they made a wonderful triangle:

'We deferred telling you earlier, for we did not want to perturb you, dearest sister but we found ourselves in a collision with a great stag in the forests of Devonshire.'

The sisterly countenance fell further at once, the tone and register of her brother's voice lending all the information necessary for suspected gravity to be confirmed. Well aware of Georgiana's tenderness of heart, Elizabeth took her hand again, moving imperceptibly closer as she did so; reluctant to give any personal information that could be furnished later in private between the two ladies, Darcy continued in scant detail to include the upsetting of the carriage; the bolting of the horses from their shafts; the spilling out of all the passengers and the arrival of kindly persons from heaven, led by one Reverend Edward Ferrars, who conducted all of them, in stages, to the home of family friends but five minutes away.

Miss Darcy, gaining strength from the comprehension that flowed through her gentle questioning, was all attention and love, yet still anxious to know every detail available under the sun. The other two members of her family insisted on meagre intelligence for the time being, their wish for the avoidance of an avalanche of emotion notwithstanding and deeply desiring to succeed in persuading their loved one that all was truly well.

'But are you both quite recovered, now?' pleaded the youngest of the three.

'We are delighted to be home again but must reassure you of the plenitude of care and attention given to us by the Ferrars and the Middleton family in whose house we were lodged,' said Elizabeth, carefully avoiding all mention of doctors.

Every fine hair was brought to bear upon the situation: the recovery of the carriage and the finding of the horses, then the return of wounded persons and belongings to Barton Park, all underwritten by a great flow of kindness and consideration at every turn.

'Do you then promise me that you are feeling well now, after this shocking event?' pleaded Georgiana again.

'We are, indeed, sister, do we not look well? A little tired, perhaps, but knowing and understanding that we must rest and go along somewhat sedately for a while,' Mrs Darcy continued.

Still uncertain of the real outcome of the overturning of the coach, Georgiana nevertheless remained calm enough in the presence of such apparent certainty of form as was presented before her.

'Come, our dearest sister, it is time that you told us of your time in London, let us ring for tea,' said the master of Pemberley, continuing, 'enough concern for one day.'

34

*T*he weeks passed slowly, time, in its ineluctable way,
healed everyone and everything. It was decided by the
mistress and master that knowledge of their loss be kept to a
minimum. No servant had been informed of the complications of
the collision and the coachmen were sworn to secrecy. Realising
that nothing was to be gained from giving excessive detail to
Georgiana, her sister nevertheless decided that her fellow conspirator in lutes must be told. A possibility for the telling came one
warm afternoon as the two were sitting by the lake:

'My dear sister,' said Elizabeth, 'I would tell you briefly of the
outcome of the collision, but I err on the side of caution for I am
so very well now. Ordinarily I would say nothing. However, you
have become my dear sister, whose love and fealty I appreciate,
nay, cherish.'

Elizabeth's hearer was delicately suspicious, was she not, she
asked herself, a sister-at-arms?

Mrs Darcy continued: 'on the morning of the collision I had
observed, after noting for a little while, that I was with child. I did
not want to inform Fitzwilliam until we were returned home.
When the collision happened, I did not feel, or remember much
for a few moments after the great noise, nor did I know that it

was, indeed, a big animal with which we had collided. Mr Darcy seemed anxious about my hip as he sat with me on the floor of the forest, but it was, of course, not my hip. So, you see, most beloved Georgiana, it has been a little journey for us both; what I have felt has been also most pointedly felt by your brother – a fact remarkable, I would have thought, for a man of these times?'

There was a desperate pause as Miss Darcy paled, then brought herself back to some colour, then wept silently. Elizabeth, now holding her dear friend's hand, could only wait through these rainbow changes which indicated the sheer and fine sensibility of her sister, especially when presented with brutal facts.

As Georgiana started to say something her sister gently put out her other hand to silence her, saying:

'My dearest, I would that you are not bereft in any way for we are well recovered. Fitzwilliam was hurt by the loss and shocked at its effects upon him, but we are both of the opinion that we shall proceed slowly and see how we go along. Why! are we not both alive and here to tell you that we have encountered one of life's difficulties and are still here?'

Sisterly love flowed between them as they sat before the magnificence of Pemberley – the day was without precedent.

'It is with sorrow that I hear of your loss, my dearest and *only* sister but please know that I will listen to the courage that accompanies the telling and learn something for my own heart,' said Georgiana softly, after some time.

'I think that I would like to take a turn of the lake, if you will, my dear fellow lutenist, which reminds me that we must again follow our hearts up the stairs!'

The two young women set off with such intimations of joy, despite all indications to the contrary provided by the preceding discussion, their horizons widened and enriched by the desire to be in truth with one another.

'Of course, I shall say nothing to my brother,' said Georgiana, as the breeze lifted her skirts a little to show the most feminine of ankles.

35

The fragrant peace of Pemberley was ruffled. Bingley's sisters had asked if they could stay for a few days on their way to visit a friend in the north. Elizabeth was silent, her husband was glum, Georgiana looked vague; all agreed that they had to recover from their prejudice and allow the intrusion – they would invite Jane and Charles also and that, at least, would bring welcome cordiality.

The days sped by quickly and the morning came for the arrival of the carriages – the Bingley sisters would come first, with Mr Hurst, of course and the dearest family only at dinner time. Elizabeth thought it a good idea to take Caroline and Elizabeth to Lambton to lunch, the Lamb and Flag was always agreeable, and Mr Hurst would be happy resting with his port. In haste, Mrs Darcy asked Miss Darcy if she would mind accompanying them, knowing of her shyness but needful of reinforcement against the barrage. Georgiana raised no objections, something for which her sister was completely grateful.

'Dear Georgiana, you are indeed perfect! I know that your inclination is not toward harsh-speaking society women!' said Elizabeth.

'My dear sister, I am perfect only in my intention to support you against would-be foes: I have not forgotten the silliness of words spoken near to you about the regiment and, after all, are we not already comrades through our precious lute?' Georgiana replied.

The two looked carefully at one another in appreciation.

Before any further speech was possible the great doorbells rang out and the entrance of much noise and bustle overturned the morning peace of Pemberley. Darcy could be heard greeting his friend's sisters and Mr Hurst; the two other Darcys hurried downstairs to further his welcome.

Thinking how like it was to the greeting of the Rosings party, Elizabeth put on her best composure:

'Welcome everyone, we are favoured to have you with us. Pray, come through and take some tea, won't you? If you would like to ascend first, Mrs Reynolds will show you your rooms, we have put you in the west wing, the views of the lake are so diverting.'

The party seemed arrested at the strongly given instructions but then recommenced their babble, feeling adequately placed to go straight to refreshment.

'Well! you look settled here, quite an accomplishment, Elizabeth, to be mistress of Pemberley,' said Caroline tersely.

The mistress of Pemberley said nothing but smiled for the tea to be poured: she was not going to court anguish this day.

'We are expecting Mr and Mrs Charles Bingley later this afternoon. Did you have a good journey?' she asked.

'Yes, we did, all roads seemed clear today and the Great North was fast; we find it commodious you know, there are a few good inns for short stops and we know where we like and who is accommodating, do we not, Caroline?' said Louisa.

'Indeed, sister. Tell me, Darcy, how is all with you?'

'We are well, thank you, Elizabeth and I are full of ideas for the future of Pemberley and Georgiana joins us at every opportunity.'

'Pray! not sharing the running of this great house with your wife! Whatever next, Darcy, are you mad?' riposted the younger Bingley sister.

The master of the great house said nothing and proceeded to the window, saying:

'It is a fine day, ladies, my wife and my sister thought to invite you both to Lambton for luncheon.'

Expecting a rebuff, he sat down where he was. Prepared.

'O charming, I am sure,' said Caroline, 'it is the like of which we never do but we are prepared to look downwards occasionally. It will be bearable. Do you not think Louisa?'

It was thus agreed that shortly after the taking of tea a small, female party would set out for the village. Not being a woman for grudges, Elizabeth had asked one of the friends at Chatsworth if it might be possible to see a little of their gardens, so she suggested such a diversion for the post-luncheon period.

'O no! said Louisa this time, we could not possibly be out of doors for so very long in this late summer sunshine, why! we shall *all* look like gypsies! Whatever were you thinking dear Elizabeth? I am sure that one little *dip* into Lambton will serve us for a long time.'

The dip was thus commenced.

Hoping that there would be few carriages going to the village today, Georgiana asked the senior coachmen to assist them in finding the most attractive route for the five-mile journey, of course, the views were magnificent at this time of year.

Arriving at the Lamb and Flag in good time, the Bingley sisters, who had barely spoken along the way, recommenced their huffing and puffing about the smallness of the place; the *perfect inadequacy* of the steppingstones through the mud; the noise of the carts putting down their wares; the great inconvenience of having stairs to mount to the dining room and the equally great inconvenience of having arrived in such inconsequent society.

'Of course, we are so very often in St James', you know, it does leave us a little bereft of good company when we are far from home, does it not, Caroline?' said Louisa.

Elizabeth, who had always observed a thankful reticence to mention the royal party on previous Bingley female visits, was a little taken aback but began to speak quietly with the lovely waiting staff who were as quietly offering a warm and sincere welcome to all.

The party proceeded straight to the dining room where Caroline began, perversely, asking for lamb!

'Ma'am, we are so sorry but there is not lamb upon the menu today, we are really still out of season and expect that there will be new lamb in a very short time,' came the reply from the pleasant lady who always served Elizabeth and Darcy on their visits.

Caroline, who was puffing even further at the inconvenience of the absence of the meat, now spoke in a louder and even more persistent tone to enquire further:

'Well, perhaps you would inform me of what you *do* have?'

Both Elizabeth and Georgiana, already a little flushed at the usurping of their role as hosts, remained silent, whilst the kindly serving lady, their friend, directed out the menu as Caroline ordered first, for herself.

Thankfully, luncheon passed without further offence to good manners and the party drove home, the Bingley women continuing their inane chatter and Georgiana and Elizabeth, seated closely in the carriage, communicating through their very juxtaposition. Upon arrival at Pemberley, the visit to Chatsworth's gardens having been liquidated, the Bingley sisters separated one to her chamber, the other to find her husband, with ne'er a word of gratitude nor even pleasantry for the outing. Elizabeth's raised right eyebrow silenced her husband as he came forward to greet the now dispersing party, one glance at his own sister's crestfallen face providing any further information that he was lacking.

'We shall see you all at dinner, then?' said Darcy, being unwilling to suggest further possibilities for the diversion of London society. The three passed silently into the library, where Mr Hurst was supping his early afternoon port, only to proceed through a door in the bookshelves, unseen. Creeping in considerable stealth past the sleeping gentleman and into the hidden anteroom where fragrant saucers of tea had been laid for persons exhausted by the insensible, the Darcy trio sat down in gratitude. Seeing the pale tea and tiny marzipan cakes at its side made both sisters weep and take one of Darcy's arms apiece: he was delighted beyond words at his wealth. Doing his best to avoid discussion of the inn at Lambton, the same later concluded, when he and his wife were alone upstairs:

'Well, my dearest, I may assume that your outing to Lambton was as ill met as the faces of the Bingley women on their return from it?'

'My love, you are in perfect comprehension,' whispered Elizabeth.

'I thought so, come, let us rest together for a while, our own dear sister is playing the piano.'

The two lay on the *chaise longue*, filled with joy for all that they had become to one another.

Soon the afternoon sun was coming round and the sound of a carriage on the drive alerted the snoozing pair back to life: their beloved Bingleys proper had arrived and could be seen looking well and greeting the butler warmly.

'Thank God,' said Darcy, 'for real family. Do let us have dinner early so that we extinguish any dangerous fires before they begin, or rather continue, if I may be as bold as to mention again the luncheon in our favourite haunt.'

'Yes! what a good idea and perhaps we might smuggle Jane and Charles up here for a little nightcap before sleep?'

Darcy nodded that special nod that he brought out in moments of *haut complicité*.

In a second, the Darcy camp was admitted to the hall and all was conviviality and the felicity of seeing one another again.

'Our dear Bingleys, please do come in, let as at once to some tea, or would you rather go upstairs first?' said the master of Pemberley.

Then Elizabeth, after him: 'Indeed! you know where we always put you, everything is just where you left it.'

The sisters hugged as if they had not seen each other for years, the men shook hands warmly and Georgiana was quickly summoned from the music room.

'We would like tea dear sister, if we may, will it incommode you?' said Jane, taking off her bonnet.

'No, precisely *not*, we are exquisitely pleased to see you, to sit with you, to comprehend all that has occurred since last we met. Come!' commanded Mrs Darcy, taking her newer sister's hand in the most lucid inclusion.

The party, now reunited after some severe recent experiences together, went quickly to the morning room, without the discovery of the other guests. Elizabeth felt that it was always a lamentable matter to witness some of the behaviour of their dear friend Charles' sisters, but she knew well how they were made and to what lengths Caroline would go to be seen as the superior personage in whatever set of personages she was present. As the youngest child of three, Charles Bingley was the opposite of his outspoken and arrogant middle sister and seemed more congruous with the elder, Louisa; yet she too was capable of the sneering banter that the younger of his two siblings seemed to adopt as her *modus operandi*. Mrs Darcy left such thoughts behind as she claimed the scene immediately before her:

'How are you dear ones? How were the lanes?'

'O we had a happy drive thank you, and you my sister, how are you both?'

'I am well, dearest Jane, and so is my dear husband – his leg simply mended as we were at home again – you see! We are both in health again and have been planning what we might do about setting a new orchard between the lake and the woods.'

Seeing that no further discussion was necessitated upon the recent circumstances in which the party had all found themselves, Jane nevertheless spoke a soft, yet warmly appreciative word to the effect of her gladness that all was gradually coming back to an equilibrium.

'And Darcy, how do you fare with your new projects on the estate?' asked his best friend Charles, the two continuing quietly as the ladies poured tea.

All was of the dearest affability between them, no one marring all that the friends shared through ignorance or consequential selfishness or wish to be first, in either speech or presence. Soon it was time to dress for dinner.

The gong sounded at a quarter to seven. Intimately connected with four out of the seven persons present, Elizabeth was in an expansive mood for the evening ahead. Casting no aspersions on her guest's earlier rudeness and indeed, all the rudeness of their history, the mistress of Pemberley came down the stairs escorted by her husband, glowing with pleasure and the sort of womanly pride that comes from knowing that one is well loved. Caroline, who was waiting in the Hall, caught a certain look between the couple as they approached the last set of stairs and Elizabeth, knowing how much the other had wanted to marry the man she now called husband, impressed upon her heart the determination to have no more detrimental thoughts of Bingley's sister.

'O my,' bethought Mrs Darcy, 'were that it could be possible to erase memories of unkindness from the past, yet we can reduce their *effect* upon us, I am sure.' She remembered the startling pain once caused to Georgiana made by Caroline's wilful mentioning of Mr Wickham.

Conversation at dinner flowed well as the Darcys placed a little *this* and a little *that* into the dynamic, avoiding all inhospitable subjects. The weather, the state of the roads and the great dilemmas facing ladies who had to make major decisions upon the choosing of the *correct* wardrobe for inner society, became the evening staple and all Darcys and two kindly Bingleys were gratitude itself for the flow of the inane river over their heads. The clock was just striking ten, however, when Caroline began to vent her irritation, a state punctuated by theatrical swipes of spite at the most harmless individuals of their acquaintance. The conversation swerved to the parlous state of huge families; the unkempt appearance and positively feral behaviour of some of the homeless seen hanging about St James' - 'waiting for titbits you know, from the great kitchens' - when Miss Bingley began to wave her arms about. Now well plied with several glasses of Chablis, she lurched to the 'horrid distaste' she felt at 'seeing so many unwanted children going about the place in town.' She continued, having thought herself very amusing on this head, making pleas for 'a veritable Pied Piper of Hamelin' to appear and wave such errors of judgement *and behaviour* (said in the darkest *sotto* voce) from the London streets; she furthered her hypothesis by standing up, in great inebriation and saying to Elizabeth, in full face:

'O, and we were sorry to hear of your *loss*, Elizabeth, but you know, there are far too many infants in the world as it is.'

Thinking this line very funny, very topical, she sat down again with a great flounce upon the cushions. There was a formidably deep silence for a moment as shock made its entry and before Darcy could say anything, Elizabeth leaned into the table and said, with great dignity:

'Well, Caroline, I may have lost our first child in the collision, but I still have the love of one of the most precious men on this earth.'

There was another, deafening silence, then the scraping of a chair which fell back with the force of its owner: it was *not* the mistress of Pemberley who left the table red faced but rather the woman who deserved the definition of its very shame.

After such iniquitous behaviour, the party was silent, Charles' face bleached white with desperation began to speak slowly:

'Dearest Elizabeth, I am beyond both shame and words for what has just occurred. Darcy, I think that you must waste no time in suggesting that Caroline leave at once in the morning – she has preyed upon your hospitality for years and this must be for the last time.'

Elizabeth looked at her husband, as, unusually, he stood up.

'Please feel no remorse on Caroline's part, dear friend, I will speak to her tonight, but I do agree that she can come here no longer,' said Darcy, continuing, 'in all my years of knowing her, I have believed that she would come through the anger that she insistently displays when she is baulked at not having what she wants but it has not happened yet. Alas. Permit me to suggest that we all retire, that she leaves before breakfast tomorrow and that we start a new day thereafter. I hope it befits me to say that we do have some mortal understanding of why this has happened. We bid you all the warmest goodnight.'

So-saying the master of Pemberley bowed to Charles and to Jane, who was ashen and swept Elizabeth out of the room; even before the first step on the staircase was mounted, the latter took her husband in a passionate embrace, which did not take him by surprise one jot – were they not, by now, come through together, as one heart?

36

*I*n moments, the staircase to the opposite wing heard the footsteps of the Hursts as they dragged up to their chamber – one inebriated into near-oblivion, the other in such an unusual distress that she could barely breathe. Below, in the dining hall, Mr Bingley was gathering himself:

'Shall we go up my dearest Jane?' he asked, 'or would you like to walk in the garden?'

'I would prefer to be outside, beloved Charles.'

In several paces they were beside the great house and before the lake. The full moon seemed to be orange – it was still early, and the air was warm, despite a little breeze. The light spun silver intelligence into all it touched, Jane felt better to be beneath its orb. Despite wanting very much to be with her sister, she knew, being a married woman, that it was to her husband that Elizabeth must now turn – they both must – especially with regard to the content of the audacious attack.

'It is with such regret that I pronounce upon my own sister, but I have never before heard anything so underhand and spiteful my dear Jane.'

The latter, who was slowly coming back to herself, surprised her husband by saying most firmly:

'I agree and how did Caroline know?'

The two turned to face one another, the hills rising before them and the shadow of the house to their backs. Charles took his wife's face in his hands:

'I cannot imagine, my dearest love, nor do I wish to investigate, but it has been ungracious, beyond anything.'

'My beloved,' she answered, 'let us to sleep now and hope that the morning may bring some amelioration of the effects of this miserable occurrence.'

'Indeed, I shall ask Louisa and Mr Hurst to leave also and, with your permission, ask Darcy whether he would like us to proceed home,' said Darcy's best friend.

'It is right, you are right, my dear one. Let us see what the morning brings,' his wife concurred.

The morning did, however, bring a wealth of change, for the whole Bingley sister contingent vanished at daybreak. Knowing the sounds of his own home, Pemberley's master heard the departing carriage, whate'er the stealth with which its content endeavoured to leave. By breakfast time Darcy and Elizabeth had walked up through the forest, with Bess and Whippet, her gangly friend who was, in fact, a thin, black Labrador with mysteriously long legs. Discussion of last night's events was no more: in the time which they had been together, the couple had manoeuvred around many obstacles and faced some most difficult circumstances, the death of their child – for that was how they saw it – notwithstanding.

In witnessing the bile of a woman weighing herself as scorned, the partners understood the origins of the spite that had spewed from Caroline's mouth, it was, nonetheless, unacceptable. Darcy had shown the Bingley sisters so much hospitality and so often, that any insult would have been unthinkable, but this was not an insult but an *assault* and should be treated with the finality of the contempt that it deserved. Both agreed that the friendship, the deeply held friendship with Charles was exempt from any harm: no blame could be imputed to their beloved friend and now brother, through association. In this, Fitzwilliam Darcy stated his allegiance to family. It was, in fact, the marking of this latter assertion that brought tears to Elizabeth Darcy – so long habituated to ill-use by her mother's tongue, that part of her was fully able to divert the potential power of words out of her heart's way, save those of her husband but then, since he had become her husband, ill feeling did not obtain.

'Let us allow the day to be kind to us, my dearest, lovely Elizabeth,' said Mr Darcy as they came into sight of the lake.

'Indeed, sir!' replied his wife, 'it is time for breakfast.'

37

*E*linor had wanted to see Mrs Jennings again for some time and since they had not been at Barton Park for weeks, she asked Edward if, when the present family guests had left, they might have her to stay? Once judging Sir John Middleton's mother as vexing, Edward's wife had, nonetheless, missed seeing the lady who was so kind to her during Marianne's illness and whose bubbling personality sounded out as an absence in her life. Mrs Jennings had given Elinor and Marianne three months' hospitality and during some very telling times – the great upset with Willoughby and her sister's subsequent illness.

It was dusk and the pastor's wife was walking back across from being with the Brandons when she sensed that someone was behind her; being a woman to whom fear was a comparative stranger, she carried on walking; her kitchen door in sight. She paused for a second, now being certain of the sound and, as she stopped, it stopped. Walking on briskly to the lit doorway she heard more voices and as she rounded the corner into the yard, could see a small group of men gathered by the door.

Gathering herself quickly she ran towards the men most of whom she recognized as being part of Edward's group. Before anxiety could release her, she saw that Edward was raised a little

153

above the group standing on the steps. As she approached, he caught her eye and carefully, slightly, shook his head – she understood at once – she was not to go there. Now was the dilemma whether to return to the Hall quickly, regardless of the noise in the bushes and the men around Edward or go back into the house via the front door – but which was locked since the servants would have closed up for the night.

She employed courage and ran as the wind back to the Hall – the Colonel was, after all, an army man.

Almost incapable of speech as she reached the door, she nevertheless pulled the bell as many times as she could muster. A flustered retainer arrived, whom she burst past, shouting at the same time.

'Colonel, Colonel, please come to help, I think that Edward is in difficulty!'

Help was at once by her side without question, pulling on a coat as he emerged running from the parlour, Marianne behind.

'Stay here!' he commanded as his wife endeavoured to follow.

Elinor and the Colonel, by now both outside, exchanged information as they ran.

'Edward is surrounded in the house yard by a group of men – some are his Barn men – he motioned for me not to proceed, so I came here directly. I think that there was someone in the shrubbery, watching me as I came home.'

The Colonel said nothing. The distance being short, they could see and hear the raised voices as they rounded the yard corner. The Colonel stepped forward, the force of his presence like a barrier behind the men and roaring out above the latter: 'Gentlemen, what ails thee?'

For a moment there was shocked surprise as the whole group, some ten or eleven, stopped, to a man, and glared at the intrusion.

'There is no harm, Colonel, the men are upset and have come to protest their distress!' said Thomas Farmer.

'This is not the way forward sirs, may Reverend Ferrars and I ask that you leave quietly.'

Now as silent as they had been vociferous, the group turned as one for the direction of the road. Above them, Edward's calm voice:

'Goodnight, gentlemen, go quickly to your homes.'

Edward, Elinor and their brother-in-law went indoors where the verbal scuffle which had arrived on the Ferrars doorstep was a discussion in the back parlour, until midnight. Word was sent to Marianne not to worry by any means and to lock the house, the servants were asked to go to bed and the three sat in silence for quite a while, recovering from the flurry.

Edward was shocked at the severity of the words and from a group he thought he knew and sat with a slight pallor till warmed by tea. Elinor sat rigidly, recovering from her anxiety for her husband; the rapid race to the Hall; the questions revolving around her head as to the nature of the presence in the shrubbery and her child within; the Colonel breathed back life into them all:

'Do not see this as worse than it is dear friends, dear *family*; they were not brandishing weapons, nor were bringing spite to you – I could see that you represent authority to them, authority who will not hear them.'

'Yes, yes, I agree, the manner they employed, nonetheless, is deeply unacceptable, why, it is dark now; unwelcome doings belie the lateness of the hour,' replied the Reverend, looking down.

'It is so, dear Edward and there needs to be some brake applied to the galloping horse of Wednesday evenings in the barn, if you do not object to the intrusion of my opinion. Good manners and safety first.'

'Yes, we agree,' said Edward to Elinor, now thinking of the necessity of reaching her bed.

'I will bid you goodnight,' said Brandon. 'Rest well, for they will not return and did not come to do you ill, remember, simply but not merely, to explode their feelings.'

'Yes, indeed, Colonel, we also bid you a grateful goodnight.'

38

*E*linor was mercifully asleep as Edward crept in after sitting by the fire a while and he was able to slip in without explanation of the end of the evening's events. Such sleep was rudely awakened, however, at seven in the morning, with loud knocking at the front door. It was a messenger for Edward.

'Sir, good day, are you Reverend Ferrars?' said the man at the door.

'I am, who may I ask is enquiring?'

'I bring a missive for you from Sir William Wick, whom you will know, is our magistrate. It is an informal warning sir and it is incumbent upon me to request your signature for the receipt of it.'

Edward stood back from the portal, now wide awake but marking the offensiveness of such a call at this time of the morning. Wisely avoiding a riposte, he signed the document, looked the loud-voiced man straight in the eye and with a brusque 'Good day', closed the door.

Deciding not to go back up to Elinor, her condition being of some priority, he stepped into the library. The upshot of the brief note was at once comprehended: he, Edward was being warned by Sir William against the 'reported activities taking place on your property, that run counter to His Majesty's policies concerning the aggregate of persons.'

Edward comprehended enough of the law on this head to know that he was not breaking it, but the point was that in only a matter of *hours* someone had informed the magistrate not only of last night's meeting but those preceding it.

'Here is the rub,' thought the Reverend, warning his own thoughts to stop them running into meanness and gossip on the possibilities of the identity of the informer. He decided at once not to share either the letter or his thoughts on it with his wife, for the moment, and the morning was put to good use by excusing himself to ride out on some paltry mission.

The lanes gave Edward great succour, mounting and lowering as they did in some wonderful countryside. As he descended towards the Abbey, he thought he might seek entry to speak of this matter to Father Mark, a man a decade older than he and of a similar outlook and sensibility.

'Yes, it was between Tierce and Sext now, he might be free to see me,' he thought.

Edward's horse Nonna knew her way into the Abbey well and chose the appropriate spot for her owner to dismount; no sooner had he rung than a friendly face appeared at the grid and admission was instant: it was a novice called Benjamin and he knew whom Edward wanted to see.

One priest was led into the anteroom of the library to meet the other. Greeting each other warmly, the two sat down. The Father could see that Edward was well but ruffled and put out his hand at once to offer support and an ear!

The energy in the room was beautiful – Edward always observed this with grateful pleasure – the smell of the beeswax polish; the scent of the candles of the same; the smell of frankincense and, these days, the tiniest hint of coffee, a cup of which was proffered and gladly received.

'I can see that something has upset you dear friend' – said the Abbot to the priest.

'Yes, but first Father Mark, I bid you greetings and ask if you are well, if *all* is well?'

'Yes, yes, indeed I am, dear friend, now, do not obfuscate, tell me, I am all attention.'

'O, Father, all is well with me, I live, as you know, sheltered beneath the kindness of Colonel Brandon; I am happily married and we await our first child; it is still summer; yet I am hunted by a lack, a lack of ability to help or ameliorate a situation that is, I fear, galloping fast beyond me!'

Edward recounted the story of his 'Barn Men' up to the events of the last night and the miserable event of the morning – he knew that it all had to stop for him, but the stopping still left the reality of hungry children and anguished parents – a reality which was not going to go away if ignored. As well as the new mechanics in agriculture there had been a cutting back in Poor Law provisions: the situation seemed impossible.

Father Mark listened with great care, the old clock behind him ticking away its own comprehension.

'Edward, these are times in the affairs of mankind when a little compassion goes a long way, it does not, however, put bread on the table. For once, I do not know what to say: the door is always open for you here, but I cannot give you a ready answer. You see, my friend, we are still in the crook of the elbow, where the men who own the land do not, *cannot* somehow comprehend how it might be to be hungry – they are sticklers for the old regime and do not wish to see beyond their noses. Yet, Edward, yet! rebellion walks apace amongst us – we are neither deaf nor blind here. In any life there are difficulties to bear but no one ever said that life should be run by drudgery and the fear of hunger and that is what is happening in many, many places. If a man works the land, he must come home to the prospect of a meal on his table.'

The two men talked on till the first bell for Sext rang, they could not conclude, conclusion was not on offer that day, but a lighter parish priest rode back up the hill, the oaks and their acorns scenting his journey and a glimpse of a herd of fallow deer lifting his heart, the size of the king stag's antlers notwithstanding.

It was sublime to reach home, to put Nonna back in her stable and thank her for her loving help and go to the upstairs parlour – Elinor's favourite retreat just now – to the comfort and compatibility of his wife.

The next day brought a trickle of revelations to Edward – as he was saying Nones himself, he gained a sudden insight into his betrayer. There had been a couple, long in employ at the Hall in the time of the Brandons' predecessor, the continuation of whom the latter particularly requested as the old gave way to the new. The Colonel unwillingly conceded, first, because he always chose his own servants and second because he simply did not warm to them. Edward's brother-in-law informed him of this difficulty when the Ferrars came but such was the new pastor's inclusive nature to which abutted a will to kindness, that he brushed off this news as something to leave alone, for now.

Over the months, however, he had often interrupted a *monologue*, let us say, in the kitchen, likewise an unpleasant atmosphere therein; again, Elinor's maid, young Jenny, seen several times evidently afresh with tears and more than once, of an evening, when Edward passed the Simpkins' cottage there were to be heard two loud voices in fierce dispute: no! he knew from where information about the Barn men came. Comprehension and action were, however, two different matters and he resolved to do nothing, at this time. Reverend Ferrars was a pacifist, always seeing and believing the best in people; like his wife he abhorred gossip, which for him was simply saying *anything* about *anyone* which was not one's own business to say. The monkey game of malice was an extraordinary thing for him, but he found himself thinking one day that Mrs Simpkins often appeared the most miserable woman he had ever met: for Edward, this was a thought barely permitted but it flew through his brain like a wind. 'O my,' he bethought himself, 'I feel like Anne Steele!' Now chuckling as he went along, it also occurred to him that the couple were like whippers-in at the hunt and they, and such behaviour, was not for him.

39

*S*eptimus Steele was an uncompromising man, a small landowner who had also bullied his way up the social scale. He was known for his dealing, thankfully not in human beings, although anything would have been possible of such a man, a century earlier. Steele's one weakness in life, a matter that set his dark, arrogant, forceful heart to one side, was his daughters: he adored them, and everyone knew it. It was strange that this man, for whom knowledge for women was a dangerous thing, should have a kindly schoolmaster as a brother, who also helped his nieces, yet he did.

Steele was conscious in his operations, he dressed his daughters well enough for them to be accepted in polite society, e'en for them to feel able to go to stay with their cousins, the Middletons of Barton Park; but Lucy's particular abilities in peeping round corners to find the very best route for herself, could not mask her father in her. Careful with language, to a fault – unlike her sister - she had clung onto her long engagement with Edward Ferrars – then a man-elect of great fortune – and travelled equally rapidly to his brother when a downturn in the former's material prospect presented itself. Lucy Steele was, however, not vicious, just calculating. Indeed, it was her best manoeuvre to find herself as

Mistress Robert Ferrars and the match was, indeed, made in some sort of place, if not in heaven: they mirrored one another perfectly.

It was then, with some trepidation that Edward appeared in 'Elinor's parlour', on the first floor of their home, one morning late in September.

'My dear Elinor, I have just now received a letter to the effect that my brother Robert and his wife will be passing by here on Tuesday and would like to be received.'

Elinor, who still blanched a little at the hearing of Lucy's name, or even of any oblique reference to it, lifted her head and put on her best smile as her husband continued.

'I know that you will not adore to receive them, but they are on their way to Exeter and would like to call.' Man and wife looked at each other and laughed.

'Shall they stay the night?' asked the wife.

'No, I do not surmise so, it is just to greet us, especially you and our child.'

Elinor, and indeed, their child, breathed a sigh of relief at the proposed shortness of the visit; she would prepare for Tuesday and excuse herself just now to visit Marianne.

Mrs Edward Ferrars indulged in neither gossip nor self-pity, much to her credit and could retain matters of an unjust or painful nature to her for long periods of time, matters that would produce in anyone else a marshalling of letters or calls upon friends, even acquaintances.

On this occasion, however, Elinor brought a request to her loving sister – might it be possible for the in-laws to partake in a small meal at the Hall? The division of labour would alleviate the rattling of any old skeletons in the cupboard which sometimes refused to budge! Marianne was all comprehension and compassion: she had lived through her sister's time of distress over Miss Steele and she would certainly not want to come within ten miles of Mrs Willoughby.

'O Mr and Mrs Ferrars! Do come in,' said Edward. Tuesday

had arrived with some alacrity. The legitimate inmate of Elinor's stomach did not like the army of illegitimate butterflies newly drafted in.

'O! how perfectly charming, such a sweet little house!' Lucy was already sounding like Fanny.

'Yes, yes, we like it, come this way,' said Edward feeling that too many mountains had already been crossed with this lady without her also now becoming a *relation*; nevertheless, he countered his downward looking, quickly thinking of the gold he had found in Elinor and how such abundance might have been singularly *other*.

'O, what a *lovely* prospect from this window, ver' lovely; how *well* you have arranged the furniture and dressed the room, which might have taken on a rather dreary aspect without the orange walls,' said Lucy. It occurred simultaneously to Edward and his wife that their sister-in-law had been spending too much time with his mother.

'Well, *apricot*, Lucy, pale apricot – the walls,' said Edward. He remembered what joy had gone on within this room so little time ago, with the 'dear brood' as he called his new family.

Mrs Dolby came in with refreshments and some beautifully fashioned, tiny pastries that she had baked herself and not, mercifully, thought the pastor, by her assistant Mrs Simpkins - one rather tart lady was enough for the morning.

'How was your drive here, I wonder?' said Elinor, who had observed, as well as heard, the arrival of the barouche.

'O, yes, we had a very good run from Salisbury, we were there with the Carwardines you know, their house is not far from the cathedral and is *so* well-appointed as well as giving on to such a well-known ecclesiastical monument. Do *you* know the town, dear brother?' she ended.

Edward marked this somewhat proximate enquiry and coloured but answered kindly enough.

'A little, we go there to see a friend of mine in the Cathedral Close.'

'O, how unfortunate, the houses are so ver' small, are they not?'

Lucy had indubitably become her mother-in-law.

It was time to walk over to the Hall. As they arrived, Marianne was in her vestibule, at a small table, ready to greet them.

'Ah, yes, this is more like it,' observed Lucy, now creating in Mrs Brandon a flush of colour at her rudeness.

'I will not answer,' thought Elinor's sister and forfeited a riposte as further evidence in her home, of ill-breeding.

All processed into a sort of luncheon, the partaking of the recent pastries notwithstanding. Lucy seemed stacked with opinion, a facility that had obviously lain dormant in her more meagre social years. Wishing to change the course of the wave, Colonel Brandon, his military powers of observation not dwindled by one iota, distilled the point of alternation at once:

'Now, sir, what brings you to our part of the globe?' he asked Robert.

The potency of the sentence's revenue was scarcely noted by Lucy - there was not even a blink of reflection nor relinquishment – only a sort of ricochet effect in her husband, who answered:

'We are about our several properties Colonel, I decided to purchase some cottages in one of the most pleasant valleys about Plymouth, you know. I was all for the coast, but my dear wife placed her former knowledge of an ideal spot near to where Sir Francis Drake was born. We found two! so I shall make one into a place simply for friends!'

'Indeed,' added Lucy, 'London life can become so exacting, I am reluctant to say, we do enjoy it, but a little simplicity is a fine thing! Of course, it is diverting to see papa and dear Anne again. Papa has new interests in the mines, so he is often in Minestock; we have to catch the moment.'

At the mention of the word mine and its geographical connection, Edward's heart sank to the reminder of his now scattered men.

After the rest of luncheon passed calmly, the two visitors

sought to escape, Robert having contributed nothing to the table gathering whilst Lucy again struck up:

'O well, my dears, we must away, I want to stop in Honiton to commission some lace and may even look at a bolt of cloth – all sorts of things in all sorts of places.'

The words seemed to propel her from the table whilst the rest of the party followed behind, the privilege of the hosts to conclude their own luncheon at once disbanded.

The whole encounter seemed played out like a game of tennis at Hampton Court – only it was not certain who was King Henry and who his unfortunate opponent. Edward bethought himself that on this occasion the King was an aggregate, all Brandons and pastoral Ferrars versus Robert and the Steeles. The Colonel headed one team, which by its presence alone overcame the demon head: '*where was* the heart in his brother and his wife?' thought Edward, inwardly concluding, 'fled over the hills and far away.'

At once the barouche was on its way and the Delaford Hall committee trooped out into a garden deliciously wrapped in the fragrance of late summer – the perfect place in which they could divest themselves of heartless relatives.

40

'The weeks have wings,' Elizabeth bethought herself. Feeling better, stronger, well again, even after the miserable intrusion of the Bingley sisters, she thought that it was time to make a visit to her lute.

The time had run carefully at Pemberley as all sorts of new thresholds had surpassed themselves in the Darcy marriage. Darcy had indeed turned into a strange bird, forever flown from the cuckoo's nest which he had inhabited for so long; here he was, a married man, safely ensconced in his much-loved home, from the upper storeys of which he could see a good deal of Derbyshire, his own county. Less happy in large company, he was a man beginning to flourish, he loved his sister and had watched over her for most of her life; now Elizabeth was the third part of the triangle, one of such pleasure and indeed, potency, that at times he dared not risk thinking about what might have occurred had she died. He had done all that was required of him as a bachelor but now his private abundance turned the key to an even more generous style within his estate.

Darcy rarely spoke to his friend Charles Bingley on that other *estate*, but both agreed that it was marvellous indeed! Despite Charles' shyness, he also possessed a forthright manner, something that his friend appreciated whilst finding it incongruous: his friend could be a strong speaker-out but in a gentle, yet firm demeanor. He had once witnessed Bingley dealing with some unpleasant behaviour shown towards a woman in a side street just off the Strand; his friend had quelled the temper of the assailant, providing him with more than adequate authority as to why his shouting and flailing must cease, finally persuading the participants in the fight to go their separate ways. At the time, Darcy, unusually bereft of words but full of admiration for his friend, could only walk with him in silence as they continued towards the Savoy.

'My beloved, lovely Elizabeth,' said Pemberley's master, sitting in his favourite chair in the morning room, the September sun flooding in around them like a grounded halo. 'You know me more than any other person, Georgiana notwithstanding – and then so differently – you also know how I have grieved silently for the loss of our child. I cannot tell you how much: this may surprise you; it has certainly surprised me. I have been a closed man. I know that you have observed my sorrow, I can hear that you can see it. E'er long I feel that we shall love another child into life, and I am so much better prepared now, upon my honour, I am,' – the smile unassailable. Then continuing:

'I never really wanted children, even when we married, yet I waited to see what I felt when one came along. When the accident occurred and I saw you in such physical distress I could see what loving truly meant, not being *in love*, as we say - I can now distinguish the two. Your loss was also utterly mine. I could not tell you of my sorrow, you were still frail and so very courageous and silent about your discomfort and your own sense of loss. And you see, a man does not always have these sentiments in his vocabulary: you have taught me how to go through my ledgers and find them.'

Elizabeth pulled herself up in her chair – she was listening intently and she knew about ledgers. Darcy continued:

'I have been all gratitude to you for this prising off the lid of my heart so that it could be permitted to speak again. I do not just mean with regard to our little one but in the time before, from our feeling, let us say, our mutuality. Coming to you has brought about a great fire in my heart, if the heart were this house, Pemberley, then it is now an inferno; it is all ablaze, from the gardens up to the attics. I am not speaking of intimacy my dearest, that would be too obvious, with honour. No, I speak of an inferno within that has burned my old self down: I am a house burned down by you!'

The speaker took a thoughtful pause before continuing.

'I am clumsy, beloved Elizabeth, and sorry to be bereft of the right words, but in this time, I have been a man in the ashes of himself. When I was a young boy, I sometimes watched Reynolds in her tasks and one day she was training a new girl in the cleaning of the hearth. Embarrassed to be doing this in my presence, she continued her teaching nevertheless, for I had stolen into her small room to see her, as was my delight. As she explained to the new housemaid the lie of the land, she told her that she must clear the grate 'unto the flour of the ashes.' At the time, I hesitated because I thought that she meant 'flower' and could not comprehend the words, even though I had in my mind some wonderful ideas to do with ashes flowering! But you see, ashes do flower, as I have come to realise, for when we have burnt them so low and so fine, when life's white fire has burned even its own ash, we are truly in a place where we can know what love is.'

As he took Elizabeth's hands, he added:

'You know of my guardian feelings for Georgiana - and I acknowledge you for all your own tenderness and concern therein – but I had never even thought possible, or credible, the manner of communion, yes, communion, that you and I share; it would have been previously inconceivable to me and for which I now thank you, from the very flour of my heart's ashes!'

Silence hung between them; within it was an extreme unction.

'O my dearest love, you are beyond welcome,' said Elizabeth softly, the smile radiant, 'I do nothing, I simply reply to your love.

You have shown to me your astonishing sweetness, a quality at which I marvel, never even thinking to find it in a man! I see it in your eyes, or from behind your eyes – it is ineluctable! - and I know not from whence it comes because it seems to belong to another world.' Taking his hands, she continued, 'and you held on for me when I was rude and undignified - and I am still astonished at how we are now, after our calamitous start!'

They laughed together, holding onto one another firm and sure.

'You know, Elizabeth, men's relations with women are ever open to calamitous starts! We are not in receipt of the wherewithal to communicate our hearts – on the contrary, from an early age we are obliged to close them. We are contained, and our love is contained and then there is, let us say, an eruption.'

'Mr Darcy!' said Elizabeth, all evident protestation but whispering something delicious and alluding to the famous legs, one knee of which she touched, as lightly as a little feather.

At this Georgiana came in, slightly embarrassed at finding the courting couple snuggled in the sunshine, her sister-in-law got up more quickly than her husband: 'Come, my dear sister, sit with us in the warm sun, it is perfectly delicious!'

Georgiana, ever sensible to atmosphere, knew that she had disturbed what she called a moment in their 'magical friendship' but Elizabeth's love took away the old self-consciousness and warmed her in a real and shared proximity – why! did they not love the same man, just differently?

'Come! we are like three summer frogs sunning ourselves before the coming of winter,' said Mrs Darcy.

More laughter and a sense around them that a wondrous painting was in the making, a portrait of three persons for whom society was not the be-all-and-end-all of life but rather time spent in a small familial group and fragrantly growing friendship.

'Georgiana!' said Elizabeth. 'I have not yet asked you to mount the stairs with me to a far room, the contents of which intrigue me. My absence from it is chafing me to recall its plea-sures, might you come with me? It is not a place for frosty old bachelors!'

'Delighted, I am sure,' said the one remaining, stretching more deeply into his chair.

'Brother, do you give us leave to be the one summer frog here, whilst we attend to ladies' business on high?'

'I do, indeed! *Mesdemoiselles – à vos moutons*!'

The two ladies linked arms and positively galloped to the door, waving *adieu* to their gentle man as they went, the one frog staying behind, bemused in the summer sunshine.

As the now-sisters climbed the last flight of stairs before the servant's floor, Georgiana held Elizabeth's arm, the former Miss Bennet squeezing it warmly in response. Just as the house was revealing its Tudor past, the older of the two turned to face her husband's ward:

'Georgiana, you are such a joy to behold and a joy to me as a friend and sister. I have, as you know, two younger sisters whose wayward lives distress and even annoy me, so I am mightily glad that in marrying your brother I inherited you!'

'O how extremely lovely, am I then an asset?'

'You most certainly are!'

Laughter rang out as the ladies pulled open the heavy oak door of what Elizabeth now called her 'lute room'. The great curtains remained open and Elizabeth remembered, with some anguish, that she had forgotten to return to them as she had been away from the chamber much longer than anticipated.

'O my, do not tell Mr Darcy of my incompetence most dear Georgiana.' They laughed again: complicit!

The loveliest thing for Elizabeth was that she was sharing a Tudor part of the house, almost left as it was – it reminded her of Tamara, parts of which had never been re-worked since the fifteenth century. Now she had to lift the lid of the chest and, like a child proud of her discovery, show her sister. Indeed, her sister was also thrilled and there was a common sense between them of delight and anticipation.

'You know, we used to come to this room when I was a child because we loved its atmosphere,' said Miss Darcy, 'I came with Mrs Reynolds, who has been here since my brother was small – she knows everything! We never looked inside the chest but just sat here, even upon it - among the Tudor ancestors! Sometimes we were very naughty and brought a little sweetmeat with us in Mrs Reynold's pocket, but we had to be most careful not to leave the slightest hint of a crumb, you know – in case of a mouse!'

Elizabeth was beside herself with joy at this confession, not only to be counted as trusted with Georgiana's secrets but to be with the Tudors in a chamber in her own home.

'Let us lift the lid, dear sister and To the Instrument!'

The equally new Mrs Darcy nearly fainted at the prospect of touching the lute, which she had only yet glimpsed, let alone lifted! Just at the second when the chest was to be opened, a sudden thought came to both at the same time: they should go down and collect that frog.

a noisy tumble into the parlour signalled the arrival of two former school room girls, their governess temporarily in absentia – in fact sacked from their employment – now known as Mrs and Mistress Darcy, two sisters exuberantly united in a common pursuit. Every day of his life, the master of Pemberley loved his wife a little more – this was an entirely new feeling, one previously inconceivable but five years ago. Whilst enquiry was being made in the top of the house, he had been sitting musing this very fact, also its corollary, the apparent absence in literature of a man deeply in love: consciousness of the masculine heart seemed to be rather thin, the work of the Romantic Poets notwithstanding! This foreign dominion, he wanted to say *destination*, was more and more within Darcy's comprehension, such that he waited with anticipation for the return of the two adventurers, who were even now bursting through the door:

'Brother, brother, we have been in such intrepid recreation!' said Georgiana.

'Come, inform me, you are positively *glowing*.'

Georgiana, going forward at Elizabeth's behest and sitting on a small footstool near her brother, began:

'Well! we have returned downstairs to fetch you since neither of us dared to lift the lute from its case – it has such an *air* about it, Fitzwilliam.'

'Yes, I remember a story woven around it, rather a sad tale, that moved our mother deeply.'

Darcy suddenly sat up rather abruptly:

'Yes, I should like to regard this instrument, I do not think that I have been into that chamber for a long time, lead me ladies, pray do!'

The ladies, somewhat taken aback by the alacrity of the masculine volition, echoed a resounding 'yes' and the party trooped upstairs like so many frogs migrating to a more favourable pond.

As the ascent occurred, the vista opened a little for the master of Pemberley, so used to being a lone man and now with a veritable store of the best company in his world. As the three processed up the staircase of the east wing, they cut a fine and comic picture – such was their new-found *camaraderie*. Turning to Georgiana, her brother affirmed:

'There was something strange about this chest, was there not dear sister? – it was said to have a false bottom.'

The manner in which Darcy articulated the last word of this piece of information, along with a raised left eyebrow, provided a moment when the group's intimate connections felt safe enough to giggle. The schoolgirls broke ranks and charged ahead.

'Well!' said the left behind, 'we appear to have dispensed with convention this morning!'

Reaching the chamber first, Georgiana carefully unlocked; Elizabeth demurred to her invitation to go first and Darcy finally arrived at the doorway, his head beneath the star among the acorns on its lintel. Elizabeth did go ahead a little to draw back the huge curtains and bring in the morning sunshine, thinking, as she did, of the exceptional summer that allowed them sunlit hours in many of Pemberley's rooms.

Darcy's recollections were slowly surfacing as he let the scents of the room bring back memory - their mother had been devastated by the tale of this chest but as a young man he had not then the wherewithal to comprehend. A further look between the ladies signalled their need for the masculine of the contingent to open the *kist* and to lift the instrument out; as he did so, they all converged upon it as a team of ancient explorers upon the opening of a vault.

Being in receipt of greater height than the others, Darcy swept the lute up with careful aplomb; it was not that it was heavy but rather that the sweeping lift rendered both its beauty and intrinsic heritage dramatic – the scent of it was audacious to Elizabeth, beeswax again, with a finer note there, sandalwood perhaps.

'I do remember more about this now, yet I received comprehension of it when cynicism about love – and what it could accomplish – brought only indifference to me. Let us clear the dust sheets and sit awhile. This lute came from a route through our mother's family, the Fitzwilliams and it deserves our whole attention.'

'I have heard that there was a very delicate story here, dear brother, yes! do tell us,' - Georgiana, sitting down upon the rug!

'I shall, I shall,' said the procurator.

The ladies, now fearless in their anticipation, cried out in unison 'then hurry!'

'I am! protested Darcy, 'and dear ladies, this is a secret matter, alluded to with discretion in the Fitzwilliam family and never published at large, you understand.'

Fierce nods of assent cut the air.

'The instrument was played in the time of King Henry VIII and, I think, within his court. In such a place, music was both central and held dear, it provided the very basis of life there and the King loved it: he was a naturally gregarious man of some sensibility and he loved it. The lute was a prominent instrument as indeed was the lutenist, for he was a means of bringing harmony and delight in times that were not without their grim difficulties – remember, the Tudors were not the natural heirs to the throne - and they fought in many ways to keep it. The lute players were in close quarters to the King and they were given protection and acknowledgement accordingly. You will know the history of Thomas More, a great Renaissance man of his time, a statesman and scholar who shared a long period of esteem at court. Now, his successor as Chancellor of the Duchy of Lancaster, was our ancestor, William Fitzwilliam, here, my dearest ladies, is the key to the chest, I believe that the lute arrived through their connection.'

Elizabeth decided that this was a story, every detail of which she had to know about. Darcy continued:

'You may have intelligence of More's erudite daughter, Margaret, said to be the most clever woman in England at that time; she was not only a great scholar but with her strong affiliation to her father, she was often around the court. Now Margaret was married at sixteen, a marriage arranged by her family.'

Here, Darcy paused as everyone adjusted their comfort, exchanging looks of eager anticipation and not a little sadness for what they sensed was coming.

'Now, there was at court, a most brilliant musician, a man of great beauty, of depth of character and with a most noble air about him. The younger Hans Holbein painted a portrait – 'Unknown man with lute' – but this was a provocative title, for the man was indeed far from being unknown. It is believed that the lute player was Philip van Wilder, a master musician, and a man of enormous grace. Now, such a man was a great favourite at court and was rewarded accordingly with land as well as being made member of the Privy Council. Pray remember that this was a most proximate place next the King and one of the most privileged in the whole land.'

The tension mounting in the room was palpable as he continued.

'My family has long been told that such a man, a gentle but powerful man, was in the heart of the Lady Margaret and I believe that it is possible, for she would have often been within the bounds of the court since her father was so well loved and significant within it.'

The two fair ladies regarded one another with great care and not a little arching of the eyebrows, their friend continued:

'We cannot know the details of this matter, it was privy to those within it, yet the story has been passed through some generations in the family and our mother said that she knew that it was not false. I had moved both the intelligence and the instrument to the back of my mind because, I should imagine, ladies, that they showed up the *lack in me* to honour love as both real and possible.'

Here Pemberley's master raised *his* eyebrows, so that his lovely charges both got up and came closer to their beloved friend.

'Our mother used to say, for she was greatly interested in this story, that the lutenist must have cut a very fine caper – handsome, clever, gentle – in every way. You know, he had come from the Burgundian court, a place of exquisite manners, elegance, music and poetry: infinite *cortesia*. Further, that he and the Lady Margaret might have been attracted to one another seems reflected in a fine resemblance in their faces and the strong presence of their very nature in all that they did. I have been to our library and there perused the lithographs of Margaret More and then of Philip van Wilder – I found that it is true, their noses were startlingly similar as was their jet-dark hair and angular faces.'

Both Darcy ladies thought that they might swoon as he went on.

'Yet! Lady Margaret was married and came from surely, one of the most famously and consequentially moral families in the land. In the circumstances, there must have been nothing to do about any mutual admiration, even longing. It is said that van Wilder and the Lady Margaret shared much together, the beauty of the music, the pleasure of a court filled with sublime sounds, with dance and with song. The tenor of such a place of elegance and charm must have been tantalising. Nevertheless, in a court where propriety was not always what it might have been, the lady in question would not, could not, follow her heart. Thus! a story, the whole contents of which are only known in heaven.'

Both Elizabeth and her newer sister were utterly quelled, their hearts rent by the poignancy of what they had heard, the starkness of it falling upon Elizabeth, especially, now a well-married woman and to a man whom she loved both passionately and dearly. It seemed barely good manners now to regard the instrument in the *kist*. The three realised this together, all feeling a lack of ease at further investigation that day, all at once exposed to their own stories and their own ideas of love. After a strong silence, Darcy spoke:

'Let us begin again on the morrow, dine and sleep on the significance of this tender tale and the comprehension that it has lived in our family for so long.' The chest and chamber were closed and the three descended to the quietness of the lower floor.

42

*E*dward did not return home from the Abbey with any lessening of spirit or will to help his men, merely a greater resolve. Yet he recognised the need for the utmost care: he had eschewed a career in politics and did not want to take one up now – sideways, like a crab! He was, further, a tenant himself and about to be a father; nevertheless, winter was not far away and hunger was greater, stronger, louder, in the cold.

Harvest had been both successful and early, and as September started to draw to a golden close, the pastor wondered when his men would like to reconvene. Of course, there were still the winter crops to sow and potatoes to pick but an evening a week might be spared, the Magdalene's man was becoming anxious, he could feel the tension mounting – at least he had started his enquiries in the hardest frost. The days went by in toil yet blessed by an Indian summer in which to bring in the bounty: the trouble was that Edward was perpetually aware that the bounty was not reaching those who helped to make it.

Elinor was aware that their baby was beginning to make a presence felt, all sorts of flutters were occurring and her husband, who had only ever wanted the life he now had, was filled with joy; as the two felt that they were going to be a family, Mary and young Margaret were about to come to stay. Excitement was everywhere and when the Dashwoods arrived with a new friend whom they 'completely adored' and who could not be left behind at Barton Park, the enormous willingness of its owners to have him notwithstanding, all was celebration.

The young man in question was a musician, a composer and conductor. Nicholas Saunders was a young man in his mid-twenties, handsome, elegant and amusing – he made Margaret laugh, and she was both eighteen and enchanted by her new friend, whom she called 'Nickluss'. Such was the warmth of presence of Mr Saunders (pronounced Sanders) that everyone mopped him up like a delicious sauce: he was a pianist; a choral scholar from Cambridge and a conductor of small ensembles and now choirs at St Martin-in-the-Fields, in London. *The* most important thing for Meg, however, was that *Nickluss* was so kind and lovely with *her*. Unable and unwilling to be formally addressed by his friends at Barton Park, Mr Saunders was loved by everyone who met him, being in receipt of the most naturally charming nature and which was *charisma* and not *narcissus*.

So it was, that the Delaford clan all came together for dinner at the Hall on an evening towards the end of September. Meg was first down, being unable to contain her excitement upstairs, having attended carefully to her dress – blue silk with a pink sash: the combination against her dark hair was stunning. Meg loved her now-brother Edward and no one could ever replace him in her heart, but Nickluss was, well, he was Nickluss and no one on the earth could replace him either. Ever watchful of her middle daughter having learned some harsh lessons via Willoughby, Mrs Dashwood observed the flush in Margaret's cheeks and quietly informed the members of her family not to be loose with their teasing. Marianne was particularly supportive on this head, having burned with both embarrassment and pain at the provocative tongue of Mrs Jennings - a memory that was not dead yet. On this particular evening, it seemed to both older Dashwood sisters that every person to be gathered around the Brandon table had undergone some previous and unpleasant, not to say miserable rite of passage in their lives. There was a discreet knowledge about the lovely new visitor to the Hall, whose treatment by a decidedly beautiful, yet arrogant and spitefully vitriolic lady in the recent past, was preposterous even to think of, never mind repeat.

Elinor called such a gathering 'a nest of souls', an idea which she put to her husband as metaphorically and practically Platonic – and despite her husband's wish to prune such a notion, he abstained and she upheld.

'Why! such nests must abide somewhere above as well as here abouts,' she thought to herself rather carefully, since her husband could, she noticed, sometimes hear her thoughts! Thus, well started up, the Delaford party came from all directions within the house and Parsonage and convened in the white garden behind it. It seemed to Elinor, as she greeted her family there, that the time of the crash and the anguish of their lovely visitors-in-need was a little way off now and she was reminded of the presence of the Darcys and that she might write to enquire of their wellbeing. She stopped herself in further comparative thought, such was her nature but, yes! she had loved the meeting with them, the tragic nature of the event notwithstanding. It was not simply that they had met in difficult circumstances which her husband had endeavoured to ameliorate, but rather that the Pemberley connection was not like the chattering members of such a class that she had so often encountered – in Edward's mother, sister and even brother. It had not taken the young Mrs Ferrars long to recover from her husband's unfortunate relatives because so surrounded by love in all forms where she lived but she could feel that it was not such a swift time for him. Nevertheless, every contact with the warm arms of the Dashwood family, especially as now extended by Colonel Brandon, helped Edward to thrive in the very inclusion of spirit that was so readily and so naturally in his nature.

'Welcome, my family,' offered Christopher Brandon, ushering

in two stewards with wine and small, delicate sweetmeats; he had also made for Margaret a fruit cup which was comical in its resemblance to an exotic forest.

'*Une coupe* à mon brave,' he said, bowing low as he brought the offering to her.

'O strawbelies!' whooped the recipient of the offering as pink as the berries she had so beautifully named in her childhood.

Everybody applauded elegantly as the cup was received - for this young woman, as her mother, trips to Delaford were a special delight, life at Barton Cottage sometimes requiring a certain and careful stoicism. It had to be said that Marianne's ever generous husband now informed some greater safety for his mother-in-law through regular and discreet assistance. Nicholas melted into the group seamlessly and with evident pleasure at being within its midst, he had wanted to play for them through the library window but was sweetly admonished for the want of his company in the garden, if this were to be so. Mrs Dashwood, in dark green, slub silk, a gift from Marianne, chatted freely with the young maestro, carefully introducing to him those whom she knew loved music:

'Colonel, I would that you meet our friend Nicholas, having much comprehension of your love of his *metier* in life.'

The two began to converse and the last thing that she heard from them was a discussion of the merits of polyphony, with which she, and most of the population were not acquainted. There was suddenly an intense *crescendo* as the Colonel's voice rose in pleasurable agreement, confirming his own interest in the music of the cloister, which had to be heard in splendid abbeys for its best effect:

'Yes, *yes*, I sometimes go to Buckfast where, it seems to me, the combination of the beeswax from the candles, the edge of frankincense in the air and the voices sounding off the pillars makes for, shall we say, an elegiac experience to Love.'

'Yes, Colonel Brandon, I do agree wholeheartedly. Why! the

sound seems to travel up the pillars!' said Nicholas who continued, with gusto:

'It is as if the shapes in the stone and the shapes in the voice were made for each other: the one helping the other upward. It is, as you say, sometimes elegiac. You might have visited Durham or Chartres? – now *there* are pillars of heaven where sound is concerned. I feel that music is somewhere above the earth and we have to bring it down; I write my own compositions and am so grateful for what comes to me – even in the middle of the night when I am obliged to light a candle to place it upon paper!'

The gathered company had become quiet in the ears of such interesting words flying about their air. It was thus Marianne who continued where her husband left off.

'It is lovely that you are here with us, Nicholas and I think that it is wonderful that you are often at St-Martin-in-the Fields - the building is so beautiful - Christopher and I have seen it on that little hill, quite magical.'

'Yes, yes, it is so well designed, eloquent, and it has been built on a site of worship for many centuries, something which I feel is important – a sort of gathering of peace,' agreed the young man, continuing:

'I feel that music has such significance for us as human beings, even if we sometimes have to grapple with its learning, or memorising, so that we can do its grace justice.'

'That is exactly what I think,' said Marianne, gratified.

Once dinner had begun, one which Edward blessed with gratitude for the fragrant friendship of the table, talk galloped straight into the planning of an outing in the warm September weather. Despite her shyness this night, Margaret was foremost with enthusiasm:

'Well, since we are in Dorsetshire, we should go to your seaside, dear sisters, I am sure that it is different from ours!'

The Dashwoods were indeed inspired to a different seascape from their own. A unanimous hum of approval ran round the plates. Nicholas seconded the idea at once:

'Yes! We need only to go straight from here and we are at once by the waves. I shall write a special little piece to celebrate our going to sea!'

A second hum of approval resounded.

'Indeed, indeed,' considered the Colonel, 'I know of a wide beach and not too occupied, there being two fishermen's huts upon it. The bay sweeps below the magnificent cliffs, as dramatic as you could ever find. We shall take a picnic, or even go to a good inn that I know at Lyme Regis - you must all inform me of your preferences.'

'Yes, beautiful, Colonel, for my part I am willing to be led by you,' said Elinor, positively sparkling.

'Hurrah!' shouted Margaret, 'We shall be your small army!'

43

Trust was all to the master of Pemberley and he trusted Bingley and he trusted Elizabeth. For a man so repulsed by gossip, or *any* giving of *any* information that was not his to give, Darcy both loved his wife and felt that he could share anything with her – he even talked of the running of the estate with her, something most rare but he did not need to have a life run by orthodoxy. One day they had ventured into Lancashire on a visit to a friend near Chorley. This town, famous for making flat irons, was now striding forth into cotton. Elizabeth was most affected by the changes being made to an ancient place and made such remonstrance during their return to Pemberley that when they reached home, she was dubbed 'Chorley'. On that day and ever afterwards, when protesting with passion about social matters that she felt required attention, the name would spring into operation. Such protestation never offended her husband, on the contrary, always assuring her of his inability to turn social reformer, he yet gave a good ear, especially where children were concerned. Elizabeth was despairing of the use of the latter in factories and especially down mines – these were changing times, with metal everywhere, where before there had been wood and four-footed creatures there was now hard metal. Unusually employing her nickname, or her 'sweet name' as he preferred, one morning of late September, he asked,

'Chorley?'

'Yes, my beloved.'

'Shall we bravely mount the staircase to the east wing? Georgiana is playing the piano and can be claimed.'

'Yes! Let us, indeed.'

'My dear Fitzwilliam.'

'Yes, my Elizabeth.'

'I am so very glad of you and glad of my life with you.'

'I can assure you, dear one, that it is perfectly mutual!'

The three ascended.

As before, Georgiana unlocked, Elizabeth drew the blinds, Darcy procured entry to the chest.

'Before we look any further, dear ladies, I feel that we must only find and return here – whatever the contents of this *kist* – it is not so much ours as in our stewardship.'

The ladies agreed.

Darcy noiselessly lifted the lute and made several paces with it, placing it on a small *credenza* to the side of the room, out of the sunlight. All could sense the occasion and lent it due respect.

As the instrument was placed down, different shades of the wood could be seen, not original to the design but part of the housekeeping of the piece and of its being played – the position of the lutenist's hands, even his body. Elizabeth thought, but did not want to say, that the lute smelled wonderful, of the wood and of the man who played it, of whom she dared not think– she had seen the lithographs. If there had been a great love in this man's life, then here it lay silent, resting in the instrument of its owner.

The group took up their usual positions, one at the head, the other at the foot, the third at the side. The sense that prevailed was one of both peace and excitement and this sense continued, its energy strong.

Darcy turned at last to the chest, he felt that he was required to be brave!

'I will not delve too deeply into this private place, even though it is in our home, yet it would be gratifying to look beneath the purple cover, which also attests to the beauty of its owner, two hundred years later.'

Clearly, the whole chest had not been regarded for a long time but then, Pemberley was full of all sorts of treasures, many of great material worth. As her husband started to peel back the cover, Elizabeth wanted to rush to stop him, or to weep, or both, such was the anguish to her of trespassing into another's sacred property.

Darcy knew at once what she was thinking:

'Let us replace everything and sleep again on this private matter. I will move the chest however, I think that it is better at a little distance from the window, even with the gauze down to screen the sunlight.'

Darcy picked up the chest, whose weight was not without substance, moving it off the rug and onto the wooden floor; as he did so, the silent observers were struck by the hollowness of the sound of wood on wood. Darcy, Elizabeth thought, made a most unusual and beautiful movement of his head as he acknowledged what they all heard – the chest was not going to let them go that easily.

'O heavens!' said Elizabeth as Georgiana gasped and the third stood stock still. It was not for several seconds that they looked at each other.

'Well, there you are: here the cavern in the chest!' smiled Miss Darcy.

'So I hear,' said her brother.

Elizabeth sat down, full to the brim with *possibility* - with a man who was a master musician in the King's court and that he might have a favourite who was too high up and too well known to return his love: she felt devastated.

'Oh, and Oh,' she said.

'May I put forward the suggestion that we return on another day? My sentiments are distinguished but quite ruffled,' said

Darcy.

The ladies concurred.

'Whatever the discovery, I would not lurch us into any public disclosure and therefore err on the side of continued – and secret – guardianship on our part. What say you, my dear ones?' he asked.

An 'aye' sped from the lips of Darcy's *ladies*, Elizabeth, still somewhat dazed by what was happening and not simply because she had realised the consequences of living in an historical archive. Darcy replaced the lute as his wife went through her curtain closing ritual - well, there were two sets *and* the gauzes on rollers: they had to be diligent, having arrived in some sort of magical garden and wishing to return to it.

44

*I*t was some days before the small triumvirate could return to the lute and the hollow in its case, Mrs Bennet had asked to come with Mr Bennet for a few days and, since Elizabeth missed her father sorely, there was nothing for it but to speak with Jane and endeavour to spread the load. Whenever the Bennets came to Pemberley, which was rare, Darcy was always most obliging and conveniently disappeared for the whole day with his steward, 'about estate business', leaving only dinner time as a potential obstacle course. Thus, Elizabeth could be with her parents – mostly her father – and they could dine in the long dining room, where Mrs Bennet and her life catechism could be kept at a polite remove. Why! it was often known for Darcy not even to hear what was being said, so far away was his seat from that of those perpetrating untruths of the vulgar kind spoken at high velocity; further, dining tables with exceptionally long armature were used so that this distance could be sustained the whole day long.

Mrs Bennet (both particularly and unusually) liked the Pemberley housekeeper, Mrs Reynolds, a kindly and obliging lady, so when asked if she might accompany Elizabeth's mother about the gardens or go to see the now blossoming attraction of the Tenants' Hall, as the Lambourn vegetable and flower property had become known. Then there was much diversion available and longer time for sojourns in the library with papa. During these days, Elizabeth, Darcy and his sister awaited their return to the lute with patient eagerness: in fact, the master of the house, slowly relaxing into a changed man every single day, made exquisitely funny motions with his eyes – to describe *upwardness* – and then a saddened face to illustrate the impossibility of the latter, which made Georgiana laugh so much that she was forced to leave the breakfast table one morning, with all manner of muffled excuses: both original Darcys had found a new and lovely way of living that was unexpected and therefore the more precious for the having.

That Mrs Bennet was heard to comment, one day, on 'the most gratifying changes evident in Mr Darcy', the latter being beyond earshot, was ironic to her second daughter: such changes being very much *not* to do with her mother. Further, the fact that the latter, the over-talkative lover of domestic theatre and remonstration, had undergone such change, was droll in the extreme: of course, all comment on Elizabeth's part was avoided.

The interim period between visits to the lute became impossible to bear and was the chief motivation in asking Jane and Bingley to take over in the parental diversion stakes; enough was now soundly, *enough.*

'How much chatter-boxing may a man take?' Darcy bethought himself quietly one morning, just when a messenger arrived to invite the Bennets *at once* to Netherfield which was about to be vacated to the new house near Ashbourne, nearing completion. Mrs Bennet was all affability and flushed at the compliment of being invited so soon and so fast and begged to be forgiven if they should leave almost at once. The idea was met with a quiet smile and a small, silent bow by Pemberley's master, his wife graciously demurred, as Georgiana, in a brand-new fashion for her, swept from the table with an 'excuse me whilst I fly to the pianoforte.'

By one of the clock all trace of any form of demanding visitation had been polished away; the sun shone; Bess was allowed into the Orangery, where a *light* luncheon was taken during which Mr Darcy proposed 'a small glass of something delicious,' to his now sacred and blessedly reduced company. Further, it was the master who told such a company that he had it in mind to invite Mr and Mrs Edward Ferrars to stay when the Bingleys came next and what did they think of the matter? Elizabeth gave a strong affirmation, following at once with the rider that Georgiana could be begged not to be shy of such a meeting, for the Ferrars were 'the most kindly persons whose family ever gave us shelter when we had been loudly thrown about the countryside' and so saying, with a little twinkle in her eye, indicated to her husband that some of the unhappiness associated with such an event had gone away, forever.

Discussion was short concerning the visitors, Georgiana was delighted at the thought of meeting persons of such calibre as those who had attended her brother and injured sister-in-law so assiduously. Elizabeth was exceeding harmonious in her relationship with her husband and his sister so that all future planning could be spoken of face to face. Thus, it was that the start of October was mooted as the date of possibility: Elizabeth would write to them as the mistress of the house.

When all was settled and done, the three wound their way to the upper floors, with barely a sound, such was their united focus on the potential gravity of the situation. Mrs Darcy never ceased to be amazed by her beloved husband. After Georgiana had ceremoniously unlocked, and the curtain drawer had drawn, and the porter of the chest had carefully transported the lute, Darcy took from his waistcoat pocket a small tool more usually found in stables for dealing with hooves. Horses being absent in Pemberley's upper floors, the ladies quickly concluded that the little hoof pic was for facilitation, were it required, of easing the base of the chest from its now visible second base. Whilst Mrs Darcy found the idea excessively diverting, she was also a little terrified, wondering to herself whether she had it in her to be a burglar in her own home. As her husband lifted the purple silk cloth, he noticed, but did not remark upon, something that looked like a small ornament which had fallen back into the chest from the silken folds. Anxious to pick the object up he yet regarded it from all available angles before silently approaching. Stooping over the *kist*, for Fitzwilliam Darcy was a tall man as well as a slender, he was suddenly, even abruptly, visited by a greater revelation than he had anticipated, for here was the symbol of his own relative, William Fitzwilliam, which even now lay downstairs in a glass case, and which was a gift from the King. Darcy well knew the signature of this small pendant and that few persons were highly privileged to wear it: as he lifted the ornament, he found himself somewhat overcome by the extraordinariness of the moment.

Elizabeth quickly noticed the sea change in her husband's face, indeed, in his whole body, and, as he stood cupping the small artefact in his left hand, she moved forward to take his right, a little concern on her own face lit by a questioning smile.

'My goodness,' he said, 'I am taken aback, a long way back indeed, for this symbol, this very symbol in my hand, was worn by our ancestor, Sir William Fitzwilliam, in his position as Lord High Admiral of England: it is a small ship's whistle, you see, a *boatswain's call*, made in gold. These pendants were given only to the High Admirals, I know this because such artefacts were the gift of King Henry VIII, there is one belonging to our ancestor in the hall downstairs!'

Elizabeth thought that she might fall over, her emotions a mixture of delight, surprise and awe!

Darcy continued immediately: 'William Fitzwilliam held his position as sea lord following Thomas Boleyn, his portrait in the library downstairs clearly shows him wearing the pendant around his neck: I am speechless.'

This discovery was a great matter to comprehend, its unveiling at once startling and, in a strange way comforting to Elizabeth, who, finding her voice again asked:

'But why, beloved, was it not in some sort of receptacle, a little box, perhaps, something worthy of the presence of such a symbol?'

'And why?' the beloved asked, 'was the King's signature gift of enormous privilege, of *dear friendship*, in the *kist* of a lutenist?'

The sisters held hands tightly, so strong was the atmosphere of this astounding conundrum. At last Darcy shared what he thought was a divulgence: he was going to turn the chest over, and he needed help. Elizabeth volunteered at once, seeing that her new sister was reeling with the emotion of this beautiful mystery unfolding in her family home. As they turned the box upside down it was very evident that the bottom was hollow – this seemed to shock Georgiana even more and she sat down abruptly; when Darcy took the stable tool to a corner of the wood, however, she started to laugh, apologising profusely but continuing nevertheless – the scene had simply struck her as hilarious. The laughter served as a breaker of tension: the complicity of the group; their wonderful familiarity and trust; the invisible compliance that they all held to the deed in hand; the concentration on her brother's face and the attention required to lever off the wood; all resulted in an urgent need to rebel! Composure was quickly gained however – Miss Darcy was well trained.

'Let us turn now, Elizabeth, are you ready?' enquired the leader.

Elizabeth concurred.

'I can see from the immediate inside that no one would have succeeded in opening any further into the chest: it is pristine,' said Darcy.

Everyone carefully lifted what had become the lid in unison, the chest now being upside down on the silk rug. Mercifully, this part had not been visited by the insect world, nor turned over for a long time. As the ladies stood back, Darcy bravely turned his attention to the releasing of the new part of the chest and there it was, a second 'lid' at the bottom of the piece. Turning the lid as he lifted it up, it was Georgiana whose intake of breath was both sharp and first. No sooner had the air from her lungs been expelled than all saw what had presented itself to her and the sigh was universal: it was an oil painting of a woman. The portrait itself was made on a long and slender canvas, for the lute case was of that size and shape; the woman was beautiful, of striking features laid out on a sculptured face, her eyes were jet dark as was her hair. She was dressed in a muslin gown, light and free for summer and a shawl of the deepest azure blue was thrown across one shoulder – she seemed very upright whilst possessing a spirit that was expressed in the placing, or rather, lack of it, of the blue shawl. The grace of the sitter was indisputable and her long, dark hair was loose – something which gave a feeling of great intimacy. On the floor before her was her Tudor headdress; lying crookedly it looked as if it had been thrown down: thus, the draping of the shawl, the loose hair and now the cast aside head piece, which was very angular, all contributed to the effect of a woman set free. To the left side of the lady was a body of books, precisely placed, as if in a specific order, the titles of which were embossed in gold on covers that were the same colour as the shawl. In this way, the books seemed strangely illuminated, even if the titles were illegible upon closer inspection.

Indicating the star above the lady's head, Darcy remarked:

'Why! she looks like the woman from The Book of Revelation, but she is also of this earth, she is both human and exalted at the same time.'

Elizabeth wept openly now, Georgiana sat flat upon the rug, her skirts about her and Darcy stood above them both, like a tower.

45

*D*inner that evening was a quiet affair after such an afternoon. Here was a possession both precious and intimate but which seemed still to belong to someone else, despite it being in what was now the home of the Darcy family. All three felt as if they were somehow executors of an eternal secret never to be divulged, the thought, even the inclination, was too vulgar, too precarious, Elizabeth thought. The owner of the lute had clearly cherished it, signs of its use were evident, but it was still in remarkable condition. Darcy sat up a little more in his great armchair, as if to make an announcement and indeed, he was, but first, in his true fashion, he was to give a little history!

'My dearest family, I want to continue with you about the lutenist whose lute, I believe, we have in our east wing: as you know, I feel that it was owned by Philip van Wilder, a man who played beautiful and complex music in the time of Henry VIII, as I have before mentioned. The court was abundant in music and its king was, since a boy, passionate about music, dance and poetry – he was always someone who loved all of the softer side of life and who filled the court with a great richness of culture and colour. All around him were brilliant men and women who were creating masterpieces constantly, even the fabric of the buildings was beautiful, inside and out; you see, my ladies: the King loved to create beauty! We must remember,' (and here Darcy made an even greater extension to his already great height) 'that as well as receiving Italians and their remarkable influence, and love of beauty, King Henry also brought in those who had been members of the Burgundian court, a magnificence of great culture, *manners* and music, especially. Now, it was from this latter court that van Wilder came, and he was greeted as a brilliant man with a good reputation as a man, as a musician and as someone who *knew beauty* – one can imagine him vowing to live his life in beauty.'

'So, it is he then, who owned the instrument we already so love?' said Elizabeth, eyes sparkling with pleasure in the candlelight.

'Yes, I do so believe and, if you bear with me, I will follow on with more of my evidence!'

The ladies applauded softly and with much joy.

'Van Wilder was born in the Low Countries at a time when it was considered profoundly necessary to create cultural courts to prompt an exquisiteness of being! It was thought that if man were to learn about beauty, about good manners, about the intelligent life of higher thinking and, dear ladies, of behaving well, then he would be closer to what Heaven really is. There was no question of ill manners or ill behaviour, they were simply prohibited, and the court was a place of human endeavour and co-operation. Furthermore,' (here Darcy took on his most didactic pose) 'the influence and significance of this successful court was great – it expanded the arts to a fine degree, to an elegant degree and Philip van Wilder was a master musician there before he came to our King!'

'Là! We admire him already and now we hear that he was a noble man in his daily being,' added Georgiana, who was clearly carried away on a cloud of devotion to the musician and perhaps, to the lady whom he could never have.

'Did you tell us earlier, dear husband, that he taught the young Princess Mary?' asked Elizabeth.

'Yes, I did say that, and he made many friends through his good nature, in fact, it was said that Prince Edward told his father of his gratitude for being visited by van Wilder. You have oft teased me, Elizabeth, about my 'good opinion, which once lost, is lost forever' but I honour those whose standards are above those so often found on this paltry earth! Our musician in the attic, I shall call him, though he is only on our second floor, was well-loved in the court, was a friend of the King and highly rewarded by him. Why! his influence was great and is said to have inspired William Byrd: our man, our very man, was most significant!'

An infinite silence suddenly cast itself, the sort of silence which can be most loud when heard, especially for the first time. Then Georgiana came forward:

'Brother, I want to ask you again about the pendant in the chest, why is it not in a special box for safekeeping?'

'I too, dear husband, for it is gold, is it not?'

'Yes!' replied Darcy to them both 'but I feel that it simply became separated, or that it was hastily put between the lining of the *kist* and the cover of the lute. I feel humbled by the story of this man, he reminds me of Edward Ferrars, it is the same stance of heart, the same quiet knowledge that there is more to life than grabbing and pushing. There is no need in these men for any of the usual deceptions of character that we employ – like my old pride – they have no requirement of such devices, let us say, that we, less noble creatures, often use to cover our vulnerable selves, to cover the old ashes of ourselves: ashes that we have not burned away or cleaned out.'

As Pemberley's master spoke, his words fell upon his family, who were startled by them, yet they knew the wisdom of which their husband and brother spoke. In a moment, the same had produced the little ornament from his pocket and showed it to them properly for the first time – it was a boatsman's call, a rather splendid whistle in gold. Both women looked at the piece, it seemed to speak the lute and, they dare not even think of it, but also, its owner.

Darcy sometimes knew the power of his being, of his own eloquence and, without the old arrogance, his real elegance: he carefully gathered his ladies to him across the end of the table, where they sat.

'My dearest ladies, my own dear family, I have deliberately saved this until now because it is so significant. When you both went up to dress for dinner, I went to our record of the younger Holbein's works in the library – heaven be praised that we have both – and I looked with some care at the portrait of 'The Unknown man with Lute' and there, around his neck upon a long cord, is the boatswain's call! What I want to impress upon you both, my most dear conspirators, is that our lutenist could easily have been given this symbol of the privilege of the King's fellowship, since the lutenist was such a great asset to His Majesty and so dearly loved by him. It was *not* that this gift of recognition only went to the Lord High Admirals, you see, does not a dear, sweet friend also have the possibility of calling in the ships, the human ships of great worth?'

All was silence. The two women sat in the semblance of a dream, so taken were they with all that they had seen and learned - the brilliance of this man of music; the honour surrounding him; the greatness of his nobility; the appreciation of his master the King and the possibility of his love for a woman whom he could never have - all matters of precious import and consequence notwithstanding, yet truly standing, erect and in the way.

For Darcy, a man who had eschewed love, who mocked its power, its owners, its perpetuators, itself, here was recognition. He carefully took his wife's hand and his sister's arm as they stood together in a moment of infinite and intimate connection. The hall clock rang the hour.

46

*I*t was agreed, then, to have an army outing to the coast on the following Saturday, weather permitting but not before Edward had a stormy meeting with his 'Men'. The weather was the first storm thus, many were able to come down to the barn at Delaford. The evening was wet and wild, the reality of Dorsetshire coming into the lanes at full tilt, but it was not cold, so a strange relation was made between the sky and the land – everything was tinged with green. The opening of the meeting was always started with a prayer said by the pastor and, on this night he would appeal for *comfort*, an inordinately normal request in most times but not this one, for discomfort gathered everywhere and Edward felt it as he walked over to the barn before any man was present.

Ned Rust was the first to appear, then Matthew Forest, Thomas Farmer and behind him, Simeon Fawke. Edward, the least judgemental man that anyone could find, was at once struck by the juxtaposition of opposites in the last two men – Thomas, the great peacemaker and Fawke a reputed firebrand.

'Good evening gentlemen, it is very fine to see you. Is all as well as it can be?' A risky question from Edward to the fire department.

'T is *not* well, Father Ferrars, we are stink tired of working hard for precious little which cannot, will not, feed the hungry mouths at our table or pay the rent on our ill-ed cottages,' warned Fawke.

A distinct chill flew around those gathered so far.

'Father, we are 'twixt and 'tween – no one save you will listen and we are sore afraid that there will be evil tempers about after this harvest if we can find no one to appeal to,' said young Tom Farmer, ever the one to stand gently whilst taking a firm line.

Edward thought of his failed attempt to interest Lord Gallhope and thought that he might soon ride again to Minestock and see how things fared there. He was further aware of the Combination Acts which outlawed meetings such as those he had set up here except that he and the men made no oaths, so he felt relatively safe and exempt from investigation. His experience in life told him that there was always someone around with a bitter disposition to a wagging tongue. Edward knew to be cautious – he was not making, nor had intended to make, a Friendly Society. All this notwithstanding, the grim situation for these men and their families could not continue, someone had to be found and encouraged to help those gathered here and in the wider environs. It was useless and dangerous to think that this was a passing moment, people could not go on working to face near starvation as a reward; further, the guillotine was within living memory: hungry mouths bred bile.

It was Ned Rust, however, who called for order, the Pastor deep in thought, as the mumbles became cries and the cries shouts and the name of Tolpuddle was heard and of those uniting under oaths and not so many miles away.

Edward woke sharply from his moment's thought:

'Yes, gentlemen, yes. This is a sounding board for you and not a sounding board for oaths and pacts. Let us remember that we are good men decent enough to keep out of violence. Let us pause and ask for guidance in what we face and help in how we face it.'

As the words left the Reverend's tongue, he knew that the situation was sinking; he was not prepared to run the gauntlet between the law, the physical reality of angry men and his heart-felt anguish for their way forward. The meeting was quickly drawn to a close and all left, astonishingly, in near silence.

47

$\mathcal{I}$t was with both determination and not a little trepidation that Edward walked over to the barn for the next meeting.

'Oh well, it will be the last for a while,' the words lay heavily on his heart.

At the same time that the Rector was opening the door, a swoop of men seemed to arrive behind him, Ned Rust at its centre; when they saw him, they went into single file. Edward did not like this show of presence, there were too many boots! Nevertheless, he welcomed them all and, as they gathered near the front of the building, busied himself with greeting those friends who worked on the fields near to the Parsonage. Colonel Brandon did not farm the land around Delaford but he was wise to all that went on there – an army man of some note does not lose his clear sight as he hands in his commission.

It was with exactly these thoughts that the Colonel toyed as he slipped unseen into the back of the meeting. Perching on a chopping log he was lower than his usual sitting height but could hear and feel admirably and he knew at once that there was trouble afoot.

Rust was quick to stand, his foot on a bale and from this commanding position beginning to tell Edward a thing or two:

'And! Reverend Ferrars, it's all right for you with your house and garden by the Hall here but we are stranded. We are BUCKLED by low wages and the price of our rents - and *still* we have holes in our rooves and the FEAR of being without food: ten shillings a week will not do for us, sir, it will NOT cover.'

At this, Rust's angry face was becoming mottled.

'Aye but this gentleman mun not be blamed Ned, it ain't his doin' – calm yoreself,' said a voice from the middle of the hall.

At this, Rust rising to an even greater height and starting forward to knock the speaker.

'*That's* not in order Ned!' – this by Tom Farmer – the gentle voice with furlongs' deep authority behind it. At the back, the Colonel sat now raised to his full height, the wall behind him.

Then more voices:

'Aye, we's only 'ere to be listened to!'

Edward, very calm as he stood before the group of men whose plight he well understood, searched quickly for words.

'Gentlemen, I *know* and see and hear your baulked spirit, your worry for your children, your worry for your wives. I have been to see the two landlords around here and they say they will consider.'

More shouts and murmurs rose and with them jostling, shouting, anger. 'Hopeless, hopeless, they aren't better than a pair of old women, supping up, whilst we does the work and *still* starve,' said Matthew Forest, twisting his cap in his hands.

'My good men and true, please, you are good men, this will not be the way forward,' said Edward.

'But how *will* we go for'ard? You muss tell us THAT,' said Rust now seated.

'I can only ask you, pray, be calm and let us see how we can otherwise raise benefits for you,' said Edward.

'Aye! Benefits, benee-fits! An' *who* gets these said benefits?' called Rust, now mercifully leaving the hall.

The men made way for the red-faced speaker who turned as he reached the door and close to Colonel Brandon thus said:

'We thank 'ee Reverend Father, for your 'elp but we 'ave to go 'igher now, make a union, make an oath to come together, stick together, we shall join with the Tolpuddle men, further afield, but by God's hand, we must put food on our tables afore the winter.'

With this a slam of the door which the Colonel now guarded, his jaw characteristically set, and a slight pause before Rust's people followed their leader out.

As his own nearby labourers waited round him, Edward knew that he had lost, saw that his anxieties for nearby farms and now further afield, were compounded. He knew that Minestock and its miners were not far behind the sentiments of these men's hearts – he wanted to say 'these dear men's hearts' because their anger, even Rust's rage was perfectly justified but not justifiable, in these circumstances.

England would not become France, the beast was different, but the beast was present nevertheless and it had to be addressed – this shame could not be left – God forbid.

As the men left, quieter now, the Colonel joined Edward on the very bale upon which Ned Rust's foot had just lodged.

'Come back to the house with me brother, let us take a brandy together. I will send word to Elinor – you do not need to go home yet with all of this around your head.'

Edward's heart was indeed still pounding, yet he was mightily grateful that Rust had chosen to walk out, even thank him, instead of a greater cacophony arising at his behest.

The two men closed the barn and walked back to the Hall in silence.

Christopher Brandon guided his friend to the comfiest chair in the house and set before him a glass the colour of sunset.

'Edward! do not harm yourself with thoughts of the hopeless-ness of the matter – a resolution will present itself. It is time now. The coming of the railways is already changing much – these men are just the start and rightly so, a man *mun*, as Ned Rust says, put bread on his table. The cantankerousness of the landowners who are utterly *oblivious* to the needs of the very men who put the bread onto *their* tables can continue no longer: it is time for change.'

'Yes, yes, dear friend, you are right, yet I do not want to salve my conscience, my awareness of what it means to suffer, simply because I cannot ruffle my own nest.'

'Indeed! but dear Edward, if you were to so ruffle there would *be* no nest because the church would abjure all attempts to put their case forward publicly and that is the next step – somehow their case must go before the public.'

48

*A*fter the misery of the barn meetings, it was with much relief that the family from Delaford Hall and its pastorage set out for the sea. The road to Lyme was idyllic, leaves had not yet left the parent plant but were coloured in every possible hue between red, rose and gold. It was agreed that the party would go to the little town first since the participants in the journey, though not long, would need a little sustenance upon arrival: the good offices of The Red Lion on the steep hill to the harbour, would be perfect. The ride through the lanes which ran down to the sea was superb, the carriage taking up most of the space between the high hedges. The Colonel always rode alongside, in the narrow places he was obliged to lead the way: he was escorting his small army.

The party wove their way down to the coast in an hour and a half and, as they went, both Edward and Elinor were able to cast off the discomposure of the last evening's events and both were heartily glad of the diversion. Today was a fresh start to life, to people habituated neither to argumentation nor aggression. Curiously, the Reverend felt that he would like Mr Darcy's opinion on the grim events of the previous evening since he had run an estate for infinitely longer than he and probably been in the business of assuaging angry men!

With the Colonel riding beside the carriage there was room for Nicholas within it – his quietly sunny presence knit together the slices carved from the Ferrars by last night's crepuscular skirmish; Mary had decided to stay at home and let the young people be together.

It was then, in a spirit faithful to harmony and gratitude that the party walked light-heartedly into the vestibule of the Old Red Lion. It was Marianne who saw him first. Keeping her composure against the shock that produces a nasty sting through the dastardly unexpected, she took her husband's hand at once. Elinor saw him seconds after her sister and remained so rigid in a facial expression just showing delight at her surroundings, that she could have been mistaken for someone having a seizure, the frozen rictus welded to the air itself. She did not turn to Edward, so many and so complex were the emotions flooding through her after seeing and indeed, *hearing* Willoughby on the night they last encountered one another - Marianne upstairs wrestling with fever and he in genuine sorrow, a dawning realisation at what he had done.

In the eldest Dashwood daughter breathed the ability to comprehend some of the myriad difficulties of love: experience and compassion are fine pedagogues. The moment of seeing Willoughby was, for Marianne, beyond mortification, her intense feelings for him smothered rather than pacified and given proper burial; there was no doubt that she loved her husband but the passion for a man whom she had believed to be her soulmate was not yet placed in an equilibrium within her heart, stoicism and practicality notwithstanding. Marianne's step started to waver; the Colonel, ever faithful and quick to assess a situation, took her arm, steering her into the resident's bar, whilst Nicholas, realising that something serious had just occurred, took the other. The whole group veered as one into the parlour of the beautiful inn and sat down thankfully. No one said a word whilst they all regulated their attention, both away from the rogue Willoughby and the remembrance of the great damage done to Marianne. It was, indeed, the latter who spoke first and with great self-command:

'My family, it is nothing, you are my dear ones and we have all come a long way from the bleakness of the past.'

This said, Christopher Brandon, seated closely next his wife, again offered her his hand, which she took with alacrity, putting it to her cheek. The action masked her own thoughts that gave substance to the idea that she was not going to revisit the site of so much pain, at least, not in public. Edward and then Nicholas, silent as the grave, quickly rallied and began to speak of ordering sustenance but the joy of the event had been murdered and the party agreed to move on swiftly to the Cobb – at least the sea would assuage their shock.

Marianne uttered not a single word as the group proceeded down the steep hill to the water, her whole being pulsing with the effects of what she had just experienced. Holding firmly onto her husband's arm, she spoke of the weather; the beauty of the setting; the elegant sweep of the Cobb; the majesty of the sunlight upon the waves, all whilst her beating heart was held savagely in her young chest.

Edward and Elinor walked a little ahead, still in a cloud of emotion after the preceding evening and now hardly daring to consider what their sister was feeling: they both gave to restoring some of the joy of the situation. Nicholas walked with Meg, who gave no indication whatsoever of what she knew. As they all reached the end of the great harbour arm, they encountered the gift of a small seal who was already endeavouring to attract their attention. Swimming toward them, his sleek, black coat shining in the sunshine, he could only inspire laughter with his whiskery face held in so many jaunty angles and the sheer diversion of an air of playful delight.

All three sisters rounded upon the small creature with grati-tude for what he was showing them – each time that they moved, he moved with them, often coming up close to the wall. Each sister had dressed for a day in the sunshine, Marianne in deep blue; Elinor in grey and lilac and Margaret in pale apricot with a red sash: the result was not only startling but attracted the sea creature to them readily. This new and be-whiskered friend seemed to love their colours and the response of their owners to him – he danced, he clowned, he swam out to sea and rushed back in again, only stopping in proximity to the high wall: in short, he disbanded the ache in their hearts. Leaving Lyme after what was almost an hour on the great arm of the harbour, all bade goodbye to their sea friend, whilst Marianne was given the dignity of shedding a tear beneath the guise of their sad departure from him.

The earlier events of the day seemed embedded in the group spirit, nevertheless, it was Marianne who again came forward in suggesting that they go further to the great cliffs a little way along the coast and walk on the stony beach there. Why! they had brought their boots with them for the sole purpose. In a moment they had all reassembled in the carriage and set off for the new location, the move providing a harbour for Marianne who could, in the privacy of the coach, dwell with her own thoughts. It was not simply a matter to her of an event having occurred in her life but rather, of having ascended (she did feel that it was a sort of going up) to a new place where she seemed wholly at one with another human being, in thought, word and deed: to her, the time with Willoughby had been a holy match. It was not merely that she had encountered someone precious to her but that her body, never mind her soul, had been taken into another form of feeling. There it now presented, like another layer, *the desolation of the idea* of never having such fineness of feeling again. Arriving at so many poetic conclusions about this state of being seemed both natural and intuitively *correct* to the lady - that she had found much to bear in the same conclusion concerning the lack of longevity of the state. For Marianne, it had been a matter of finding someone in a soul connection, but the connection had been dashed: here lay the source of the grief.

Further, all of this was not a mere matter of opinion – hers or that of anyone else – it was a simple matter of fact, entailed in and lived out in her body. She would not stoop to comparisons with her devoted husband - her feelings there were conclusive concerning the generosity of both his material provision and his true kindness - but she saw, in the journey to the great cliffs, that one could not simply dissolve an orientation to a first and precious Other, whose breath had been her very own. On this head she had to ask silent absolution from what she was thinking in such close physical proximity to both Christopher and to *Love*, wherever that dwelt; and she knew that both Byron and Willoughby could confirm such a place: there was the fatal rub.

She found her voice speaking from some distance as it took charge of her:

'Let us therefore walk upon these ancient stones and admire the cliffs and watch the gulls diving,' it said.

No one wanted to challenge this invitation for it was a day when all their several sorrows seemed to unite and provide the great benison of understanding.

The Colonel carefully took his wife's hand, asserting a tender comprehension of the distant plea which her silence had provided. Here, a man still able to live within the core of his natural sweetness, despite years of demanding self-preservation as a military man and, indeed, a hero. The look between them was of softness and a form of understanding that emanated from his being previously harmed by the events of his own first love; her according of honour to the hearing of his own 'broke heart' and the promise of ensuing longevity of loyalty, e'en to death.

The walk at Bridport Bay provided exactly the right conditions for the amelioration of much. The three men and Margaret set off up the near-vertical path to the cliffs, firmly ushered by two wives keen as mustard to put the day into a better frame down on the seashore. It was Elinor who, barely out of earshot of the cliff expedition, burst out:

'My beloved sister, how can it be with you?'

'O Elinor, my heart seems to be an inferno, without any voli-tion on my conscious part: all of my components are fiercely taken aback. Yet! I am not the girl that I was then and am given a man whose love is profound and I cannot, will not, allow what we have become to one another to be damaged – there has been too much suffering on both sides.'

'My fair Marianne, that is wise!' said Elinor with such gravity that they both smiled and the former continued.

'It is a sort of impeachment of the soul, when it cannot be with the one it prefers, I think. It is not a matter for the head, it is about the heart and the body – the body knows: all of it.'

'I am in accord, dear sister,' said the other. 'When I feel the fluttering of life within me, I ask myself whether the little soul has yet arrived: we do not know at what time the soul enters that small body.'

'O Elinor, only you, or you and Edward, could be thinking of souls in unborn infants!'

49

Florence Fawke resembled her father in everything, save the love of her mother, whom she fought against with a will that seemed to belong to another earth. Steadfast and true to the man who had sired her, little Flo' was indomitable at five; eschewing the commands of her limpid mamma she stalked through her world as if it were her place of dominion. Interested only in what her dadda said, did and thought, she was detested by her siblings, with the exception of the baby for whom she had often to care. Seen amongst the cottages dragging the wee child along or pushed under her arm like an old rag doll that had seen better days, she was fierce, fighting her way through life valiantly. Visiting the older ladies of the dwellings for scraps which implemented her meagre and lacklustre diet, Florence was yet loved by them, the only real source of comfort to her.

On Thursday 26th October she decided that she would follow her father to the Barn and see for herself what happened there; she had frequently heard of what went on and found, in her ample imagination, a place in which hope dwelled, as an oak leaf ready to fall from the parent bough. Dadda came back from the fields early on Barn nights, as he had done the day before, but this day, this one day, she had heard him say that he would 'be up and

215

away there' before dark, 'as the owl on the swoop'. In such words she found no meaning but watched her own opportunity present itself, even as she was determined to take it.

In the brief moments of supper, she sat as still as a windless night, mopping up what was said and what was not said with her grey bread into the lifeless mess of green water set before her. Well versed in subterfuge she slipped away as soon as she could, without telling mamma that she would take her sister with her: the real dolly was pushed under the arm and the two went along together as they had done since the baby's birth.

Setting out on the top road, the two bowled adequately along. The high hedges kept them well covered, the small places within, where the badgers had their entrances, providing bolt holes if the necessity for bolting presented itself. A cart that veered unexpectedly around a corner gave the bigger girl a fright, so flown were her thoughts in an eagerness to find dadda's Barn, that she almost dropped her smaller charge. The baby was also doing her best to cling to her only source of security, as the occupants of the cart created havoc in an otherwise silent landscape, their shouts and cahootings loud in her tiny ears: like any small animal frightened by the unexpected she put down her head deeper into the shoulder that gave her shelter.

Walking apace now, the pair found the way to Delaford top, as the Hall was called, plain as could be. Despite the increasingly crepuscule nature of the evening, the sky darkening in seconds, the two made an inelegant sight, like the two foundlings who they really were. Hoping to reach the barn before dadda got there, Flo' put on a push to make the possible real.

Rounding the corner of the village where the parsonage could be seen, the elder child saw the barn at once, recognising its location from the many tales told of it by her home fireside. Thankfully, the small door within the greater door was open and the girls pressed through it. The immediate aspect was pleasing – far more welcoming than any description could have provided – and Flo' imagined her father, 'commanding the show' as he said, standing afoot a bale, and telling the Pastor a thing or two about the plight of the working man.

The child was not prepared for the smell of the building, its corners well swept and the bales in neat rows behind the few benches, like a church, she thought. The straw of the bales looked enticing, their scent and the warmth of the closing evening notwithstanding and it was not long before the two little girls made a cosy bed between the cobb wall and the few hay strands that provided an exquisite rug for a small slumber to await the arrival of dadda.

Even as his daughters were in the higher lanes, Simeon Fawke was running along the lower pastures, the bundle beneath his own arm of less calibre than that of his own little mirror. Waiting all day for the opportunity to present itself, Fawke had extrapolated from Mrs Simmons all the information required as to the whereabouts of the persons of Delaford Hall and its rectory: 'O yes, gone to Lyme for the day, it's all right for some,' she had said, eyes green and glinting, 'gadding and flouncing in the carriage whilst folks like us stay behind to clean up the mess.' This was said with such feeling that the renegade's own eyes positively shone with the grim delight of his way made plain. The same eyes did not notice that the regular nature of the barn's layout had been disturbed somewhat.

Moving as silently as the grave Fawke moved amongst the bales, quietly lifting several on top of each other and to shut off one window whilst preparing the other for a hasty departure with a small pathway for his escape. The great door was barred and to this he added the smaller portal, clicking the lock across, to make exit impossible.

Carefully sliding through the narrow inlet which he had prepared before the second window, the grim face regarded all around it with the putrid pleasure of revenge and, finally covering his tracks, lit the tinder box in his hands, witnessing the crackle and rush of dry grass as he did so. Closing the window behind him could not mask the delicious smell of the hay igniting and then the straw in the bales and then and then. The pace of the man running and rushing in the dark held nothing against the sleep of his bairns in a cocoon of smoke, wrapping around their chests, the gentle hand of death mercifully conducting them away from the real perils of their inadequate lives thus far.

50

*A*s Fawke left the high lanes, his departure marked the arrival of the coach and six carrying the returning Delaford folk. The evening was now so drawn in that the sight of fire was unmistakable to them and the two men within the coach, alerted by the sight and smell of the flames and the forward charge of their friend and leader, Colonel Brandon, leant out with horror at what met their gaze. The sight before them was at the same time both mesmerising and terrifying, the flames now leaping high into the night sky and the smell flooding toward them of a powerful and acrid nature.

Both women were silent, held in by what was happening and Margaret, a young woman now coming into her powerful femininity, involuntarily clasped the arm of Nicholas Saunders, who placed his own capable hand on top of hers.

As the coach ground to a halt at a safe distance from the danger for the horses, all could see that it was too late for intervention and the men, including the Colonel, whose building it was and whose military life had well prepared him for such an eventuality, stood as one before the enveloping flames. The barn was isolated enough from other parts of the Delaford community to contain a fire that did not spread but the old retainers of the

Hall had already begun to form a chain of buckets from the well and the flames were being staunched by their loyal efforts. Mary Dashwood, returning from a friend in the valley, could only stand far behind the men, unable to move a muscle, her face lit by the light of the inferno.

Feeling that she might faint, Elinor quietly took herself back to the parsonage, accompanied by Marianne. Only Margaret stood alone beside the carriage, the horses now led away to the stables, and would not be drawn to any dwelling whilst her friend, along with Edward and the Colonel, was baling buckets against the flames: by midnight all was rendered calm and the two stable lads and one of the coachmen volunteered to keep watch against any rogue elements re-igniting. Everyone else retired from the scene.

As the dawn came, Edward, still unslept, came back out to the Barn, his able mind unwilling to take cognizance of what had happened. The big door of the building was still standing, as were the walls but the roof was gone, and the windows bore little resemblance to what they had been before. Wary of stepping into a place of lesser safety Edward stood for a moment by the east side, his mind in as much turmoil as it were capable of, when he realised that there was a sort of bundle between the wall and what remained of the burned rushes. Failing to comprehend the formless shape and indeed, presence of the bundle, he stepped forward as his senses began to convey to him the horror of what was before him and whose grim details his mind did not wish to comprehend.

First moving backwards against the potent possibility that was slowly making itself real to him, he yet could not, would not, go forward to conclude the information given by his senses. As his body moved out of its gridlock he realised, with the full cognizance of a loving man and a parent elect, that the bundle was made up of two little girls, one almost a baby. The latter was wrapped around by the elder of the two, whose long hair, once beautiful, was now frizzled. He stood aghast above the children, a dereliction hovering around them yet one completely overcome by the certain smile spread across the face of the girl, whom he thought to be about five years old, and whose look was only what he would call ecstatic. Edward, a man living his whole life and against all odds, within the parameter of his heart, was not a jot surprised by what he saw. The arms of such a child were so tightly wrapped around her sister, that anyone being out of comprehension of the gravity of the situation might have thought the girls sleeping peacefully after a long journey: the smoke had mercifully killed them.

Nevertheless, in a profound paralysis of both body and spirit, the realisation spread through the priest that the fire had taken more than the vitriol of a furious man. As Edward turned to run to the Colonel the latter was walking swiftly to him, his own feelings of apprehension the fierce harbingers of early rising.

Whilst the two men stood together, the sun just rising, the proximity of knowledge seeped into every crevice of their consciousness and they turned toward one another with the name of *Fawke* on their lips. It was not many minutes after that found the two now-brothers on horseback and on their way to the small cottages in the ley of the high lanes. Their correct presumption made the task of enquiring and then confirming the truth to the Fawke parents. The Delaford men thought that it was the hardest matter they had ever had to convey and to see Fawke's face as he realised that he had murdered the only being who truly loved him, was no recompense.

Colonel Brandon agreed to superintend the responsibility and cost of the funeral and the Constable was not called – another illustration of his character and calibre that did not surprise anyone - and the two men left as quickly as they had arrived, devastation in their wake: love was not just the privilege of the upper classes.

51

*I*t was not till the evening of the day after the fire that the inhabitants of Delaford could come together. All remained profoundly shocked at what had happened and Edward and Elinor, now recovering from an amalgam of previous events, agreed not to discuss the day until later, when there would be more perspective. The Reverend Ferrars found himself feeling crushed by what the fire had done; as was his wife, whose mind was struggling to find composure after the fatality in the barn. Grieving for the loss of the two little girls, she wept for them and the feral nature of their father; the unnecessary tragedy of their deaths; the misery of their mother and the life left to live in between.

Set next to the wake of the barn fire was Elinor's concern for her sister. Quick to register the need for mercy within her own life, she tempered her natural anger with Willoughby, or rather, with his deeply thoughtless actions, against the man that she had seen emerging over a short but significant period. It had taken, she felt, real courage to talk to her as he did that night and she also gave way to recognising the change in him after his inappropriate marriage and some valuable realisations about masculine desire. Both Ferrars saw that the distress at the Old Red Lion was countered by the seal, the sturdy magnificence of the ancient cliffs and even the sea itself, so that there had played out in the day, an incomparable balance to the heart's grief, shot through as it was, in the morning arrival at Lyme. Neither Edward nor Elinor could settle and their choice of avoidance of all desperate thoughts, let alone subjects, was instigated by Edward:

'My beloved, how is our little one, in all of this buffeting swell?'

'Wriggling and snoozing, and then, I should think, dancing!' said Elinor, endeavouring to be bright.

The arrival of Meg to say would they please come to hear Nickluss play ended any further enquiry.

'We shall be delighted,' said Edward gratefully and the trio set off toward the garden.

In the Hall, the Brandons were in an upstairs sitting room where they could not be overheard. Both were devastated by the deaths of the two small children – scapegoats of their father's temper – and the futility of so many weeks of endeavour on Edward's part. Claiming little distress for the loss of his barn, the Colonel showed only the solidarity with his brother-in-law which had first brought the men to the Barn and all that they had done together to alleviate suffering families. Agreeing not to speak of the grim matter for the while, the subject of Willoughby inevitably arose.

'It had to happen, my beloved Marianne,' said the Colonel as they both came to be seated, 'would you like to talk, or would you like solitude, or just to sit with one who knows your turmoil on this head?'

Mrs Brandon opted for the latter, next to whom she settled in proximity made strong through their mutual sorrow at the fire. There was no question that she could talk to him of the confusion in her heart concerning the man she had seen in Lyme – and with strong feelings that she thought to have quelled – but she did not wish to sit alone in the desert; anyway, she had made a decision to love this man. Why! they had not long embarked upon their marriage, awaited the possibility of children and she did not care for a life of uncertainty and instability. No! Marianne Brandon lived as she enjoyed: it was inconvenient to have been caught in an unexpected storm, but she would have to recover: the calibre of her husband and the great fealty to love in his own heart made her feel ashamed of the lack in her own. Even she could see the events of the day slipping away – now she must allow them to recede. Yet, reclining in the arms of a strongly loving man, she could not prevent the conversation going on between her head and her fevered heart. At last, she bore upon herself to desist:

'If I were a fishwife, what has happened would not obtain, but yet, I am a woman spoiled and wrapped in luxury, not to mention real care and comfortably seated next its provider. My heart must be still – I may never again meet the man who moves it so strongly for another twenty years!'

Colonel Brandon, his own stoical and long-suffering heart aware of all that the morning had exposed, would yet not compromise the prospect of a fine marriage with a woman whom he loved and whom he had fairly won. Further, a man who had already learnt something of the agonies of love was doing his best to wrestle from the power of its past and settle into this, his own second gift from destiny's fair hand, without looking back. He dressed quickly, and beautifully, for dinner – which he frankly welcomed as a diversion. The gong sounded as both appeared from their separate dressing rooms and no one regarding their descent of the stairs could have guessed the conflict unexpectedly created at the start of the day.

The trouble was, for Marianne, that she had brought the art of seduction into the cold light of her day, an art much practised and perfected by a man who was desirable in many other ways; the fact that she had further placed the pleasure of their coming together within the container of eternity was both complex and something not easily countenanced in everyday reality. Marianne knew of the tragedies both of Mary Shelley and her stepsister, whose suffering at the hands of magnetically handsome – and famous – men, was both extreme and consequential. Further, she was not a fool and knew already of the difficulties – and often misery – of reduced circumstances. As she sat, then, with her husband, she conceded to herself that she was not the girl she had been at seventeen but also that too much of incalculable content had passed by since that time. Willoughby had been a huge love, of that there was no doubt, but she was not the selfish and proud young woman that she had been in his presence and she saw that he was the spectre in a mirror that shone back at her.

'Care,' she thought to herself, as the miasma of emotion swelled around her, 'I will conquer this, for my *head* knows the facts.'

Discreetly signalling to her mother, as they met later in the hall, that she would like to meet before breakfast, Marianne led the way into dinner, which was a decidedly convivial affair, the rest of the day rescued and made what its start had promised. Margaret and Nicholas - who was also beautifully attired for the evening – looked demure and elegant by turns: a tantalizing combination. A young man bursting with talent and wrapped in a deal of humility is a rare thing and the Brandon family both recognised and appreciated him.

'Mama, we had such a walk up the cliff, it was nearly vertical,' said Meg greeting her mother after the day.

'O yes, the size of those walls is unfathomable,' said Elinor, 'they must be as old as time itself.'

'Yes, yes, we had to haul ourselves up the last few paces but the grand vista at the top is worth it, we felt like Mr Turner!' said Edward, shining within the warmth of his real family after some more trying hours.

'Or a musician! I have made a little sea story for us, for after dinner, if you would like?' said Nicholas calmly, as if he had just noted down a list for the grocer.

The dining parlour had taken on an air of exquisite softness, the sun still strong outside and the candles lending a further *douceur*. Everyone was able to breathe again. The walls were apricot, for the small parlour was used chiefly in the warmer months so that the late sunlight, and the candles rendering the room's walls doubly muted, provided the most sensitive cup for the communion which flowed between all gathered at the round table.

The Colonel had found a delicious wine for them – every detail attended to with the marriage of military precision and a fine sensibility. It was thus, that wellbeing seeped into the very bones of all seated together, that eve. There was silence for a little while, then Margaret burst forth with a genuine delight, forgetful of the preceding distress:

'And mama, we saw a seal, he was adorable and performed many tricks and antics for us.'

'You must listen for him in the music, Mistress Margaret,' said Nickluss, with a smile to melt all hearts.

Mrs Dashwood, who was well enough experienced in reading all the signposts in an atmosphere to do with her family, knew that something of a serious nature had occurred within the day, even before the fire in the barn; leaving this aside, she sat grateful for her enormous fortune in being here around a small table in Dorsetshire with those she loved. The illness and loss of her beloved husband; the over-prompt inhabiting of her home by Fanny; the arrival of Edward; the swift removal from Norland and the move to Devonshire, all followed upon by Marianne's illness, constituted the great wave that had built up, crashed down and was now reforming into a still, smaller sea of fragrant wellbeing, the grim reality of the lost children notwithstanding.

They all withdrew to the library which Marianne had filled with late summer flowers before they left for Lyme and now, in the light of so many beeswax candles and the intoxication of their marriage with the floral overture, their new young friend played them his sea poem. Only those who were at Lyme really compre-hended the discreet cadences of the day's journey but the moments of desperation and the role of the small, master-diverter, could not be missed. The great cliffs and the magnificence of sea, sky and rock were before them in the music - the *crescendo* of all that had formed the day was incandescent: the music, the fine company, the perfume of the flowers and the contribution of the bees made it so.

When the last note sounded, it was Edward who stood up, his face alight:

'Nickluss! We thank you with all heart, you have been a dear painter of magic for us in a sea of despair.'

52

*E*veryone had at last settled for the night. Meg was delighted to be staying with her elder sister, at the latter's behest, after such a busy day and on so many fronts and was in an extremity of bliss. Love had arrived for the first time and here, a young woman of exuberance, natural charm and wit, all abutted by kindness, was doing her best to fly away to sleep. In the greater scheme of things, she was aware, as her sisters had been, of the precipice along which she walked as a young woman without support of a certain kind, lacking since the departure from Norland. She never dwelt on what had been before, never gave herself permission to think of her father, forever fled from his youngest daughter; never felt less than anyone else because surrounded by the love of her family and the wondrous provision of Sir John Middleton and now the Colonel. She knew that she owned an effervescent spirit the energy of which could not be placated. It was time now, she decided as she lay there, to pass through a certain gate, to insist to the gods, wherever they were, that it was time to bloom, like a flower, even if its roots had been moved to some rocky crevice on a cliff top. Why! the small sea pinks at home were ravishing and they flowered in rain, storm and wild wind. In this state of insistence, she grew deliriously happy and fell into a fathoms-deep sleep.

Further along the corridor, Elinor and Edward were talking softly – about the day, about the truths of love and the grim truths of agricultural life not so far away from them and now pushing forward into public comprehension. All was silent save for the gentle call of the one owl, flying on to the Hall's elegant chimney pots after retrieving its mate, when the sound of hooves on the drive startled Elinor out of drowsy restfulness. Edward was just turning toward her in enquiry when the jangle of the doorbells brought them both up.

'O good heavens, whoever can that be at this time? It is almost midnight,' offered the Pastor, pulling on his dressing gown whilst sweeping toward the landing, his wife following at a more reticent pace, yet certainly in pursuit. As he arrived in the hall he met with Mrs Dolby.

'Let me, it is rather late for visitors,' he called to her, just as the key was being turned in the old lock.

Outside, there was a fresh-faced man with a letter, toward whom Edward stepped, thanked for his late delivery with a coin, and bid a warm goodnight. Elinor arrived just as the housekeeper disappeared into the kitchen.

'Whatever can the matter be, it is past twelve?' she said.

They both sat down on a settle put there for the purpose, inches into the hall.

Before opening the note, the Reverend Ferrars moved his whole being toward the angle of his wife, intimacy was not just for the bedroom. He read aloud:

Norland, September 24th 18…

Dear Edward and Elinor,

I am afraid that something very grave has occurred, and I must ask you if I may come to Delaford on the morrow. I am travelling at this very time on the way from Norland to you.

I ask for your assistance because Fanny is very ill and is quite disturbed about many things; she is at present with her mother at Berkeley Square but will be returned home to us shortly.

I would be grateful for your assistance.

Please expect me around noon of this day.

Yours…

John Dashwood

Edward put the letter into Elinor's now trembling hand. They both stopped and looked at one another and then moved, as one, toward the kitchen. Mrs Dolby had already put the kettle on.

As dawn broke Elinor finally went back to sleep; Edward got up and fed the chickens who were already well awake and flapping. He felt a deep sense of fear in his stomach – breakfast was out of the question – and realised that he had to surrender to the inevitable. Fanny had been impossible with the Dashwood family, rendering Mary, Elinor, Marianne and Margaret a miserable and penny-pinching existence, only ameliorated by the goodness and kindness of a man they had never even met, family or not. Doing all that he could to avoid prejudicial judgement, the Pastor nevertheless knew a little about how Love worked and which required a certain devotion to it to comprehend. In the easiest way unimaginable and with a terrible sweep of the cat's paw, his sister had made intolerable the life of the Dashwood family immediately after the loss of Mary's husband: he wondered what news would be brought at noon.

Mr Dashwood had been, like Edward's own father, a loving and gracious man who oiled all the wheels of his estates so that at his death, those delicate and invisible sources of motion ground to a fast and terrible halt. The similarity of their fathers was not lost on Edward; further, reasonable though he was, he could not ignore the unhappiness caused to his wife and her family by Fanny, nor her influence – which was another indubitable matter – upon her husband who had reneged on his promise to his father upon death, to care for them. That his brother-in-law could not rise above the controlling mania so consequentially evident in his wife and give vital help where vital help was due, was something that left Edward only glad that he could stand back and observe. Observation and judgement notwithstanding, however, he had also been in receipt of Fanny's spiteful tongue and her singular lack of compassion and support for his now mother-in-law, stood as fact. Indeed! he did not condemn his sister, but he could not fail to notice the way in which life sometimes turned round to face the greater misconducts of persons in a way that could have been written on Belshazzar's proverbial wall. Fanny's obstinate lack of respect; her ferocious stance taken in a situation of gravity and against helplessness and despair; her rigidity in claiming *her* rightful entail in Norland whilst adding substantially to the exclusion and near downfall of her own brother; and the grim removal to a cold cottage in Devonshire for the Dashwood women, all sat upon Edward's passionate altar for fairness. No! he would always love Fanny and did not condemn her, but she had made, in this Pastor's book, a schism in all that he held dear and he acknowledged no lack of surprise that the wind had changed. He waited sadly to hear what calamity had befallen his sister to precipitate the arrival of a dramatic message in the night, followed by the coming of her husband – whom they had barely heard from in five years.

Just as he was sitting down to breakfast, both Elinor and Meg arrived at the table, the former having apprised the latter of the night's darker activities, the prologue to the tale of John Dashwood's arrival.

'O my beloved Edward, it is still early, we may all thankfully sit together before our household experiences any abrupt change.'

Meg, who was always first to say what everyone else was thinking but dare not say, held nothing back:

'Aunt Fanny! well, what a surprise…'

For once Elinor did not upbraid her young sister but coughed a little as all three looked down, somewhere below the vista of the floor.

'Shall I go to the Hall, as soon as we have eaten and tell Marianne of the message of the night, or would you like to do so, my dear Elinor?' asked her husband.

'I think that we should all go,' she replied in a whisper.

Scarcely had the little party returned from the Brandon household, where their embassy was met with the compassion and not a little frankness on the part of Marianne than John Dashwood's barouche arrived with a skeleton livery. Only Edward and Elinor met him at the door and he was shown forthwith into the small morning room off the hall: Delaford Parsonage had once been a Tudor manor house and this room, in particular, still had beautiful, carved beams.

'Please, sit down John, we are so sorry that you have been obliged to visit us in difficult circumstances: may we offer you tea at once?'

'No, I am perfectly fine, thank you.'

'Then pray, tell us how we might help you,' said Edward, still standing.

As John started to speak it was evident that he was in a great distress, his face seeming to approach a rigidity and pallor that they had never witnessed before.

'I am sorry to tell you that your sister Fanny has a dreadful canker and it is likely that she may not survive.'

Both Ferrars sat in silence.

'I have been advised to come by my wife herself because you see, she is quite broken. Quite broken.'

Both Ferrars now sat back in their seats, Elinor catching her breath.

'In the last weeks, she has been doing her best to come to terms with the fact that part of her tongue has had to be removed – a ghastly education, I mean *operation*, and one from which she may not survive: the shock alone has been grim.'

Edward stood up again, walking to the fireplace where a small fire burned.

'And is it certain that she cannot survive?' asked the Pastor.

'We do not really know, of course she has availed herself of the best physicians, close by in Harley Street but the *effects*, shall we say, of the illness have been mortifying to her.'

Elinor, whose imagination was always expansive, did not like to think that her brother-in-law had chosen a very telling word in his exegesis.

'Please tell us whatever you can and how it is best for us to help,' said Edward, mesmerizingly still.

'I realise that you have your own life now, but your sister is going through a mental disorder which accompanies her illness and, it is my unpleasant duty to tell you that she has delirious times, rather like nightmares in the full daylight, in which you feature, Edward. With all the good will in the world, I cannot convince her that you have been looked after by your wife and by Marianne's husband and are well. I know that you are not a hard man and will have forgiven her for how she has been but worse, she sees herself in a pit, in which she is trapped and out of which she cannot climb: she screams and cries and shouts to us, but we cannot help her, the laudanum only makes it worse. Please do come to her, if you have it in you Edward, and on Elinor's behalf too, because Fanny keeps trying to tell us that she has 'crippled Elinor.'

At this the latter begged leave from the room and left the two brothers-in-law alone.

'I will come back up with you to Fanny,' said the Reverend Ferrars, his own heart now beating fast.

'If you but can,' said John. 'I will return at once to her, she is so truly pitiful, that to be the carrier of good news will be uplifting, *alleviating*, I dare say.'

The two men sat before the fire in silence, the one visibly relieved, if only temporarily, the other mindful of the enormity of the situation.

'Of course, I will come. It behoves me to insist that you stay with us the night, John, it is too much to contemplate setting off again without rest and sustenance – you must reserve some strength for young Henry,' said Edward.

'No! thank you, Edward, I will rest better in the carriage, knowing that you are coming with me and pray, do you forgive her? Shall the others forgive her? She is chained to a memory of her behaviour and I beg that you will cut the chains, for they grow apace.'

'There is no question of harbouring grudges in this household, John.'

The latter agreed to partake of some luncheon in the little parlour, its own history and beauty holding and strengthening him to make his way back home.

At the end of the repast John Dashwood asked bravely if he could see his mother and sister whilst remaining where he sat: Edward bethought himself that this showed enormous courage and silently fetched them, excusing himself from their delivery to the parlour. As he closed the door, he saw the terrified faces of the women who had loved John for so long, as the latter burst into great sobs, the volume of which could not be muted and which were carried, even in the wind, to Delaford Hall.

Realising that he had to leave almost at once with John Dashwood's departure, Edward prepared to travel up to London; his emotions were mixed but they were clear and fair. There was no question of hesitation in forgiveness, at least on his part, he could not speak for the others. Both he and Elinor agreed to confer after his return; there had been too much flux in the last few days and they both needed to allow it to settle – his whilst he was travelling to his wife's old home and hers to be expressed, perhaps, in discussion between the Dashwood women when he had left.

Elinor, now heavily with child, could only affirm to her husband that she loved him and, whilst certainly being too wary to admit it to herself, had done so from his arrival at Norland! It was, she said, without doubt, that she was better off by far to be his wife, in a place they both loved and without any inheritance, than a spinster going about gratuitously *in a barouche*! He quickly avowed that he too had never, as she well knew, wanted the blessed *barouche* and in allowing his life to take a different, even opposite course, had managed to be the better, the more hospitable and greater self for it. He bade a short goodbye to those remaining at Delaford and asked the Colonel and Nicholas Saunders to keep the spirits of the Dashwood ladies as high as possible – the musician having been pressed to stay until the start of his London season, for 'a friend in such times is a friend indeed.'

As the sun was coming round to two o' clock, the Reverend Ferrars left the parsonage to see his sister. His head was clear – judgement was nothing to do with him – but he felt fearful of what he might find when he saw the result of it.

53

The brothers-in-law barely spoke on the return trip to Norland. Given that John had already had a hard, two-day journey to Delaford without time to repair or renew his strength there, he did very well. Edward felt sustained by all that wrapped around him: his Elinor; their home; the great delight of attending their first child; their familial neighbours and all that was shared between. For a man who was still young, the parson of Mary Magdalene had found much for which to be grateful when his prospects had felt and looked very different. He could not go to Norland relishing what was happening to his sister, his persistently unkind, vicious-tongued sister. Seeing her in this horrible place would not help him in any way: he was not a man who delighted in revenge - even thoughts of revenge had never occurred to him - he was simply not a man who cared to repay that which had been visited upon him.

In two days, the carriage travelled with both velocity and grace, the state of the roads being in its favour. In one inn at which the travellers stopped, all was amiability and good service – it was as if people knew that the two men were on a mission of mercy. Norland was soon in sight; it was not a vista that attracted Edward much - the last time that he was there he had met Elinor, began to fall in love with her, only to see her ousted from her life-time's home by a singular lack of compassion that was both heart-less and unnecessary. Why! there was enough room in the great house to hold five families who would scarcely meet one another in weeks, not to mention the great loss of security to a woman starting the second half of her life.

'And now,' he bethought himself, 'we have overcome many hurdles, including my engagement to Lucy.'

It was then, without any hostility that the rector of a 'small country parish' arrived from Dorsetshire to find how his sister had fared.

'Come this way,' said John, striding straight upstairs to one of the smaller morning parlours. Edward was suddenly beset by nerves. As the door swung open, nothing could have been worse conceived: Fanny was sitting in a small chair, a nursing chair, surrounded by flowers. The fact that she was dressed in grey and lilac, somewhat slouched into the even greyer cushions that supported her, seemed to create a surreal effect for which he was unprepared. Her skin was sallow, her cheeks quite emaciated and her hair lack lustre and brushed back into a sort of tight *chignon*: the scene was beyond description.

'Come in, Edward, pray be seated, I will find some tea for you,' said the now master of Norland.

There was movement in the back of the room and a small figure rose from it – Fanny's nurse – and left with John.

It was several minutes before the priest recovered his powers of speech indeed, he was remembering that he *was* a priest. He stood quietly before his sister, waiting for her to focus upon him.

'I do not know what to say, Fanny.'

A grey slate came out of the sleeve of the chair, the patient wrote upon it clearly:

'At least you can!'

This unexpected wit shook her brother and he started to weep – what came from him was a flood - a flood expressing all that had gone before them since he was a child, for he had been his father's son and his father was gone, indubitably gone. His sister had always favoured his brother, Robert, the two were physically alike – in looks, in attitude and the possession of a form of superiority that never gave way to anything or anyone. *No one* could ever dent Fanny, she was inviolable; for her, conscience and good will did not exist; people were simply part of her game to get the best for herself and everyone must hurry! It was her frame of life, this agitation to have everything that she wanted, and such a position was precipitated and maintained by her mother and her younger brother.

In all the time that Edward had been aware of his sister, he had never seen her ailing, now she was like a wounded animal and he did not know what, or how to do.

'Fanny, write down what I can do,' he said, still weeping, wavering in the sight of the drowning woman.

Silence and then a sort of gagging noise from Fanny as she started to write.

'Please FORGIVE me,' spoke the slate, 'I have been so blind.'

'Fanny! There is no question that you are not forgiven. I bear you no malice and I am sure that I speak for Elinor, she is not a woman to bear a grudge: it would not serve her, it would not serve either of us.'

Struggling to keep his own composure, Edward sat back a little and then leant forward to take his sister's hand: she started to weep.

The slate came forward:

'I cannot see my son – I feel unable.'

Silence fell again.

In the moments that intervened, the two looked deeply into each other's eyes: the same eyes, brilliantly blue, their father's eyes. Through these windows the brother spoke without words to his sister – to tell her to forgive herself; to tell her to bring in peace; to ask Love, wherever Love was, for that peace.

'I cannot pray in a conventional way for you, Fanny but I ask you to include yourself in the mercy that you now see was lacking for those whose lives you affected. It is the only way to be free from the ordeal in which you find yourself. I speak as a man, as your brother and as a minister of a church that is watched over by a woman who is one of the greatest forgivers of all time.'

Silence.

'I am lost. Lost!' spoke the slate.

'No! Fanny, you are *not* lost, it is not possible when you practise being the opposite of the woman that you have been.'

'I am not religious, like you!' came the reply.

'Fanny! I am not religious either, I feel that there is only and ever Love and everyone, everyone knows what that is. Time will heal your mouth; for now, let it rest and with it your thoughts.'

John returned at exactly the moment that Edward realised that his sister was exhausted:

'Edward, breakfast has been laid in the morning parlour downstairs. We have put you in Elinor's old room and there is hot water there: please feel able to rest now.'

As he stood, the lilac-grey figure wrestled to get out of her seat and came slowly toward her brother, a hand outstretched; as he turned to her, she fell backwards, hitting her head on the corner of her chair. Both men saw her bite the tongue that remained; both men rushed to pick her up. As they lifted her, her head fell back, her mouth flooding with blood; every attempt to help her breathe was defeated against the flow; an incredible flow that would not, could not be staunched.

They realised that to fetch help was impossible: there was no time. Just as the clock in the Great Hall was striking nine, Fanny died in the arms of her husband and beside the brother of whom she had always been so proud, yet so inexplicably jealous.

There was nothing more to say and nothing more to be done.

*F*anny's funeral took place a week later at Highgate Cemetery, where she was buried in the family vault, with her father. The Dowager, Mrs Ferrars did not come, could not come and sent Robert and Lucy, and her sister Anne Steele, whose sunny and sound presence went far to heal the shock brought to the whole Ferrars family. Lucy too, was with child, so the requisite changes to the family had the possibility of being implemented: in the future there might be different laws and kinder persons to solve the misery of entail. The party from Dorsetshire went up to London together, staying at John Dash-wood's house, from where the procession to Highgate left.

The day of the interment was brutally hard on young Henry, who despite certain spoiling from his late mama, resembled his father's warmer spirit and missed the reality of a mother, what-ever her foibles. Margaret, who had left Norland, five years ago, thinking most noxious thoughts of the boy, was desperate to share the understanding that she thought his due: had she herself not lost her precious papa when just a girl? The party took great courage to their bosom and they cleft together as one, all enmity vanished in the tragic circumstances. Both Elinor and Lucy Ferrars were now sisters-in-law, with the same name and both attending their first child: 'it will be interesting to see what these new little cousins make of each other,' Elinor thought, with grace. Forming a quorum of those with greatly different views from the Old Guard, as Edward called them, was essential to him for the progress of the Ferrars family; perhaps Robert, his sparring partner having left the earth, would show a different side of his character.

Mary Dashwood came back from London to Norland, courageous in the coming and found strength to see the old home again, without resentment, pain, or an overblown sense of grief: she had found her late daughter-in-law difficult. Mary came with Elinor, Marianne and Margaret, and with Edward, her warmly affectionate son: in each one living a memory of the consequences of Fanny's power mongering. Yet! Yet, they all grieved for her; for the waste of a life less well lived; for John, faithful to her and long-suffering to the end; for Henry, left behind whilst young and for Norland Park itself, unnecessarily bruised and moved about in its own spirit. The place was a community of people who worked in both estate and house and who had become used to being disillusioned by their futures there. All turned out for Mrs John Dashwood and bade her farewell: Highgate was the perfect resting place for her – she could chat to the rich and famous eternally.

It was almost impossible for the Dashwood family to speak, collected again in the family home, as they were, and feeling the intense shock of Fanny's death. Mary, no stranger to grief, felt deeply for her stepson, with whom she had so recently found such painful astonishment at his lack of practical help and compassion for her, and with great consequence. Mary pondered to herself, sitting on the same terrace that she had loved for so long, that John's gentleness had gone before him all his life. The trouble was that owning a disposition of essential kindness did not protect him from being influenced by those nearest, those who were able to override the gentility of spirit through a certain persuasion. John had born the death of his mother, the remarriage of his father and then the birth of three daughters from him, very well. The second Mrs Dashwood had always loved him and endeavoured to include him and his position as the only male, and therefore heir, was frankly encouraging to his confidence – indeed, how else could he have made a match with Fanny? Nevertheless, somewhere within such a man there lived an absence of courage whose progeny was often a deficiency of principle, one which came to the fore in the face of bullying: it was as if there were a small hole in the gentle spirit, which let in its obverse when pushed by force. John had simply buckled at his wife's constant pushing and pressing and then there was no way forward except to concur, a miserable obsequiousness created in the place of true collaboration and the maintenance of compassion.

For a woman so used to loving, it was unthinkable to Mary to allow another to press so hard against the intuitive spirit that it fell apart, permitting all manner of convolutions extreme, not to say corruptions. The fact was that John had been worn down by Fanny – by her irrepressible will to involvement in everything beneath her nose and to jealousy of any person being centre stage but her. This husband's natural gentleness and generosity had been destroyed by his wife's incessant will to power over those who threatened her own. If but Mary's stepson had found a way of holding up against the dam, a means of staying true to himself in the force of the battle waged against his profoundly good heart but no! Mary Dashwood knew *exactly* from where the source and force of judgement upon her had come and after this very day would never allow the thought to come through her heart again: it was closed, this door of exclusion.

The grim wake over and the family gaining peace from resting in a gracious house, John asked his stepmother to meet him in the library. Such a beautiful room, saved from recent 'restoration' and still smelling, Mary thought, as she walked into it, of her beloved husband – 'where now, his thoughts and words?' she wondered as she passed through the door. She was first to arrive, John came into the room very slowly and she could see that he was devastated by what had happened to his wife and, indeed, how. His stepmother started up to say something, but he motioned for her to stay seated.

'Mary, I just wanted to speak with you before you left.'

'Of course, dear John, pray, be seated.'

As he sat, he began to weep copiously at once and his hearer felt that these were somehow the tears of a younger man, one whom she had encountered many years before in similar circumstances: the loss of the woman he loved. She sat very still, allowing all that had to flow out to be able to do so.

'Mary, I have been unable to look at what happened in our coming to Norland; it was done in the face of being swept along by Fanny's tremendous wish to live here, God rest her soul: I think that she thought it would change life in some way, you know, like a princess living in a palace.'

'I, I do want you to know that it is all forgiven, John,' said Mary with great gentleness.

'Before you say any more, dear *mama*, for you have always cared for me as one, I feel that I must tell you swiftly that Henry and I will not stay here, cannot stay here and we would that you return to your home if you wish. There are more than adequate funds in the estate by which you may live until your own life ends and there is too much sorrow for us to continue in how things were.'

It was impossible for Mary to speak; she was not the woman who had left Norland for Barton Cottage and she felt a great sense of gratitude that she had survived there. Further, she owned a long list of people who had helped her to live again after two consequential losses.

'John, I want you to be sure that this is what you and Henry want – it is ordeal enough for you both – you must be certain that you want to live back in town.'

John sat forward quietly:

'We are certain now; it is not so very long since we were living the town life and we feel that we are better placed for distraction in a busy place.'

Now it was Mary who wept. Both parties looked very frankly into each other's eyes. John spoke first:

'I would want you to have your beautiful home back and feel that, if you agree, we could come to you often, asking you to help us rebuild a new way of being, as you have been obliged to do yourself. It must surely be the way forward for the family to have their Norland returned, even if only to visit and to rest in again, knowing that all is come back to them: as is their right.'

Mary was determined not to weep again – here a man before her devastated and fractured - but she said softly:

'Thank you, John. All that you have offered us is beyond my imagining and I accept with pleasure. I am sure that Meg will find your offer miraculous too.'

55

*M*rs Dashwood sat very still in the library of Norland before leaving again for Barton Cottage. In the time since she had departed from her beloved home, she had given scant attention to thinking about what she had left behind – it was simply too painful. It was not that she lacked courage but there had been so much to deal with upon Marianne's illness and then the coming-right of her daughter's life with the arrival within it of Colonel Brandon. Whilst Mrs Dashwood was well aware that she was not 'in attendance' as she called it, during certain painful moments of her being, she was, nevertheless, conscious of her true lack of comprehension of Willoughby, he was a libertine – but she knew in her deep heart that this side of him was not all. Being almost as taken as Marianne with his appearance; his energetic address to every situation; his fine and able physical attributes which, exceeding every lady's hope for a handsome man, seemed to have become even more illuminated through his abilities in music, dance, literature and horsemanship, she stopped pondering on the anomaly of the man. In short: it was unsurprising to her that he took up Marianne's heart and held it somewhere beyond his own previous ministry of libertinism, yet what he found there seemed to overcome the ill-gotten gains of seduction – and this is what she wanted to remember.

It was not possible for Mary Dashwood to forget the distress of Eliza Williams and her child, but she wanted to make more solid within herself the view that Elinor took of Willoughby, a view which was kinder, fairer and more compassionate than her own: she knew this, she saw, in her older girls, the precise need to defer judgement and she saw that they were right. Margaret continued to dub Willoughby a rogue, but all the sisters possessed loving hearts unused to being covered over by either shame or device and their mother must follow suit. If Mary Dashwood were as taken in as her middle daughter, it was not for want of intelligence (in both uses of the word, she felt) for she was neither a cynic nor a conspirator against love.

In considering Willoughby, she marvelled at the manner in which Elinor failed to judge him cruelly when he had almost killed her sister, the near-death of whom had taken place before her own eyes. Knowing of the conversation that was held between Elinor and the repentant seducer, Mrs Dashwood was able to stand back from prejudice against a young man gone down into some dark alley, a veritable *cul de sac* of the self, out of which he failed to climb: until, that is, real, affectionate loving came to present itself to him.

Further, there was the salient realisation that she had been a good mother to John Dashwood, yet he had fallen, in treating her and her girls with the most abhorrent lack of care. Being a woman who had loved her husband with both passion and comprehension, she did not, could not, understand the moment when the heart's will to love turned into some sort of abrupt mechanical matter in the linen. Stopping herself from thinking any further on this shocking subject, she bethought herself that she would brook none of this libertine business and thanked God for daughters.

Nevertheless, Elinor was right when she was careful not to condemn Willoughby in behaving in a way that many men had taken upon themselves as their *modus operandi*.

Sitting there, in the library, a place that held so much and so fond for her, the re-possessor of Norland was able to investigate within herself a few of the spaces in her memory over which she had embroidered a fanciful tale. Yet, she was not harsh upon either herself or the loving spirit that lived within her. That she had been obliged to learn much about survival at Barton Cottage, was indubitable and she acknowledged that she had learned a good deal and that none of it was wasted.

As she sat in her new, old place, Mary Dashwood felt that she would like to hear Nickluss playing something beautiful there – he was such a gift to them. At that moment, as if hearing her mother's thoughts, Margaret turned the door handle and was delighted to see who was sitting there.

'Come in, dear Meg,' said Mary, 'I was pondering on the enormity of events just now. Perhaps you might enquire as to the presence of your sisters and bring them both here?'

Ordinarily someone to keep surprises until a later moment of prepared delight, Mrs Dashwood decided to eschew the demands of her orderly nature and furnish her daughters with the news that their brother had offered her the return of Norland. She was more than conscient that she had not asked them about a return but there was no question that she would spend the rest of her days in a sea cottage in Devonshire when she could find again the home that had been lost to her. All three of her family came into the library so immediately that she felt they must have been nearby.

'Come, my dearest daughters! Pray, do not have a worried countenance, I have some good news for you,' she said, beckoning them in to sit around her.

'O mama! is it really good news? it seems that we have been a little beset by the converse,' said Marianne.

'It is, indeed, my love, I can tell you that its import took me very much by surprise.'

All made their inquisitiveness comfortable as Mary continued:

'In the last days, John has felt that the great turmoil that was

Fanny's illness and, let us say, departure, has prevented any further wish to remain in this house: he and Henry would no longer like to be here at Norland.'

There was a splinter of suspended breath through the three daughters as their mother continued:

'Further, that if I would like, Margaret and I could return here for the rest of my life. Meg, I am so sorry not to ask you first, but I answered him in the affirmative for me, saying that I would enquire with you and that is what I am doing now.'

'O mama! There is no need!' said her youngest daughter, laughing and weeping at the same time, 'I love you and I could think of nothing more wonderful than to return to our home!'

Such joy that arrived in the Dashwood camp was as sudden as a breaking wave below their cottage – visible and palpable over the essential feelings in the container of the time in which they sat.

'Good heavens, mama!' said Marianne, always the first to allow the flow of language out from a maelstrom of emotion. 'Permit us to be proud and happy that our brother has found it in himself to comprehend the measure of our reduction!'

All were found wanting for a moment, in the way of words – Mrs Brandon had summarised *exactly* – when Elinor, who was often the last to say anything when a major event was occurring, began discussion again:

'But mama, is it quite fine with Henry, is he able to bear to leave this house to which they had so relatively newly come?'

'Yes, it is, Elinor, my first sentiments exactly but John says that they have both missed being in London and both will be equally glad to continue in their home there, endeavouring, as best they can, to start a different life, without Fanny.'

Resplendent in their intimate connection, the four women sat together on the window seat, all with the respective memories that the room lent them and now with the hope and sheer joy of returning to a place which they loved so well.

'Well, I am sure that Elinor and I will be delighted to bring our husbands home!' said Marianne.

'Indeed,' added Elinor, 'and our new little ones!'

All agreed, with love and felicity, that such a thought was sublime.

56

*I*t was, then, with much gratitude, that everyone arrived home to Delaford late on a September morning which still held the warmth of summer. In a quiet front parlour, the Dashwood ladies sat together, two with their respective husbands and an air of pleasure and gratitude about them. In the meantime, the Hall had been delivered of condolences from the Middleton family and an invitation to be received at Barton Park as soon as they felt able. Christopher Brandon, who read out the kindly letter, suddenly thought that such an invitation might be made in reverse – as coming from them; quickly drawing Marianne aside to ask her opinion, he resumed:

'I realise, dear family, that these last days have been impossible to imagine, let alone to bear, so I offer a tentative possibility that you might like to have the Middletons here, I think without the children, in this instance. Please do consider together and give me the intelligence of your decision.'

It seemed as if there were immediate assent, but the little group nevertheless did as the Colonel had suggested and agreed to parley later. In returning from Norland to Delaford a watershed had been reached for Elinor, Marianne and Meg as well as for their mother and, of course, Edward: all had been delivered

of a blow in their lives and the person who had been instru-
mental in its delivery was now gone. In every individual so
affected, there had been growth, recovery and renewal – each
one could feel, as well as see these elements and they knew
them in their hearts too. In this way, there was no fervour of
revenge, nor any complacency on the part of the five - their plea-
sures in life were not taken at the expense of another's loss.
They did not speak of that loss nor the release of it, only felt it
together, knowingly, like a great, wide shawl about their
communal shoulders.

What *was real* for them, however, was the deliciousness of the
freedom felt at having crossed a threshold that miraculously
allowed them to breathe again: their loss was honoured and they
could go home to Norland. Being unwilling to join wholeheartedly in the formal aspects of her husband's work, Elinor gave
herself leave to investigate Plato and had decided that somewhere
in the inchoate distance, just about where the Absolutes lived,
there was a grand Court of Love, with its own life and laws. It
was to these latter that her fine heart appealed when she was
doing her best to struggle with St Paul, for example!

It was in one of these days, awaiting the arrival of the Middletons, that Meg was sitting in the *Orangerie* at the Hall, next to one
of the recently fruited lemon trees that always seemed to bear just
in time for the equal arrival of the colder autumn nights and their
possible death. As she drew in the scent, she was transported to
Granada, to a palace that she had heard of and whose history
seemed to be evoked in the small blossoms before her. It was still
Spring in the *Orangerie* at Delaford! Sitting in a sea of scented
green, she closed her eyes to think of the greatness and civilisa-
tion that she had heard of, when Nicholas came in and she
jumped out of her reverie as she opened her eyes to find him
standing there.

'O, I am so sorry to disturb you,' said the welcome intruder.

'Please do! I am in a sort of trance, taken far away by the
lemon blossom – I was in Spain, I think, at the Alhambra. Pray,

join me, if you would like,' said Meg, offering the wicker chair next to her.

'Thank you! If you would not mind my presence in your palace?' said her smiling friend.

It was several minutes before either spoke again. The scent of the blossom; the delicious warmth of the morning sunshine on the leaves of the still-blooming geraniums; the great felicity of knowing that the family could return to Norland and now the sheer delight of sitting next to an intelligent young man whose male beauty quite scared her: it was, indeed, a good deal for a young woman to take in all at once.

'Tell me, Mistress Margaret,' said the seemingly far-away voice of the young man in question, 'tell me, if you would like, how you are.'

Margaret, falling faster and faster into a sort of heavenly paradise, pondered for an instant before replying.

'Well, Nickluss,' she said very softly, 'we were all so afeared when we went up to London - it was not easy to be present at the funeral of a person with whom we had not had a very nice time. Yet we all realised that we were there, together, to support our brother and especially Henry. It seems only a moment since we waved goodbye to them as we left to come down here, but it has been five years almost exactly.'

As she ended these words, her hearer sat forward a little more on his chair.

'I am so very sorry that you have been to such a place of difficulty and not a little alarm,' said he.

Again, the thought-filled pauses.

'Please, do not be perturbed, do not!' said his hearer, 'we are all so certain that the land we had to cross with such sadness is not a place of contempt for us; we are a loving family, despite our quips and nips.' She regarded him thoughtfully. 'Perhaps Marianne and I express more, in our ways, that is louder, or quicker in opinion than our mother, or Edward and Elinor (and certainly Colonel Brandon) but yet, we realise the dangerous pitfalls of ill-speaking and, I suspect, ill-thinking: it is my eldest sister whom I must thank for this learning, you know.'

'I agree, it is a dear learning to be silent when silence is required,' said the musician, pausing, then continuing, 'I wanted to ask you, Miss Meg, if when I go back up to London, to St Martin's, whether you might come to some of my evenings there, when we start in earnest? You understand, I am just beginning but I have long grown out of worrying about how it will all be, so I invite you to come and see. And hear!'

Margaret blushed from the base of her neck to the tips of her ears and then laughed, quite loudly, replying:

'I would be most honoured if you should allow me to come to one of your performances, but I must ask mama and perhaps stay with Uncle John, whom we could ask to be my chaperone.'

'Of course, of course!' said Nicholas.

Both sat in a small envelope of pleasure, their innocence unpunctured.

'Perhaps I can write to you when I return and know the dates and programme of what we shall play – and sing!' said the burgeoning *maestro*.

'That will be very delightful,' said the far away voice of Margaret Dashwood. In the late morning sunshine, not far from the sea and near the bottom of England, sat two young people blessed with the knowledge of having come through and found one another.

57

*I*n the meantime, the Hall had received from the Middletons a warm letter of acceptance for the invitation; further, that they would come in three days' time, if that were acceptable and a messenger was duly sent straight back to say, 'yes please!'

At breakfast, the day after the encounter in the *Orangerie*, the news was announced that Delaford would be receiving visitors of a certain calibre on the morrow in time for dinner: at this, all was joy in profusion. Nicholas was delighted, especially since he knew the Barton Park family so well, indeed, had sprung from them to the Hall, and Edward and Elinor also found themselves content about the arrival of such jovial and kindly friends. After breakfast was over it was agreed that the menfolk would walk towards Chard, with its fine vistas of woodland and forest, and the hope of catching sight of some roedeer and bucks.

This walk was a particular favourite of Marianne – to walk to Forde Abbey – which she loved - but on this occasion there was a little to say to Mama and besides, the men perhaps needed to be together. The walkers set off under clear skies and with no prospect of rain: they left about one o' clock – the weather was kind, the ground not yet muddy – all was well. As the land dropped down towards the Abbey, the pace of the party brisk and bright, Edward apologetically brought up the subject of the fire. Starting in a quiet tone:

'I wanted to thank you both for your courageous help during the night of the fire and your support in dealing with its grim results. Colonel, I do feel beholden to you for being so very generous with the Fawkes and, indeed, for the absence of putting forth charges to the Constable for the loss of your barn.'

'Edward, I cannot say that it was *my pleasure*, but I certainly felt it my duty, not in any legal way, you know, but in the sense of one human being in a good position in life to another who is not. I have a certain fealty to my own good fortune, even if it were both hard won and in the extraordinary context of war. I bear Simeon Fawke no ill will and the ill wind that he created unfortunately blew back at him with terrible consequences. It remains to be seen what happens next, but we are both now exempt from the necessity to feel any further obligation to the cause for which his men fight – our hearts' compassion for the reality of that cause notwithstanding.

'Thank you, dear friend and brother,' replied the pastor quietly, 'your knowledge and success as a military leader helps me greatly, as does your status as a man living in goodness.' He turned to the younger man: 'tell me what you think Nicholas.'

'You know, sir, my life is very pleasant now, but it has not always been so, and it is only two generations ago that my family suffered very much indeed. What my heart feels, alongside the reference to my history, is that your men needed someone to hear them out and you have provided that; in the weeks that come they will need someone else, someone freer in their familial situation, to persist on their part. The most important thing, for me, is that you were there at the start with them, listening to their real and consequential grievances.'

'Thank you, thank you, both! said Edward, feeling better. 'You both know that I could not become a political tool. These may be times of rebellion but there is much corruption in the law, amongst the magistrates and in parliament and it would only take a snuff of the candle for these men to be transported, or worse. I could not have that on my conscience but at least we have tried. It is a delicate line between their progress forward out of the miserable ignorance of their masters and the possibility of dying here or in the New Colonies.'

'You were in a cleft stick, dear Edward but it is one from which you may now graciously slip,' said the Colonel, putting his arm across his brother's shoulder.

The three men walked on in amicable silence the air very thin for the time of the afternoon. The sun, still high, burned across the brown fields beyond them, even now dotted with the shape of men working to prepare the land for the next year. The sea gulls were circling, anticipating what was being unearthed as the tilth became finer. Edward bethought himself that he could even hear crows in the distance.

58

*T*he dinner gong was soon clanging out against the noisome arrival of the Middletons: Delaford was in full flow! It seemed that all roads converged in the wake of the gong and all friends met in the Great Hall, appearing from many directions and various. Meg did not appear from the library, as was usual but slowly walked the length of the staircase in the magnificent splendour of a new frock – deep pink with a purple sash and the tiniest dash of emerald in a brooch from her late grandmother. Everyone seemed to know each other, the length of time of such knowing not obtaining; this familial group had already heard the chimes at midnight.

'My dears! Well, well, well, we meet again!' called Sir John, beaming from ear to ear, Lady Middleton beside him and his mother beside her, who continued:

'Indeed! It is with such pleasure that we are here and all together again!'

Both the Colonel and Marianne bowed to their friends from Devonshire, as Mrs Brandon proclaimed their welcome:

'And it is marvellous that we are all here at the same time, come! If you would like to prepare for dinner, it is nearly ready, and your rooms await with hot water!'

Shortly, the Colonel and his lady led everybody into the pretty summer dining parlour at the back of the house, its open aspect to the garden a certain fillip. The scent of the first autumn flowers had already flooded in, lending the room a masculine character – the Michaelmas daisies, the sedum, their heads like so many small, red cauliflowers and the glass vases of tall golden rod behind them. In the background, the trees in the *allée* of oaks had started to shed their leaves and the aroma was strongly woody; Meg, who loved the outdoor world, exclaimed as they were all entering:

'O just smell the autumn everyone! It's the drying of the leaves and the falling of the oak cups!'

Mrs Dashwood smiled to herself, her youngest daughter had always called things by her own vocabulary – and oak cups were oak cups! All murmured in accord with their family member who helped any occasion – happy or sad – with her own version of the *mot juste*.

'Lady Middleton, Sir John, be seated here, if you will,' said the Colonel, who guided everybody to his mental map of the table: Edward was next to Nicholas, who sat facing Meg, with Mrs Jennings on his right – were they not old friends?

Everyone quickly fell into conversation, whilst Marianne was keen to declare their pleasure at having the Middletons, and for sending Nicholas to them, 'who fits in amongst us as if he were family and is now!'

Sir John quickly brought everyone up to date on the flow of life at Barton Park: the visit of the hunt; the fraternity meet on the moor; the significance of the coming rutting; the abundance of the apple harvest; the start of the potato picking and the salvation of everyone being together again – Amen!'

'Sir John, you are wonderful company and we appreciate you!' said Marianne, further explaining, 'how happy we have been to meet Nicholas, whom Meg calls 'Nickluss' and he does not seem to mind!'

Sir John continued: 'O but you are so welcome! Nicholas has become part of our family and now come to you. We are very blessed!'

Poor *Nickluss*, now quite pink about the ears, was beyond delight and Mrs Jennings, who positively burst with affability and joy, was second in the glowing stakes and asked her son to explain how they met the young musician:

'Yes, indeed, indeed, we are so happy to inform you, with his permission.' A nod from Nicholas gave the speaker assent to continue. 'As you may comprehend from the maps, we are in great proximity to Cornwall and have acquaintance with many families there, one of long standing. This family is in the sea village of St Mawes and lives there on a steep hill above the town at a house called Braganza. Such a house, by the way, was called after a ship that carried Byron to Turkey, his poem there, written on board the Falmouth Packet in Falmouth Roads, on June 30th, 1809, with its stanza 'On Braganza'. Once we made our friendship with this family, we did not want to lose it. But yet! I will ask Nicholas to continue, for the story is, as the Colonel would say, *remarkable*.'

'Thank you, ma'am, and I would start by saying what Mrs Jennings omitted in her good manners, that the lady of the house called Braganza was my beloved grandmother.'

The table insisted on leaning closer, to a man, since they were already so intrigued and delighted by the gift to them that was Nicholas and who continued:

'I have to say that not only did I adore my *nonna*, but that any musical ability I have, has, I believe, come from her. She would play the piano and sing to me, just the two of us, and her voice was singular because she was Russian – well, she was not Russian, she was Polish but the part of Poland in which she lived was, over centuries, strongly interlinked with Russia, sharing a mixed language, culture and history. You may have guessed that her land was what she called Biélorusse her name was Zoscia, or as her family called her, in the softer diminuitive, Zofsia, which means 'Feminine Wisdom.'

'O what a *lovely* name, Nickluss!' said Meg, her heart shining bright in the fire of her imagination.

Nicholas continued: 'In the middle of the last century, the alliance between the Polish people of my grandmother's area, the Lithuanian people and the close-by Russians, was broken. This shattering was both serious and consequential because the leaders and the gentry of Belarus at that time spoke Polish, so very much was lost in the war against the bigger neighbour, Russia.

My Zofsia's home was beautiful, deep in the forests – it was a sort of *dacha* but bigger than the usual cottages. Her family was well-educated, musical and with a big circle of artists from Europe coming and going because there was much in the old alliance that drew people in from the artistic backgrounds of countries abutting Belarus. It was soon all to end, however, for the bigger neighbour, now no longer a friend, came as an enemy and many people fled, my grandmother being one of them. Sadly, she came alone. Her husband, of course my grandfather, was killed and her brothers were lost too, as was their beautiful home, which was completely burned down. She came to England and, by some linked friends came to Cornwall – St Mawes - and that is where my mother was born.'

Everyone present was at once fascinated and filled with the sympathetic comprehension that was their trademark as a family. Nicholas continued:

'So, you see, I owe my passion and any abilities I have in music and, indeed voice, to my Zofsia, whose own magical, rather deep voice I can still hear today.'

The whole table was silent for a few moments and then burst into a soft applause, the warmth in it real and palpable. Nicholas blushed with pleasure in the gratitude of being upheld: a young man with a certain story in his make-up, that he had not often told. He played to them at the end of dinner – the sea poem with its secret content of yesterday and then some musical thoughts on the walk to Forde Abbey. What remained for everybody, however, was the power of a child's love for his grandmother – one who had died when he was a still a small boy - and how her influence shaped him so very well, as a man.

59

*M*eg found her way to town through the generosity of Colonel Brandon's carriage; ever there for the most necessary of private and unspoken requests, the Colonel and Marianne thought it perfectly appropriate to send their lovely young sister straight to John and Henry Dashwood under their guardianship on wheels. Being in whole cognizance of why the visit to London was being made and in full approval, the chaperoning of Christopher Brandon's sister-in-law and ward notwithstanding, Meg set out in early October after a lovely summer spent at the Hall. Given the nature of the visit and the youth of the lady making it, it was decided that Marianne's maid, Anna, would accompany her.

In the moments during which she travelled, Meg reflected on this, her first long trip alone: she was aware of the route that she had taken from the house in which she was to stay in town, for it had belonged to her father – something which brought with it the anxiety of returning. Endeavouring to imagine colourful days of parading about the garden as a small soldier, her beloved papa sweeping her up upon his back for the canter, she eschewed all thoughts of recent times filled with the great proximity of Fanny and her new regime for them all. In hauling up the past she decided that she would take out all the grimness in her heart's gallery and replace it with a new set of pictures; for not only was she now turning toward Berkeley Street, but it was lit, in her mind's eye, with a picture of a lovely friend whose presence she appreciated and whom she found deeply attractive. In short, she was in the very opposite place to the one in which she had left it!

As the last years' distress fell away from her youthful being, Meg was reminded of the potency of friendship and the magical qualities of love within it. Unlike her middle sister, she was not given to sweeping fancy, she was forthright in a different way from Marianne, with a quality lit by a whimsicality that encompassed the droll but not the destructive. Further, she was doing her best not to roar into passion, its cost having been clearly illuminated to her at first hand during the Willoughby administration and the devastation that followed.

'Come in and welcome young Meg!' called John Dashwood from the top of the terrazzo steps that marked the way into the town house of the family home. As a child, Meg had thought that the steps had the most practical of patterns, fit for all sorts of games and imaginary journeys – the following of which inevitably ended in some sort of tumble, with bandages. In entering the house, she had expected a certain scent, for Fanny's perfumes were always in evidence, along with her forbidding presence. But this time there was no scent and no Fanny and for a moment Meg was decidedly compromised, even stammering a little as she started to greet her brother and his son:

'Hello John. Why, why! Henry, you are infinitely grown!'

Henry thought it very amusing to be infinite in his growth but nevertheless returned the spirit from which it was said and bowed to his aunt.

'Has your journey been satisfactory?' said the infinitely grown.

'I think so, Henry,' said Margaret, thinking that the recent turn of his life had brought visible change to her relative, change to which she was neither insensible nor a stranger.

Settling herself and Elinor's maid into their rooms, the young woman up from Dorset thought of her past home - there was much to ponder on concerning the time that she had known there. Despite all that had occurred, it was not truly within Meg to be mean-spirited; when Henry was a younger boy, moving into Norland as her usurper, she had deliberately regarded him with contempt; now with both the intervening years and the loss of his mother, there was a different picture to behold: 'everything has a price,' she bethought herself.

It was agreed that Mr Saunders would call upon his friend from the south west and that morning tea would be an appropriate time. Having made herself as comfortable as being in a house with her brother and nephew who had just gone through a severe and shocking loss, would allow, Margaret set to finding a suitable place in which to entertain Nicholas. That she was nervous about the encounter, to boot, only extended her discomfiture. Deciding to ask John for help, she detained him after breakfast and before the real start of the day:

'Dear John, I wonder if you might advise me of a small corner in which I might offer Mr Saunders tea and which will not incommode you?'

'Of course. I think that there is still sunshine left in the conservatory, or you might like to resume to your favourite room in all houses – the library!'

Meg was grateful of some diversion in conversation with her brother, she had never been drawn to Fanny but resisted all attempts to follow into any ill thought of her now that she had gone. It was hard to know what to say, or when to say it. Besides, the house was decorated in a new way, one which was youthful and colourful, even catching an air of exuberance in some places. In her late sister-in-law there had lived a feminine spirit of fun; it was a dear pity that such a sense had somehow become entangled with spite.

The great houses of the squares around the old family home were built with extravagance in mind and Meg found them stimulating to regard in this, her first true venture back into the London world. Finding herself alone with Elinor's maid was not an unpleasant experience - Anna was older than she and filled her time with reading when not occupied with the human aspects of her work. In this way, there was adequate content for discourse but the warmth so present at Delaford and the easy rapport between herself and her sisters, wove into Meg's delight at being in town to see a young man she found rather wondrous.

A long time was taken in dressing and 'flouncing' as the Dashwood younger daughters called it, when they felt able to sink into the luxury of finding time to make themselves beautiful. Marianne's maid was extremely capable with hair, so more minutes were used in dressing it to maximum effect, the day-light and a morning tea appointment notwithstanding. The doorbell rang at eleven on the dot and it was with some trepidation that Margaret sailed downstairs, hoping not to betray the enormous number of butterflies within her middle: a new experience for someone used to being a little boyish in her communications with the world.

'Nickluss! Pray come in, it is so lovely to see you again,' she called from behind the butler. She had not expected to feel so exhilarated at the prospect of her *maestro* and she could see by his eyes, which seemed to have been cast over by faery light, that her own state of apprehension lived in them too!

'Miss Margaret are you well after your journey from Dorset?' the maestro asked.

'I am indeed! Come through to the library, I am supposed to call upon Anna to accompany us, but I am sure that it will serve to sit amongst the books.'

The two walked slowly into one of the most beautiful rooms in the house, still pregnant with many of the late Mr Dashwood's favourites and which had not followed on anywhere after his death. The smell of polish in the warm sunshine decided their fate, for the welcome feel of the books, the beauty of the mahogany furniture and now the arrival of both the housemaid with a tray of tea and scones, followed by John Dashwood himself, made a setting both private and proper.

'John, this is Mr Nicholas Saunders, our friend from Devonshire and to whose concert you are kindly taking me tomorrow: Nicholas, my brother, Mr John Dashwood,' said Meg, her ice starting to melt through the effort of speaking.

'How do you do, sir, pray be seated and welcome here,' replied the host.

'Thank you, Mr Dashwood and for allowing me to enter into your home in such times,' proffered Nicholas.

John bowed, as was correct, whilst leaving the room.

The Dashwood library had remained surprisingly unscathed after its invasion by Fanny and her will to change everything within her sight. Voluminous striped curtains in red and pale ochre had been put to the windows where before were only the wooden shutters, and the finer seating covered in the matching fabric. Every corner did seem rather *de luxe*, Meg thought, but it was not nasty, just bright. There seemed to be something left, in the making, on one of the small tables near to a wing chair, a sort of bricolage of pictures and some notes, written around them in Fanny's big handwriting: it was sorrowful to think of her sitting there, perhaps planning her next inroad into the house's modification, only to be struck down at a moment's notice and then to die.

'Marianne would have gone boldly forward to look,' thought Margaret but neither she nor her friend moved a muscle, even an eye, to investigate this apparent oversight further. Perhaps it had been left on purpose – a little bit of someone dear left behind and whatever the Dashwood sisters may have thought of Fanny, her husband loved her.

There was still a smell of sandalwood about the air, as in all the Dashwood papa libraries. Meg was not sure whether her late father used the oil on his hands when he was with his beloved books, or whether he just smelled of this beautiful and delicate scent when he was in his best place: whatever the case, the greater effect was charming and a little provocative, say, to love.

'Please tell me how you have been here in town and how the preparations for tomorrow evening have come along,' said Meg, whose pale blue dress, with a red silk sash, seemed to harmonise with Fanny's reworking of the decoration of the room, the remaining of the shelves and books, in situ as they were, startlingly withstanding.

'We are pleased, there is one more rehearsal, this afternoon and we shall be fine. I like my choir very much and the ensemble is playing well; I shall say little more, lest I spoil your coming!'

The resistance they both felt to being together in a small and lovely place yet being unable to speak naturally, began to recede:

'It is always a pleasure to sit amongst the books, do you not think Nickluss?' asked Meg.

'I do! and sometimes there is the bonus if a library has a pianoforte – then the marriage is indeed fragrant!' proffered the composer. A small silence ensued.

'I am so happy to be coming tomorrow evening and pray, have you been writing anything new or has this time been occupied in rehearsing?' said Meg.

'There has been little time for much other than preparation, but I do so love this town and as I pass by the river on my way to St Martin's I acknowledge its great and, I think, often ferocious history. I am always glad to be beside the water and I have been given rooms in Cheyne Walk, so, there I am! I know that your family has been here for many generations, do you love any particular places?'

'I do! I remember and love the parks! St James' and Hyde Park: the paths are wondrous just now as the *oak cups* are starting to fall,' said Meg.

'O yes! *the oak cups*!' said the maestro, dipping his voice and his eyes, most tantalisingly. 'How I appreciated that evening with your family, Meg, if I may call you by your family name: is it preposterous of me?'

'O, I think that you already have! It flew in naturally within the heart of my family, which you know has secretly adopted you!'

'O they are lovely, I am so very happy to have met you all. And as for the parks, perhaps we might walk in St James' since it is not far from here? We may perhaps ask Anna to walk with us?'

A warm silence fell between the two.

60

*F*riday suddenly arrived and Margaret Dashwood found herself dressing with particular care – there was something quite dashing about being in Berkeley Street and going out to St Martin's to hear and *see* Nicholas. She felt apprehensive again, so every hope of looking and feeling lovely was to the fore. She thought to herself that finding a special place where she and her composer might talk, was important – it was a matter of dignity and protocol, she knew - had she not lived through the difficulties of Willoughby and Marianne?

When the carriage came round to the front of the house it was time to stop thinking and feeling and enjoy the bustle of crossing part of the town – she loved London and there was much to see. The journey to the church took little time and they would therefore be early at the concert, so that a tour along the Strand was necessitated to alleviate any sense of bad manners. Both Dashwoods (Henry was not in attendance) bethought themselves that the road upon which they travelled to extend their time of arrival was very handsome and both noted the new and freshly built.

Whilst Miss Dashwood had been to many evenings in London, they were always within the context of her family; in this instance, however, she felt as if she came alone – this was a propitious occasion for her. To have been enveloped within the arms of her mother and sisters, whatever and however their circumstances, was indeed a benison and, for a moment, she held that unspoken gift to her heart. She and John were welcomed into the church by the Rector, Reverend Holden Pott, who kindly showed them to their seats for he knew her brother from his doings in the parish. Margaret had been to St Martin's before and remembered it as being simple and beautiful, particularly at night. Candles were lit at every turn and the light from them reflected off the shiny, dark pews; the combination of the candlelight, the many and colourfully dressed patrons and the ambience of the seating prepared for the players was enchanting. Looking around her, Meg could see that she really knew no one and then suddenly, the musicians filed down the aisle to their places and she was obliged to point her head in the appropriate direction for all concentration was now forwards. In doing so she was held back a little, being no longer able to look out behind her for her *maestro*.

In seconds, the ensemble was seated and she was just busily occupied with the dress of the musical participants when Mr Saunders came to his podium, not from the back of the church, as she had expected, but from the side to the right of the altar. Suitably taken aback by this arrival and in a direction which she had not anticipated, Meg found herself ruffled, her hopes to see him further dashed when his entrance, and the small ovation that he received in making it, was almost obliterated by the feathers on the head of the lady seated immediately in front of her. John, who was doing his best to concentrate, for it was his first social outing since the death of his wife, was at least heard to ask her if she were 'all right' behind the barrage of so much finery!

The Reverend Holden Pott was by now next to Nicholas and was, Meg suddenly realised, well into a small oration as to the calibre of his musical guest and his ensemble – her little fluster over seeing or not seeing him and the small, baulked expectation of where he might enter had diverted her from more important matters: heads were silly things! Sweeping round to bow to the glittering audience and thank the Reverend for his words, Nicholas, *her Nickluss*, suddenly caught her eager eye, now radiating from a glowing face: the eyes spoke - there can be no words for these incandescent moments. The real music of the evening was thus suspended somewhere between these two key participants in what Elinor so appropriately termed 'The Absolute Love'.

The first pieces were from Haydn – *Serenade* – and then Hummel – a beautiful *kyrie* from his *Sanctus*, during which Meg thought that she might weep out the very pit of her longing heart. Then there was an intensely fast Mozart and a lovely Beethoven ensemble treasure for strings. Margaret loved the violins but always, and especially, the cello, its magnificent depth carving into the very soul. Just as she was starting to settle to the normality of this strange occurrence, Nicholas, whose anterior form she had been studying minutely for the last two hours, left his place at the centre of his players and proceeded to the pianoforte. Wishing not to seem conspicuous with her concentration upon him, Meg glanced away at the very moment that he stood next the instrument to commend what was to follow.

'My lords and ladies, it is without precedent that we include this next small Handel piece, which is a *particular* favourite of mine and which I equally dedicate to someone who is that same to me.'

Impossibility met the full fathom of fearlessness as Meg looked straight at her beloved friend, just as he started to sing 'Did you not hear my lady…?' By the time the word 'blackbird' was reached the intrepid traveller in a new land felt that she was somewhere high above Wren's wonderful dome: London had never been like this before. The beautiful song rang out through her heart and into every part of the town; into every steeple of every church where love had ever dwelt and it was met with rapturous applause: for the intelligible sweetness of a male voice held in such perfection; for its diction and pitch; for the gentle accompaniment of the same to its best harmony; for the intense

delight communicated from song to hearers and the simple pleasure of male love held out for all to share. If Meg had thought that
she would burst with pride then she was about to become incendiary, for as Nicholas bowed low to his audience, as a veritable
Warwick to his Elizabeth Queen, he caught Meg's eye with such a
flash that she felt that everyone must have seen it: the sumptuous
feast was thus, *announced*. The lady receptor was exalted: never
had anyone informed her of the energy of shared fealty and its
gargantuan effect.

'I think that truly hits the mark, do not you, dear Margaret?'
said John, in obvious ignorance of the proximity of the person for
whom the song was intended.

'I feel so,' said a nearby voice somewhere in a church in
London, 'I feel so.'

The last pieces of the concert could have been played
anywhere - Miss Margaret Dashwood was not in any place near
to them but far, far away, somewhere in a golden meadow. The
voices which sang and the piano which played could not reach
her until, at the very last moment, the cello spoke to her loud and
clear. With the authority of its magnificent depth, it told her to
pay attention, to hold onto real feeling, to include reason and
protocol and to know that with care in these respects, love's
container would not be harmed. Hardly daring to look in the
direction of the conductor of such an exquisitely prepared and
executed evening, Meg waited with her brother for him to attend
to the drawing together of his players, observing the gratitude
that was evident in the young man and the style with which he
praised everyone, excluding no one. Soon the church was almost
empty, with the Dashwoods remaining behind.

Realising that there was, indeed, something beginning
between his sister and the man of the evening, John did not hesitate in inviting the latter to join them at home the next day: the
response was both immediate and positive.

61

*M*argaret Dashwood's allegiance to sleep was slight that night, bound only by Queen Mab herself. She did not even care for the vanity of a tired face upon the next day, the necessity of reliving every note of the evening was preponderant.

It was no dream that a messenger came to the house as Meg was descending for breakfast with a letter for her; one which she took directly from Hough as he was answering the door. Seeing that no one else had responded to the sound she slipped into the library unawares. Growing anxious to gain comprehension of what was inside the missive, the warmth and delight for her of her favourite room, notwithstanding, she sat in the window seat, sheltered by the voluminousness of the striped curtains pulled about her person. She observed her own fingers trembling as they moved to open the pages at the red sealing wax.

Cheyne Walk,
21st October 18…
Dearest Meg,
Please might I call you by your family name? It is with such sadness that I write to you, yet all propriety requires that I do so before I come to Berkeley Street later this morning.

I cannot explain to you in the way I would like best, but I need to tell you that you are becoming dearer and dearer to me at every sight – I think that it began when we men all made you scramble up the cliff at Dorset beach and you were so very gracious and amusing, making us all laugh at your own expense. If I thought that we might continue along our way together – pulling ourselves up vertical cliffs notwithstanding - I would fall down with gratitude but I must inform you of a time in my life about which I feel very unhappy and this fact must now be for your perusal.

I am so very aware of the difficulties that have, I want to say, traduced your life in the last years and in which you have been not only good natured but turned the more difficult moments into humour made at your own expense – as on the cliffs that heavenly day.

I would never behave without propriety, but I need to tell you something about my life, that whilst it being common knowledge is, nonetheless, a matter of someone else's impropriety affecting my own future.

Meg, when I was a younger man, you know that I am seven and twenty now, I walked out with a young woman – please do forgive my even mentioning this indelicacy to you – who was a little older than I. We were not real friends, as, I think you and I are, and I was at an age where I was learning about life and about my place within it. I mistook my feelings for her and, whilst I did not ask her to marry me, her parents assumed that was the way of our relationship. Time went by, perhaps longer than I had realised, and we seemed to see less and less of each other, whilst at the same time, her parents seemed to want to see more of me.

It was only when I stood back enough to see that as the many months rolled on into almost two years, we did not see each other in any different light, nor did we claim a real acquaintance.

After this realisation, I hastened to talk to the lady in question and went to the house one day, unbidden. As I was rounding the corner, I saw her getting out of a barouche and into the arms of a much older man, whom she kissed goodbye and then went into her home. You may imagine that I was astonished and somewhat confused, as well as deeply shocked. I had the presence of mind to pull the doorbell, intending to face the lady and ask what the meaning of this event was, when the door opened and she came out, accompanied by her parents. I was quite beyond myself and demanded comprehension of the situation at once.

We all reconvened inside the house and there, in one of the anterooms off the hall, I was informed that I had become some sort of horrid 'cover' for their daughter, whose real love was, indeed, for the older man whom I had seen and who was at last free to be with her. My indignation, nay, rage at being so ill used, was great. I left the house that day, never to return but what had occurred was to me a lifeless charade of all that I had thought love to be: I was left with a very strange perception of it, indeed.

To this time, then, I have not looked at anyone, nor even contemplated the looking, until our ease of friendship and the kindness of your family brought me to realise that I might love again and be safe in the doing.

Please, most dear Meg, do not be offended by what I have told you. I am ashamed of this time, that I could have lived with such unconsciousness and stupidity. Whilst there was no engagement or even talk of it, I felt the censure of others — their judgements formed out of conjecture and prejudice and which probably continued after the event was closed.

I shall still come to you this morning, as John's invitation to me last night but if this letter sets you against me then I beg you to return it with a messenger, forthwith and I will understand, in a moment, that all is at an end with our dear friendship.

In amity and respect,
Your Nicholas

Realising that the proximity of her fragrant wishes was close, Meg sat silently, shaken, the fingers now wrapped so tightly around the pages that she consciously relaxed her grip, their precious content not to be crushed.

Any questioning about the state of being happy was something that had never come before the youngest Miss Dashwood. Aware of the grim truth of losing her father at thirteen, she was yet saved by the protection of her mother and sisters and the manner in which they lived as a small family. In all the time that she had been in this feminine harmony she had never questioned her position within it; now she was set aside from them for a moment and able to consider what it was to be close to someone so upright, even with a certain moral fastidiousness about him, as well as being talented, kind, funny and loving. This, indeed, was the stuff of happiness! That Nicholas, especially after the success of last evening, could even contemplate that the news of this letter could offend her, was not to be borne. Why, the young man was exemplary! and did he not see that she loved him already? There was no possibility of censure in Margaret's Courts: in this she was in *complete* accord with her sister Elinor - and Plato.

Realising the time, she quickly wrote a reply, the while thinking that she must put her dearest and already beloved maestro out of his misery:

Berkeley Street,
   21st October 18…
   My dear friend, for you are my dear friend, there is no prosecution for you stemming from my lips.
   I embrace with honour your will to veritas and incline myself to a walk in St James' after morning tea, as we had arranged.
   With immense sincerity,
   Meg Dashwood

Spinning out of the library, the curtains left in their pucker, she ran straight into her brother.

'John! May I just send a small note to Nicholas on Hough's hand? He will be with us at 11 o'clock, as you kindly asked last evening.'

John averred, a small lump in his own throat rising as he met the shining eyes of his sister: before him, a young woman unmistakably at the start of a great love.

62

*J*t was still early Michaelmas in St James' Park. The morning had flown by in the library with John, Henry and Anna continuing a stream to mark the necessary boundaries between two young people becoming acquainted. The park was thus the perfect place and the most scintillating beatitude to the advent of love. Elinor's kindly lady expressed both comprehension and discretion by walking at least ten paces behind and certainly out of earshot: the couple was grateful and felt released from the tension of the presence of others. The first paces were silent, each being careful beyond measure, then Nicholas began:

'Mistress Meg, I am so delighted that you could come to St Martin's last evening, I was extremely glad to have you and your brother with us.'

'It was a delight dear Nickluss, we were so pleased to come, the evening was a treasure!' said Meg, looking at him fully for the first time, this visit.

'O, you are so kind, people are so kind. We have been together for quite a short time, but we are all able to play several instruments and it makes us sensible to one another for the nonce!'

'It was astonishing to hear you and see you with your colleagues,' replied the young lady.

The walk passed the back of St James' Palace and small pleasantries were exchanged about the ghosts that must surely run amok there; the unseasonable warmth of the day; the passing of ducks, swans and even *pelicans* in the waterway; the rush and bustle of the squirrels and,

thought Meg, 'the life everlasting' – so desperate was she simply to sit with Nicholas without enormities of slight chatter which they both disliked. No sooner had she bethought herself than the *maestro* rendered her thought into action:

'Come, let us sit for a while, I am sure that Anna will accommodate herself appropriately.'

Meg, her heart now cantering into a meadow of frustration, concurred.

In the instant that they became seated, words fell from each one as if the fountain stopped had been unstopped – something which both found very funny – the great benison of laughter solved all: the way forward was both easy and plain.

'Thank you for seeing me today, I was desperate that you would not be prejudiced against me,' started the young gentleman.

'But Nickluss, it is with certainty that I know that life changes things and that these miserable times, whilst sometimes continuing for a bit too long, do pass. I am so very sorry that you were caught in someone's unkind net, but this happens and then one day, one single day, it all stops. Why! we are all returning to Norland after this visit to London – how little any of us even dreamed of such a possibility!'

'Persistence is a fine habit, I know,' said the lover, 'oft times the demon route shows itself as such and we know that there is nothing that we can do but persist in removing ourselves from the anguish. Allow me to tell you something lovely.'

'Please then, do tell me, yes!' the breeze lifting Meg's dark hair into a frame around her face.

'Meg – are you sure that I can call you by that name?'

'Yes, yes! Did I not but say!' laughed the voice behind the hair.

'I am fearless then! *Meg*, I have been without my parents for ten years now, they died within weeks of each other, which at the time was very devastating, for I loved them both equally and very much.'

(A sigh from the lady.)

'In that time, I have been the ward of my mother's sister, who is elderly by now and a dear friend to me, as well as my aunt. She lives alone in Bath, to which I flee when in need of rest and a place in which to compose. I have been able to continue with my music through her, although I will inherit from my parents next year: it has been an unusually long time for me to wait because of the value of the investments involved. I only say this to you because I do not wish you to think that I am some sort of musical gypsy going about the place without substance.'

Meg, now close to being beyond herself at the news of more deceased parents, held onto Nicholas' arm, keeping as much length from it as practicable and within protocol, Anna's presence notwithstanding.

Meg was now awash with tears – she was not sure whether of sheer delight or the hearing of the comprehensible misery of her friend – it did not matter. They both sat in silence as squirrels wove back and forth; the breeze grew into a wind and back to a breeze; the air seemed amassed with pigeons and even sea gulls and Anna continued talking to another chaperone, with smaller charges.

'So, dearest Meg, you are informed of all that is crepuscule to do with me, or which could be inclement in our dawn.'

Meg, herself in a growing seesaw of emotion, could not speak. After some minutes, Nicholas, now anxious that he should not have brought his extraordinary situation to bear so soon upon the book that was now being written between them, spoke quietly:

'Say something to me, my dear, sweet Meg!'

'Amen, I say! Let it be over for you now, the miserable time with the lady and the strange man; for it is *nothing* to me, except in that it has hurt you so very much.' Fresh tears now started to flow in runnels down Meg's cheeks. 'In the greater scheme of things, you have done nothing wrong. I suppose that there was talk, as there is always talk and that you did not like its projected shadow upon you but for me the past is inconsequent upon the manner of man you are now.'

'I did not like the talk, yes, but gradually there came about a realisation that all had not been what it seemed and thus a recognition, if you like, of the innocence of my own part. In fact, the family concerned went to Germany to live, in one of the emerging cities – the older man was a Count!'

Margaret Dashwood's face crinkled with laughter:

'O well,' she said, with her usual candour, 'what a surprise!'

'Please know, dearest Meg, how glad that I am to be sitting with you and laughing with you, these smeared pages of the ledger cleared.'

In looking into each other's eyes all was lucid. Reason is not always sweet, its marriage with passion uncertain but in this autumn day in an old London park, two innocents came together, to begin their lives again.

---

hen Elinor's maid returned to Delaford it was with new eyes, for she had witnessed first-hand, the genuine sunlight between two persons of a mutual persuasion. Whilst not sent as a spy, nor being herself of an inclination to be one, she nevertheless informed her lady of the correct and sensible manner in which Miss Margaret and Mr Nicholas had conducted themselves. Further, for someone who had not visited the capital before, she was delighted to have learned so much in such a short time.

Margaret was full of life and with eyes that said, 'I have been especially happy.' Edward was the first to observe her demeanor, their friendship, existing over a little time now, rendering him a facility to see all sorts of information and, indeed, pleasure. Ever the man to be delighted with others' success, he found in his young sister-in-law a new *gravitas* that was always there, merely waiting for the moment to assume its proper place: love works in many ways. Arriving in the kitchen after a short morning ride on Nonna, he was delighted to see that Elinor, now most aware of the seven or eight weeks left before her confinement, was downstairs and waiting for him to return.

'Good morning, dear husband,' she called, as he came in

through the porch, 'I have been thinking of a little treat that I would like to put to you before our life has a definite new look about it!' As Edward came to the table, putting his head close to hers, she smiled: 'well! you smell like a forest!'

The intimacy in which they lived had not ceased to bring Elinor both pleasure and amazement, the long months of peace, the scuffle with the barn men notwithstanding, felt to her like a reprieve after the tension and difficulties of grief at Barton Cottage. Ever the practical daughter, even over her mother's view of life, she had still found the removal from Norland an increasingly larger event than she had thought. The winter months had only prolonged the feelings of separation and the terrible, seeming finality of it all. One wintery February, the challenge of entail and its consequences upon so many women had created a futility which ran counter to her usual spirit of overcoming the obstacles of life. At that time, she could not see how the Dashwood ladies were going to go forward, so increasingly bereft of funds were they and so aware of their dependence upon the beneficence of others.

Then, of course, the turn of events that had brought Edward back to her: he was indeed, an unimaginable luxury! Now that Norland was being returned to them, also something unimaginable. On the autumn morning in which breakfast was being shared at Delaford Rectory, there was one outstanding matter that she could not omit and at variance with her usual common sense she approached her husband:

'Dearest Edward,' she said.

'Yes, my equally dearest Elinor,' said he.

'I have been thinking about something that I would really like to do before our life changes.'

'Then tell me!' said the recipient.

'I would like to go to Pemberley!'

'My goodness!' replied the husband, 'do you feel up to the drive?'

'I do!' said the wife, 'if you would not chastise me for the doing of it!'

'I would!' said Edward, 'I am inordinately fond of you, not to mention wanting the safe arrival of our child! However, I think that we could invite Pemberley to come to us and perhaps enquire of your sister whether the Hall might just accommodate Mr and Mrs Darcy on our behalf. What about that?'

'Well then, we shall ask!' said Elinor, her unusual quest for adventure quelled by the happier possibility of the northern party coming south.

'And' added Mrs Ferrars, 'I would request if you might write on our behalf to ask them to come and if it would be too painful to see me in this state, given the origin and nature of our acquaintance.'

'I shall, my dear' replied the one to the other, 'I shall do so forthwith, starting with our neighbours.'

64

*A*nd so it was that Pemberley was invited to Delaford in the late autumn of a year in which the Darcys were doing their best to remain in the sheer pleasure that life had recently granted them. Georgiana was making immense progress with her piano and had been walking out with a young Russian man whom she met in London and who was most *sympathique* in the sharing of many mutual interests, especially music. Elizabeth had spent time on the estate, some of it with her husband, to the inordinate surprise of the steward. Darcy was over the moon. The invitation from Delaford arrived in the middle of what could only be termed 'harvest gratitude' and Elizabeth and Fitzwilliam agreed at once to accept. They were very touched at Edward's gentle hint that his wife was a little larger than usual and he hoped that this fact would not distress them in the light of their origin of meeting. When Mrs Darcy wrote back to thank them and accept, she expressed the pleasure that she and her husband were anticipating in seeing them and that nothing could mar such joy.

It was then, after much rain and storm that the October sun shone again and the Fosse Way was found to be dry enough for safe travel, that the Pemberley couple set off for Delaford Hall in Dorsetshire. Traversing the Pennines to meet their long road south, Darcy always felt that the Romans had built such a road for him, his frequent enough visits to the south west being perfectly accommodated along its back. All that the Pemberley couple had to do was to travel to Bath and then follow the road to Ilchester, turning off it for a very few miles directly to their destination. It would be a delight to stay in Bath – a place they both loved – and to go at a slow pace, recent experiences notwithstanding. At the outset there was no fear about matters of the past – inner circumstances had changed much for both the master and mistress of Pemberley. In the months that had intervened since their last encounter with the south west all manner of acceptance had occurred in both partners and it was with delight and all demons demolished that the trip was started.

Such was the pleasure of both travellers in the possibility of stopping at Bath that it was agreed between them to stay there for two nights, resting after the long drive. Both Elizabeth and Darcy liked the town and knew it independently of their marriage, the former loving the new shops around the Pump Rooms and in Milsom Street, and the vista of the river along Pulteney Street. When Mrs Darcy was Miss Bennet, she sometimes ventured south to visit second cousins and whilst loving its sparkle, bustle and beauty, the great luxury of it sometimes made her ponder on the penury of her financial state. Never being one for devoting herself to the art of fashion, the shops, with their great array of silks and the sheer range of delight given opportunity by them, only served to exacerbate further the feelings of lack with which she had often lived at Longbourn. Now, when she could have almost anything she liked – for her husband had secretly laid upon her a monthly annuity – she was reticent to purchase, preferring to look at the possibilities on offer and refer them to her husband at intervals in the day where necessary. Elizabeth had not lost the pride of independence grown and spoken out in her family home, but she so loved the harmony and companionship of her husband that it was not worth striking out over matters that only resembled rebellion for the sake of it – any way, it seemed so rude.

Darcy, himself long the recipient of a family tailor and outfitter in St James', also loved the cut of the chase, as he called it: the ability to promenade a very little in one or two lanes giving off the Abbey and which positively shone to anyone in possession of curiosity. Even Fitzwilliam Darcy enjoyed ambling with his wife among streets that resembled an Aladdin's cave, the ability to pay for such delights notwithstanding. That Elizabeth could again taste the delight of Sally Lunns and with the possibility of any tea, newly arrived from far reaches of the world through Bristol, promoted not only an extravagant sense of wellbeing but a fierce reminder of her pirate days in Falmouth. Her husband equally enjoyed thoughts of his wife in her smuggler's kerchief, something which gave rise to a further seamlessness in the loving joy they had come to know in Cornwall.

Conceding that this trip to visit the very same persons who had helped them in a dark hour, the man who had kept his heart concealed by the mask of arrogance and separation could only praise heaven, wherever that was, for the great advancement that his life had made in falling in love with Elizabeth Bennet. That the two had found only fortitude and thanksgiving in a time of despair said much for them and here they were, safely delivered through the fog and on their way to see those whose kindness had helped a different sort of delivery. Indeed, to have come to this realisation was a source of great comfort to the master of Pemberley and that no life of inane chatter contained in a continual tour of the socially enhanced could begin to replace what he had now. That which Darcy held dear was walking beside him in a side street at Bath – there could be no gainsaying the truth of this knowledge.

Finding themselves in similar locations regarding the vista of memory, neither spoke but each knew the great worth of finding peace with the other:

'Chorley?'

'Yes,' said Elizabeth, mindful of the intimacy of the moment when her sweet name was used.

'I wanted to tell you how very glad I am that I did not lose you in our debacle in the forest and that whilst we strove, on that day, to keep ourselves from falling or fainting, or even dying, we did extremely well and now we are here today, amongst the shops! I love you extremely, dearest Chorley and I use that name today for you are innocent and lovely in wanting a meagre *Sally Lunn* when I feel able to offer you anything that your heart desires.'

'Ah but you see,' said Chorley, 'all that my heart desires is you.'

65

*A*rriving at Delaford in the late afternoon sunshine, the party of two was delighted to discover that the proximity of the Hall to Ilchester was great, so that having left Bath, Mr and Mrs Darcy wove their way in near silence, going along well to see some very significant friends. They had sent on a messenger from Bath, to give the Ferrars an idea of the time of their coming and, true to form, their arrival was within the quarter of the hour.

Edward, who was walking from the Parsonage to the Hall, heard the carriage and, as he swung round, in one of those magnificent turns that seemed to encompass his very essence, Darcy took him as the first sight of Delaford Hall. In that moment, the master of Pemberley saw all that he had recognised in the pastor and he was deeply glad to have come.

'We must celebrate this time of happiness after the storm,' he bethought himself, climbing from the carriage to greet the man with the kindest of eyes, even before helping his wife down from the coach.

'Reverend Ferrars! Why! we have arrived from the north in a better state than our last arrival from the south!' Darcy exclaimed.

'Mr Darcy and Mrs Darcy! it is with such pleasure that you are welcomed here. I hope that your journey has been kind. Come, let us go inside.'

As Elizabeth got down from the carriage, she knew that she was walking beside a man who had truly saved her life – and a small tear fell through her lashes as she looked towards him. Despite Delaford's relative lack of grandeur, a small array of servants lined up before the Hall. In the moment that she regarded the people, Elizabeth could only really see Edward and, in the instant that she held out her hand to him all the grief and confusion – and loss – of that time vanished away. Speaking warmly to those smiling eyes, she said:

'Reverend Ferrars, it is with such pleasure and not a little gratitude that we have come to be with you. We appreciate your invitation to us and look forward to seeing Mrs Ferrars again and of course, to meet and thank Colonel and Mrs Brandon, our kind hosts.'

Just as she had finished speaking, the latter came forward from the portico in welcome of their guests - all was affability and grace - and then last, walking in timidity for the knowledge of what she had *not* lost, came Elinor. As she stepped forward, the two small lines of retainers stepped back, even as the Red Sea, as the two women faced one another between them. There seemed to be a small second when Elizabeth saw the reality of where she might have been had not the collision occurred but then the thought was dispersed and she moved quickly toward Elinor, gently offering her hand and inclining her whole body toward her in genuine affection:

'Dear Mrs Ferrars, we are so glad to see you! If it were not for your husband's prompt action, I hesitate that I would be here today; we thank him and we thank you and the Middletons, for the kindness you showed to us in that recent time.'

At this, Elizabeth curtsied low, as if to a monarch, and her husband bowed also - a moment in time when all barriers were crossed, all prejudices exceeded and replaced by the indemnity of real human affection. As Mrs Darcy rose from her fond greeting to

Elinor Ferrars, she felt like a woman coming home to herself and as both made to step back, they simultaneously fell forward into an embrace as if between sisters. All overlooking the scene smiled whilst secretly gasping a little at what a common experience of a sensible nature can create.

Having rested for a while, Elizabeth asked if she might make her way to see Elinor via the garden. All was possibility and since both husbands were themselves in the *Orangerie* of the Hall, Marianne took Elizabeth across to the Parsonage. The former lady had not played a great part in the events of the collision, yet the ease with which Mrs Brandon felt able to speak with Mrs Darcy was evident, the knowledge of the degree of suffering the latter had undergone sufficing as a bedrock. It was not the way of the Dashwood ladies to gossip but they had shared between them the grim calamity of the stag and the carriage, and they equally rejoiced in the recovery of Mr and Mrs Darcy and now their arrival at Delaford.

Conversing as they crossed to the pastorage, Elizabeth and Marianne discovered their love of Bath: the way that it is couched in a cup of hills; the views from their summits; the tremendous rush of the river at the weir below Pulteney bridge; the Baths of course, and the colourful and tantalizing nature of the shops. On reaching Elinor, who was waiting for them in her small upper parlour, the realisation of mutual friends was confirmed by Marianne's sister, who was acquainted with a family in the spa town through Mrs Jennings. Not wishing to stay when there might be so much to say between Elinor and Mrs Darcy, Marianne left whilst expressing her happy anticipation at seeing them at dinner.

Both ladies sat together in silence for a moment and then Elinor began to speak:

'Mrs Darcy, it is so kind of you to come down half the country to visit us, but I had it in my heart to see you before any more time ran along behind us.'

'Yes, I too wanted to see you again and might we call each other by our first names in the privacy of this place and conversation? When we experience some event that makes a mark upon us it is not always the case that we wish to revisit the site but both Fitzwilliam and I have wanted to meet you again and not simply, with respect, out of our gratitude, which is great.'

'I know that is true for us, too, Mrs Darcy.'

'*Elizabeth*,' said the other.

'Elizabeth! said Elinor. We are so pleased to have you here.'

Both sat for a long, restful while, exchanging that which was able to be discovered in the silent mutuality that comes from having together traversed a disaster.

'We shall meet again at dinner, Elinor, and as before, we are indebted to your husband in finding us in the first instance. Why! we could have been lost in the forest forever!'

Upon that light jest on something dark, Mrs Darcy requested to find her way back to the Hall alone through wonderful shrubberies and beds ablaze with dahlias striking out among long flushes of pampas grasses at their back. Reminding herself to ask about the gardens at dinner, she was again at the Tremayne's and on her way down to the river, every step healing the gash of the collision and removing the private splinters left behind in her heart.

66

*I*t would never have occurred to anyone seated at the Brandon's table that night, that the Hall, or its occupants or tenants were less than the master and mistress of Pemberley – it was all a matter of what Edward called 'the heart's pronunciation.' In their coming together that day among the pines there was no time for status or protocol – Elizabeth may have died and in such a moment it was neither prejudice nor jealousy that saved her. When a man is down and his wife bleeding on the forest floor, there can be no room for ignorance of the perennial truths of life: how many times had the master of Pemberley thought this since his collision with the stag – further, the symbol of the great creature was not lost on him: 'if one has to encounter death then why not through nature's majesty?' he bethought himself.

As the party sat down together in the summer dining parlour at the back of the Hall, it was evident to the Darcys that they were amongst special friends. Whilst all the usual protocol was observed at table, there was in evidence the most delicious freedom to speak to one another 'between the pages' as Elinor called it. No one was playing a part and no one finding fault or creating censure since such boundaries had long been breached:

here was a delightful and liberating experience. Laughter rang out as the friends found mutual topics and curiosities, least of all and ever so lightly, the friendship that had come out of adversity.

'Colonel and Mrs Brandon,' said Darcy, leading in, 'it is a great pleasure for us to be with you and to stay here, thank you.'

'You are most welcome!' said the Colonel, 'it is an equal pleasure for us to have you here, is it not, Marianne?'

'Indeed! We are delighted. Pray tell us, we know that you have comprehension of the far south west, but do you know this area? perhaps the Dorsetshire coast, it is close to us,' asked Mrs Brandon.

This time it was Elizabeth who answered: 'Mr Darcy! I have never enquired as to your knowledge of these environs, do tell us. For myself I know Sidmouth a little.'

'I too!' asserted the recipient of the question, 'in my youth we visited this area, staying on Exmoor and found the area of such beauty, even if there were rather too many stags…'

There was a small rush of panic across the table, but Darcy's raised left eyebrow denoted the tone of the message which was deliberate: the group smiled and found itself able to relax together, the past mastered.

Marianne, who had not yet set out on her road to motherhood, gallantly continued the theme of visiting the area: 'if you might like to see any of the nearby sea towns, we would be delighted to direct or take you to some pleasant places. For us, we love to go to Bridport Harbour, it is an exceeding busy place and filled with all manner of shipping and then it is lovely to go on to Lyme Regis.' The table quivered again at the mention of the name and its historical ramifications, but the speaker continued boldly as if to go to Lyme were both a commonplace and constantly charming activity: 'it is possible to spend a pleasant day in these places.'

Piecing together these delicate areas of conversation, the observer would thus appreciate that strides had already been made through potential explosions and that all was well: an atmosphere of warm friendship providing the bulwark against, if not the antidote to the promotion of difficult memories.

Soon Bath came up for attention and the feminine contingent found much to put forward concerning the town as a favourite and, in some respects even more elegant than London. The great pleasure of the table was talk of music and the Derbyshires spoke of the lovely evening which they had spent at Truro with Mr and Mrs Bingley and their friend Colonel Fitzwilliam. Of course, at the mention of the name, certain discreetly leading questions were asked, and Colonel Brandon at once professed a knowledge of his acquaintance – a perfectly logical conclusion given the careers of both men and any way, Colonel Fitzwilliam had a remarkable and ubiquitous presence!

All was delight at the coming to intelligence of the facts and another tale was embarked upon concerning the kinship of Mr Darcy to the Colonel; their many years of friendship and their recent and serendipitous discovery of him at Truro Assembly Rooms. Mrs Darcy continued where her husband had left off, introducing the splendour of the summer's evening in the sea town; the veritable Progress down the leg of Cornwall and via (she hardly dare mention for blushing) the Old Jamaica Inn, about which her husband teased her sweetly, the presence of the company notwithstanding. Indeed, so vivacious was Elizabeth's regaling of Truro, the life of the quay and the musical evening in particular, that its colourful expression gave much amusement to the party. In this way, step by step and in the most amicable of circumstances, a veil was drawn over the unfortunate collision, such that the profound basis upon which the friendships of the table were formed could rest without anxiety, all fragile bridges crossed and reupholstered – if bridges could be so.

As the evening ended it was agreed that the table would reconvene tomorrow, at the same time, when a friend of the Delaford community would be staying for one night on his way from the south west to London and whose company they felt the Darcys might enjoy.

67

he next evening the gong sounded out gently so as not to clash with the delightful music rising past it and up the stairwell to the guests dressing for dinner.

'Why! that is a beautiful piece of playing my dearest, lovely Elizabeth,' said Darcy, briefly verifying his appearance in the looking glass before descending.

'It is somewhat ravishing I would say, my beloved,' smiled the beloved's wife. 'And I believe that you have caught the sun a little today: I shall have to hide you when we return, lest the household should think that I have been consorting with the gypsies and returned with one!'

'Sauce!' levied the recipient, placing a kiss upon the brow of his critic.

As the two were taking the stairs at what could only be called an ambling pace, a young man flew by at their conclusion, sweeping into the dining parlour and being heard to ask there for the whereabouts of Mrs Brandon. Hearing that the latter was about her sister, the gentleman swung lightly back, catching the eye of the guests as he did so:

'Good evening!' said Darcy, moving forward to offer his hand to the young man, 'I am Fitzwilliam Darcy, and this is my wife, Elizabeth, we are guests here.'

'Good evening to you both, I am also a guest, Nicholas Saunders at your service.'

'Delighted. We are sure. Was that your touch at the pianoforte that we heard?' asked the master of Pemberley with the eloquence of genuine interest.

'It was, indeed, sir, I was looking for Mrs Brandon, to ask her if she might play a duet with me this evening after dinner.'

No sooner was the sentence spoke than Marianne appeared, a red rose in hand, so that a small conglomerate was now gathered at the foot of the staircase:

'Ah, there you all are!' she proclaimed, asking, 'has the gong sounded, am I late for my own dinner table?'

'You are not, ma'am, nevertheless, we were all just seeking you out!' said Nicholas charmingly.

'Then let us fly into the garden and call Edward and Elinor, my husband is bound to follow apace.'

In doing as they were directed the little procession made a merry picture: first Marianne and Elizabeth and then Darcy and Mr Nicholas – the latter beginning to sense the same feelings of kinship that he had met once before in this house, except that this time someone most dear to him was missing.

As the group moved into the white garden – still beautiful in early October – they were met in one direction by the Ferrars and diagonally by the Colonel.

'Greetings all!' said Edward, looking singularly refreshed by the sight of his *dear crew*.

'Greetings!' said Elinor, at the same time regarding the Colonel quizzically and asking, 'why! sir, from where do you stem this early evening, have you been to the village?'

'I have, dear Elinor, I just wanted to feel my way through a small difficulty but not one that cannot be transposed, like a piece of music, onto Monday morning.'

A flash of concern travelled across Edward's face, for he could easily guess from whence the difficulty came but yes, it could wait until after the great pleasure of this evening.

'Do I see that you have already met each other, Mr and Mrs Darcy and our friend the composer?' said the Colonel.

'We have sir, and are delighted, for we heard his beautiful creation as we were dressing for dinner and we have not heard such music before: it is positively enticing,' said Elizabeth from the part of her that was indubitably a pirate.

'It is, indeed,' applied Marianne 'and we feel *most* happy to have him amongst us, for he expresses whole days that we spend together in musical notes and then plays them back to us, like a magical picture show!'

'How remarkable!' said Darcy unknowingly stealing the Colonel's favourite adjective and with aplomb, 'we should like to learn more.'

The garden seemed to gather up the dear crew, now encompassing the northern arm and the autumn light fell upon them in her beneficence. Darcy particularly noticed that there was no shortfall in this light, it seemed to bless 'him who gives and him who takes' and he was at once mindful of his own life, his own mercy and the effect that being within Edward's circumference seemed to have upon his sense of it. 'This is a most particular group of people,' he bethought himself, all expressions of explanation withdrawing from him, even the necessity of considering why. Darcy, a man who had spent so many lifeless years, whatever the degree of his material wealth, had always chosen to be on the edge of a society whose presence he neither craved nor enjoyed. Yet here, in a country house not far from the sea, he felt more at home than he had for a long time – apart from being at Pemberley – or indeed, Tamara. Wanting and meaning to speak to his hosts, he asked as they all walked into dinner:

'Tell me, Colonel Brandon if you feel able and willing, how you find your life after being with your regiment?'

'I find it utterly splendid, Mr Darcy, thank you! at the time I did all that I could as an officer far from home in the East

Indies, but they are done. In those years I felt able to do my best and it was, in a sense, only that it was at such a remove from life here, that I could do it with adequate ease. I served my men as they served both me and the King and I pressed forward with all that was needed to be done there. I suppose that it was only when I returned to England and some personal family matters that rankled with me, that I acknowledged the great service that the experience of being a soldier in charge of men had provided. That I had to keep in check some rather strong emotions, at one point, was a matter which I only realised through the discipline of my past command and, indeed, my will for peace. I am always glad that I did not rise up in anger, even though the events which goaded me were both serious and painful.'

Darcy felt humbled to be in the presence of such a man and said little in response, for that moment, except to honour what he had been told and to ask, separately:

'I see from your library that you have many volumes that I own myself and many musical manuscripts; do you play Colonel, or is your wide interest in appreciation and admiration?'

'I do play a little, but I love and study the manuscripts as if they were stories, which of course, they are! Here is part of the reason that I appreciate my wife's musical ability – a great benison to our home and our life together – and to our friend Mr Saunders' widely mounting accomplishments, why! he has just been playing and conducting in London.'

At this moment, the whole party had come into the Hall and were now regrouping in the small dining room; the autumn light, now deeper and as if more mature than its summer cousin, slowly setting on the apricot walls. It was as if the party consisted of returnees from some strange diaspora, so easy was their conversation, marked by a certain intelligence of one another that lent it an exquisiteness of sensibility.

'Why! this is a beautiful room and lends itself so well to this time of the year,' observed Elizabeth, taking her husband's hand in a small fervour of appreciation for the pleasure of being in such a place and such company with him.

'It is really Marianne's doing,' replied the Colonel, 'when we married, she took on some discreet changes and this room was one of them: I have been able to leave the house completely to her light touch!'

'O, my dear one, you speak so kindly, but you gave me *carte blanche* which I both valued and wanted to honour,' came the swift reply.

As the evening travelled along, it became evident that a certain indelible *camaraderie* accompanied it, each person seated at the table feeling both able and free to contribute in a manner which gave back to the whole with a sense of what could only be called equanimity and grace. Such a concept was nothing to do with material status, or rank but rather with what was known and shared by these friends, Darcy was particularly pensive upon this head:

'How ridiculous have been so many of the gatherings of my life,' the master of Pemberley bethought himself, 'and here I am with my beloved wife, a woman whose family I criticised with a brutality not infrequent in my vocabulary of that time and yet who has brought me to the deepest pleasure and *significance* of evenings like this.'

Indeed, the beloved wife was at that moment observing her husband and how he was evaluating where he was and perhaps who he was, anew.

'I would not wish for that collision to have happened,' she thought quietly, 'yet it has brought us real and affectionate friends, whilst at the same time dismantling the very obstacles to their formation in the finding.' Briefly skirting the thought of the Misses Bingley in their home at Pemberley, she bethought *herself* that she would rather spend an evening in a broom cupboard than be required to negotiate another dreadful time in their presence.

So palpable was the dear relief on Elizabeth's face that her husband turned to her, across the table, enquiring of her well-being whilst secretly thinking 'my beloved Chorley looks beautiful this night.'

As the evening was close to its end, the Colonel gave out an invitation to those gathered to adjourn to the library where, with their permission, he would ask both Marianne and Nicholas to play for them.

Delighted to a man, the party moved seamlessly to the comfort of thick upholstery and a glass of port wine without the prejudice of separation. Marianne began with her best loves and which had now become family favourites – all sat in amicable and appreciative silence and applauded forthwith at the end. Yet the wonder of the evening was truly brought by Nicholas Saunders, who had held back in conversation throughout dinner, preferring to observe and listen, given what he could see was happening between the Pemberley visitors and the residents of the Hall and the fact that he was a new boy in the latter. When he started to play his own sea poem, a rendering so personal to Marianne that he had obtained her permission previous to its playing, the party was elevated, as one, to a place of some sort of communion in which words could not and should not obtain.

The candlelight on the apricot walls held nothing to the delight of the faces, the holding of hands and the frame of what Mrs Mary Dashwood would call *real human affection* - spun in a light invisible to anyone reckless enough to be near and without a heart to feel it.

At the end of the piece all was silent for several seconds and then applause flew softly over the assembly like the peace dove that it was.

'I do thank you so much,' said Nicholas, with a certain timidity, continuing softly, 'and may I thank my hosts for the day which inspired such a composition.'

Observing the presence of something most precious in the young man's own face, Edward and Elinor looked across at each other, knowing of course, of Marianne's encounter with fear on that day but also of the now known as inevitable arrival of love in two hearts in the very same hours.

'We hear that you are playing in London and conducting also. Are you very excited, Mr Saunders?' asked Elizabeth, the first voice to be heard after some little time of appreciative silence.

'It pleases me very much, Mrs Darcy,' answered Nicholas directly.

At that moment, Elizabeth and her husband asked the same question:

'Mr Saunders, do you play any other instruments?'

The table was amused at the spontaneous synchronicity which they had heard.

'Yes, yes, I do – I play the viola,' said the young maestro, 'and sometimes other stringed instruments.'

The look between the Darcys spoke volumes – volumes of lute strings.

'I wonder, then, whether you might come to Pemberley to look at an instrument that we have from the seventeenth century?' applied Mrs Darcy after a nod from her husband as to explanation, 'it is a rather beautiful lute. We would be thrilled if it might be played again, retuned and played again,' said Elizabeth, her dark eyes shining in the candlelight.

'It would be perfect if everyone here might come to such an occasion,' thought Mr Darcy aloud, his wife nodding in acquiescence:

'Perfectly thrilling,' she confirmed.

As the clock struck a quarter of the hour from midnight, Edward held firmly onto Elinor's arm, feeling their child stir as the arm rested upon her own expansive frame:

'This is what life should be like,' he thought, gratitude coursing through every vein of his body, 'it is as if we were all singing the same song: it is all so very simple.'

68

It had never occurred to Elinor that she would want anyone but Dr Jago to attend at the birth of her child but as she waved goodbye to Elizabeth Darcy something in the pit of her stomach told her, in no uncertain terms, that she must not let her go. As is the wont of humans, led as we are by our heads, that is exactly what Mrs Edward Ferrars did and she witnessed the carriage go with a growing and palpable fear.

Doing her best to distract herself from what her heart was sounding out loudly, Elinor spent the morning hoping to allay the fear, but it would not be banished and by noon she realised that her time for confinement was fiercely upon her. Sending for Dr Jago was foremost in her mind but predominant was the first requirement to send out a messenger to ask for the return of the Darcys. Mercifully, Edward was able to comprehend at once, he had felt apprehension in his wife's body before and he was not going to ignore it this, of all times. Reeling with a rush of emotion, the like of which she had never felt before, Elinor felt suspended somewhere between hope and disaster, but she kept before her the need to have her new friend with her, why! had this woman not almost died on the floor of the forest. Bereft of any sense of panic, the wife of the priest of Mary Magdalene took herself calmly to bed, having sent for hot water and the rest of the known paraphernalia for giving birth.

As the doctor arrived and shortly announced that he must turn the child, Elinor knew that she had made the right decision in recalling Mrs Darcy.

'This is not the time for husbands,' decided Jago, shooing Edward out of the chamber, much to his great irritation, for he was a man whose love for his wife was profoundly ignited and thus in some conflict with the mores of his day. He too felt Elinor's need to be with an older woman and not the sister of her own family, who was yet passing from love's beckoning into another ward. Again, the summoning of Mrs Dashwood would take longer than that of Mrs Darcy, the former in London with John and young Henry. Like his wife, Edward knew that the mistress of Pemberley would not mind returning, had he himself not witnessed her own spirit of love?

Within the hour the sound of horses announced the return of the great carriage into the drive of Delaford parsonage; thankfully the Brandons were about their business in Exeter, so there was no need for referrals and mannerly entreaties. Darcy looked touched by the request and Edward seized him at once and bade him to privacy in the *Orangerie* at the back of the Hall, where they were close enough to help. Elizabeth proceeded straight upstairs, thinking as she went, that she would not be sure whom to ask were this scene to be her own – her love for her own sister, who was not yet a mother, notwithstanding. As Mrs Darcy entered the chamber, Elinor's first thought was that here before her was a woman whose own near-public loss of a child embodied the courage and heart of this moment: she was, indeed, the right companion.

Holding her hand out to her friend as she came into the room, Elizabeth, a woman now loved into a new form of herself, was still Miss Bennet as far as dear sisters were concerned and here was a dear sister. Elinor smiled as Mrs Darcy's prompt arrival provoked a tear for her own hopes of a safe delivery. Still shaking from the acute discomfort of Doctor Jago's turning the infant, here was a sister in the throes of a territory she had not before encountered, yet here was a land without milestones and Elizabeth came forward feeling the distress of her friend at once:

'My dearest Elinor, I am here, I could do no other, we turned about at once with Darcy's full comprehension and approval. What may I do for your immediate relief?'

'O believe me,' Elinor continued weeping silently, 'the weight of your presence alone is incalculable - the doctor thinks that the cord is around the child's neck.'

Elizabeth endeavoured not to flinch as her most ample imagination made headways into the situation:

'Do not be fearful, dear friend, for I have heard of many babies whose entry into the world is not straightforward. We must keep our thoughts away from anything grim, I am sure that all shall be well, we must rescue ourselves from downward looking.'

'I shall try, Elizabeth, I shall try. Pray tell me about your home again.'

The next hours were spent as the mistress of Pemberley carefully painted a portrait of its position; its aspects in the land; the views from the lake; the views from the hillside and even from the crags of Derbyshire; all the while administering love and attention to the weary and anxious brow:

'There is something beyond life, in these moments, is there not dearest Elinor? It could be likened to being in some sort of corridor.' The squeeze of the hand ineluctable coming as the reply.

The companion continued,

'As I lay on the forest floor, I knew that it might be all up with me but there was a strong feeling that all would be fine again, that I was wrapped in fearlessness, despite the seriousness of my situation. It was not simply the presence of Fitzwilliam, or the stillness after all the great noise and confusion but a more profound sense that there was nothing that could not be overcome. Even with my husband's distraught face, I felt a seamlessness between myself and life – it was like being on the edge of a great, yet calm sea, a place of silence where earth and air meet. Strangely, I was not afraid.'

'Elizabeth, dear Elizabeth, I am often there now, in deep but quiet water then fear intrudes within me, or near to me and as it comes up from my loins, smashing, or trying to smash all in its path, my body hurts more, claims more. I am hoping to be bigger than this lion!'

Taking Elinor's hands in her own, Mrs Darcy felt the sheer fineness of the moment as she breathed love into the frame of her friend's body, as Darcy had done for her. It was not a physical breath but an infinite outpouring – if she could feel its colours, they would be aquamarine and silver. Elinor's face seemed to say in reply, 'I am going along better.'

The women could hear a sudden breeze outside the window and which momentarily distracted them both enough to leave behind the poignancy of the moment, for Elinor was clearly faint. The birth seemed to her like the opening of a door, and it was indeed, such an opening but the fear returned as she felt something sticking on the lintel above the door and as the sticking became pronounced a fever rose up steadily.

The afternoon wore on, Elizabeth sent to the Hall for ice and it came quickly and with small white rosebuds scattered over it - the two mused from whom the buds had come since Marianne was not at home. Mercifully, the fever was coming down. Elizabeth held her patient's hand, stroked her head, put ice on her forehead, even sang a gentle lullaby until she realised that the child had not yet come. Then bethinking herself that it was yet a good idea to be born to soft singing, imagined that if Nicholas were here, he might play a little gentle Brahms in the parlour below: were they not rich as a family with all these truly gentle men?

The clock ticked on relentlessly – they always seemed so loud, these clocks, when something was difficult or wrong. As the evening started to pull in, Elinor was wracked by increasing pain and the slow, dragging feeling again – the door stuck on the lintel. Dr Jago thought that there would be an arrival before midnight, he had just returned as Elinor was urging her dear friend to seek refreshment when there was an enormous surge and the boy was born. The doctor could see the tightness of the cord around the neck at once, but his strength was manifold and with one strongly deft manoeuvre he pulled it away and over the head. The agony of the intrusion was beyond explication for Elinor but at last the door had come off the lintel and she almost sat bolt upright with the relief. Elizabeth, who had privately hovered between hope and fear for her friend and her baby and their lives, felt the energy of the small body enter the world and she was amazed and in awe: what was this passion called birth?

Then all was over and a moment of silence sounded out as all waited to hear the cry of the child claiming its right to live – and the cry came, e'en a clear shout which proclaimed 'I am here!'

The two women hugged one another and wept openly, each almost mesmerized by the other and the delivery, not only of a child but of a release from the grim prospect that had waited around the bairn like the predator that it might have been. The small, creased face held fast to that of his mother, whilst the friends, new yet deeply proximate through shared adversity, laughed at the strong fists and saw that this child, a beautiful, dark-haired boy, was truly alive and intended to claim his inheritance to life, regardless of cords or lintels or even the great lion of pain – for the irises of his own eyes were black with fear.

Outside, the early winter weather drew in as a prayer of gratitude was felt, the spectre of loss vanquished. Elizabeth stood back as Edward came into the room, anxiety leaving his own grey countenance as he saw that his wife and child were safe and well. They could all hear Darcy whispering at the foot of the stairs and the three giggled at the wonder of the Master of Pemberley talking with the maidservants. Indeed!

And there was not a soul in the chamber who did not acknowledge the possibility of the situation being other and raise eyes to an invisible heaven that there had been no death there this day.

To be continued.

ACKNOWLEDGMENTS

I thank the dear friends who have made a long journey with me, the result of which is this text:

To Suenel Brewer Holloway, for fine editing; to John Morris for the initial reading and criticism of the text and the same by Ann Branson and Lizmarie Morson; to Rose Kent and Rob Lieper, in whose home I was locked down during Covid and whose guardianship of it became the possibility of my writing this book. Thank you to Alyson Guy, for her inspiration and work on the front cover and Mike Hancock for the same. Thank you to MYeBook Publishing Team for their patience!

In alphabetical order, I thank the following dear friends who supported this endeavour: artist Edna Fourie; Patricia Hall and her husband Arjan Bogaers; Julia and David King; Judy Krige; Gillian Lord; Nicholaas and Christiaan at Old Village Lodge; the Schutte family; Catherine van Alphen. Also, the loving staff of Temenos, McGregor and the same of Volmoed, Hermanus.

To Africa, for all that she has taught me about Love and for Love's gift of this writing.

To the alpha and omega of my life, my sons, Alexander and Nicholas, who have bravely born their mother's great Spirit!

Summer 2022

ABOUT THE AUTHOR

Marella Santa Croce is a passionate academic –

BEd; MA;BA;MPhil – and has written many theses; taught Creative Writing in the University of Warwick School of Education and English and Comparative Literature in many schools and colleges in the UK.

This is her first novel. She has two sons and three grand-daughters.

Printed in Great Britain
by Amazon